Over the Garden Wall™

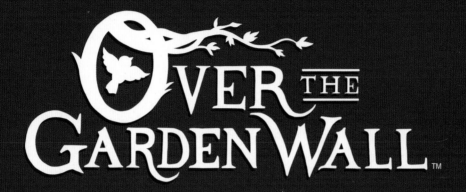

VOLUME ONE

OVER THE GARDEN WALL Volume One, February 2017. Published by KaBOOM!, a division of Boom Entertainment, Inc. OVER THE GARDEN WALL, CARTOON NETWORK, the logos, and all related characters and elements are trademarks of and © Cartoon Network. (S17). Originally published in single magazine form as OVER THE GARDEN WALL No. 1-4. © Cartoon Network. (S16) All rights reserved. KaBOOM!™ and the KaBOOM! logo are trademarks of Boom Entertainment, Inc., registered in various countries and categories. All characters, events, and institutions depicted herein are fictional. Any similarity between any of the names, characters, persons, events, and/or institutions in this publication to actual names, characters, and persons, whether living or dead, events, and/or institutions is unintended and purely coincidental. KaBOOM! does not read or accept unsolicited submissions of ideas, stories, or artwork.

A catalog record of this book is available from OCLC and from the KaBOOM! website, www.kaboom-studios.com, on the Librarians Page.

BOOM! Studios, 5670 Wilshire Boulevard, Suite 450, Los Angeles, CA 90036-5679. Printed in China. First Printing.

ISBN-13: 978-1-60886-940-4, eISBN: 978-1-61398-611-0

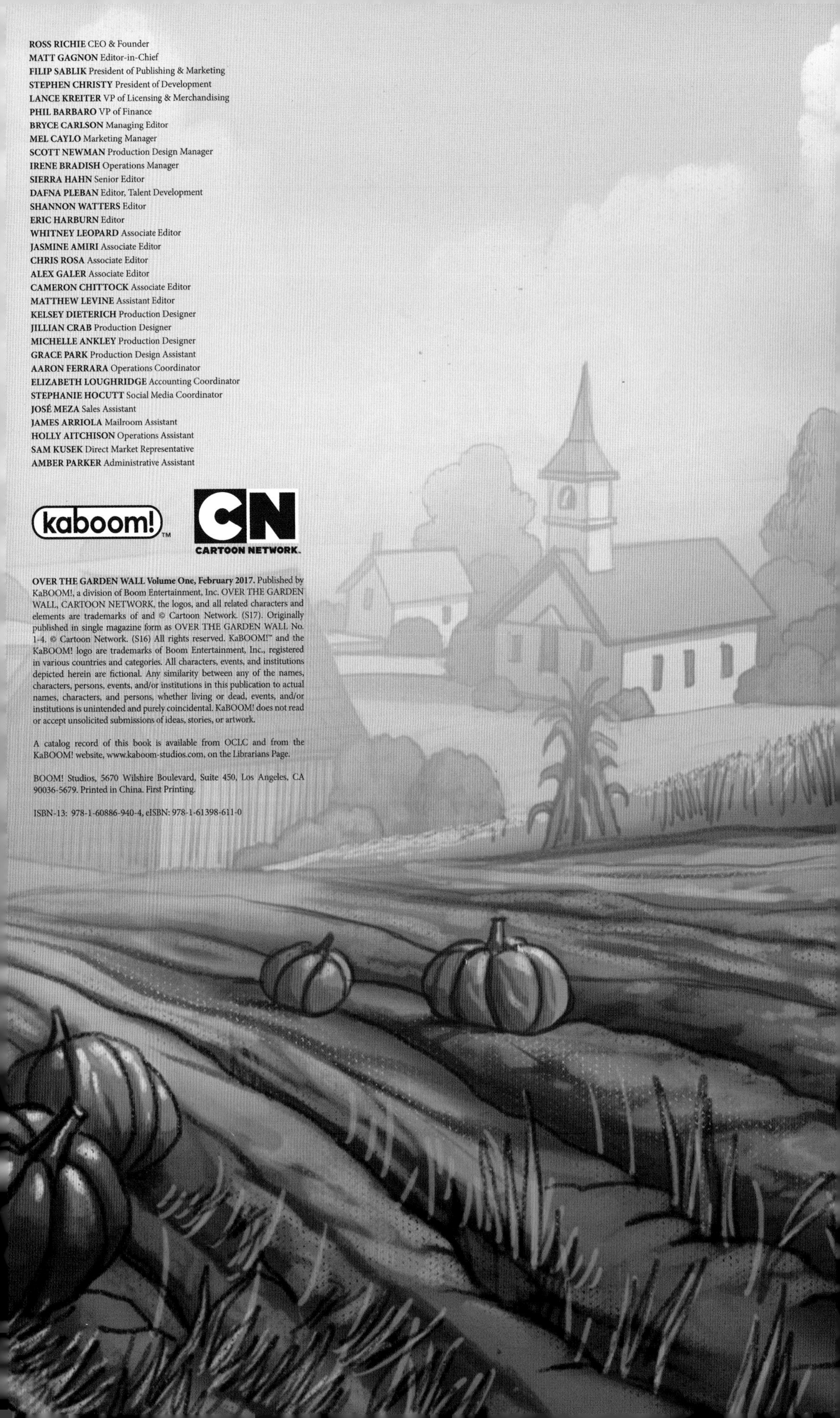

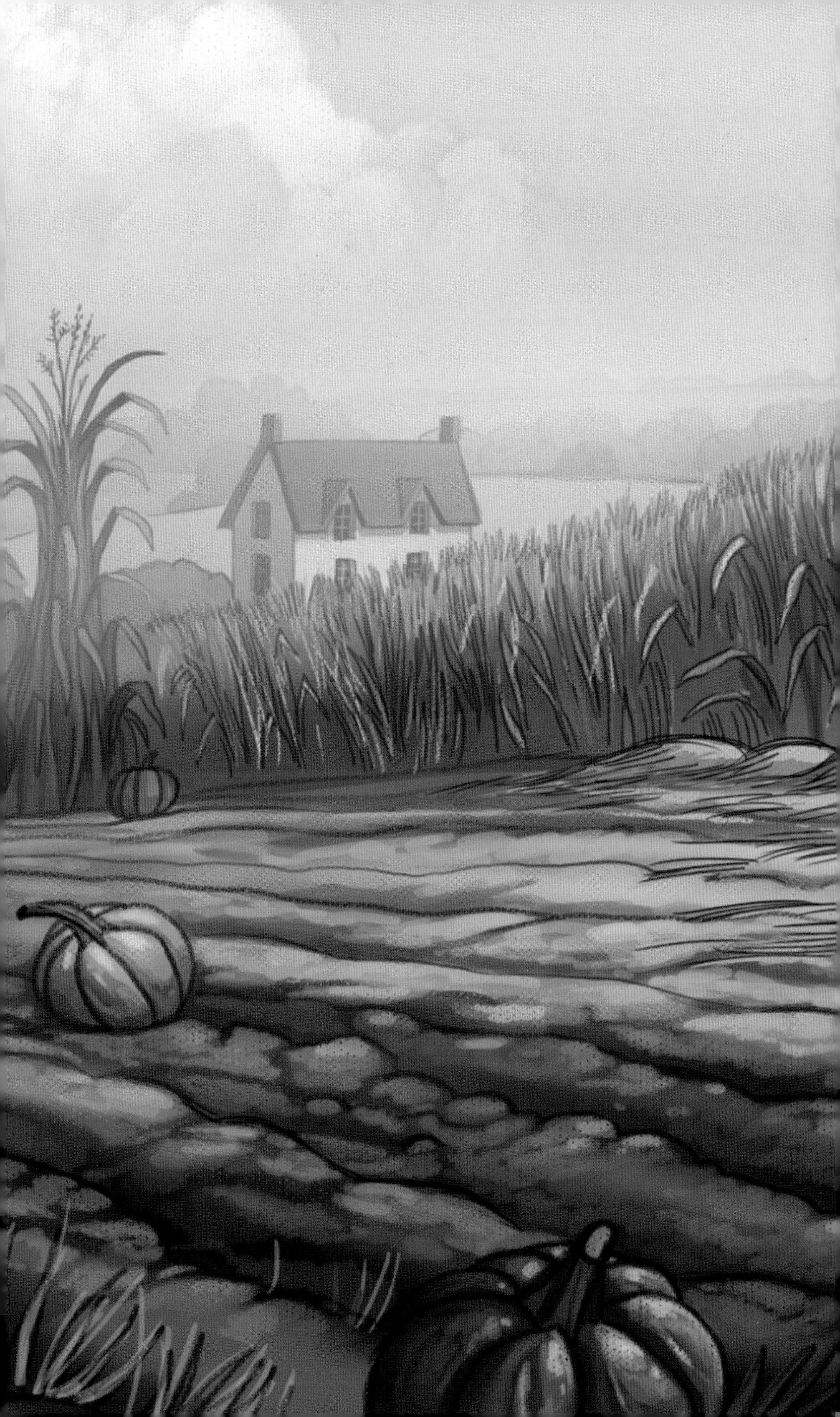

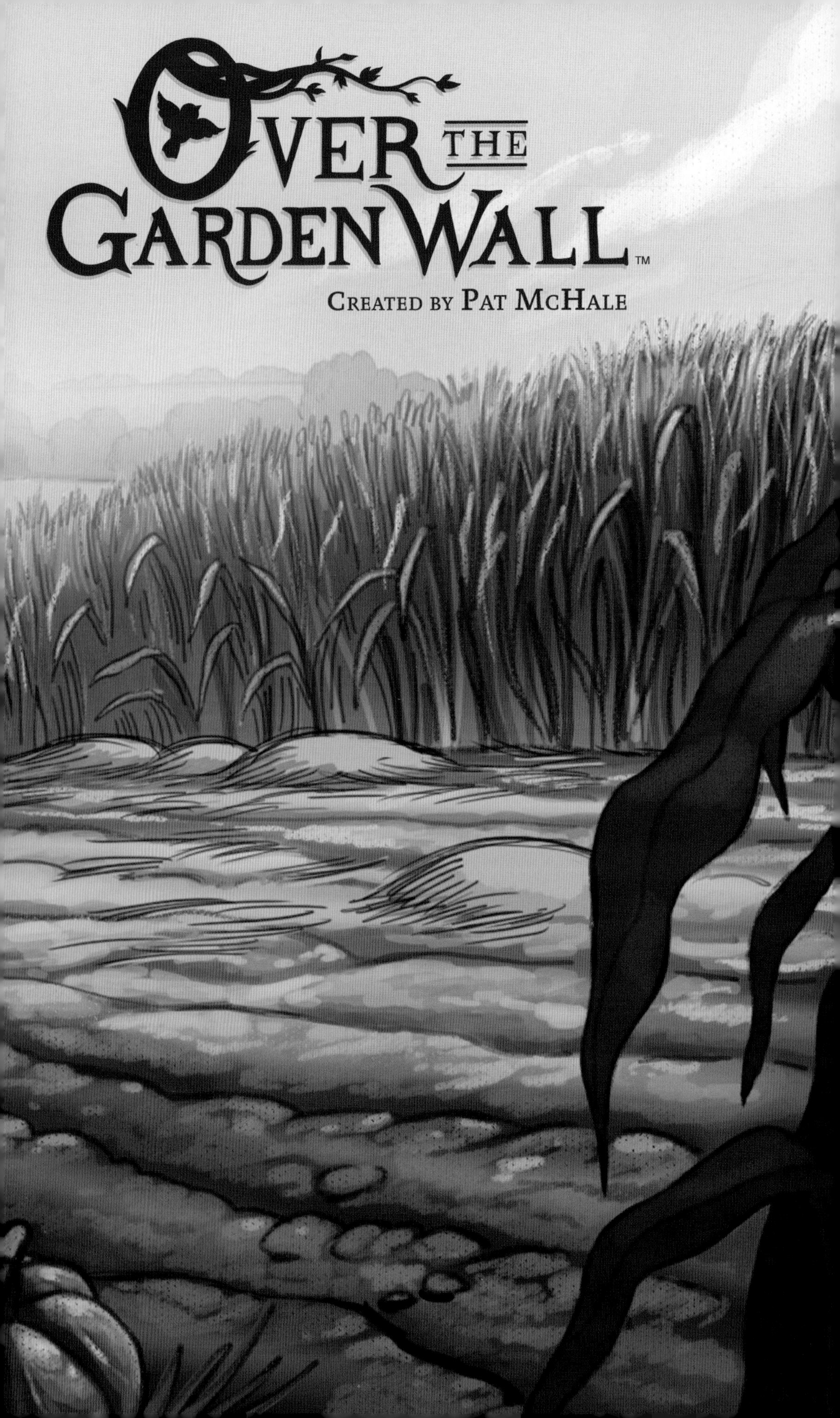
OVER THE GARDEN WALL™
CREATED BY PAT MCHALE

"Dreamland Melodies"
written and illustrated by Jim Campbell
with Danielle Burgos

"Homeland"
written by Amalia Levari
illustrated by Cara McGee
colors by Whitney Cogar
letters by Warren Montgomery

cover by Jim Campbell

designer Kelsey Dieterich
Associate Editor Whitney Leopard
Editor Shannon Watters

With Special Thanks to Marisa Marionakis,
Jim Valeri, Jeff Parker, Laurie Halal-Ono,
Nicole Rivera, Conrad Montgomery,
Meghan Bradley, Curtis Lelash and the
wonderful folks at Cartoon Network.

DREAMLAND MELODIES

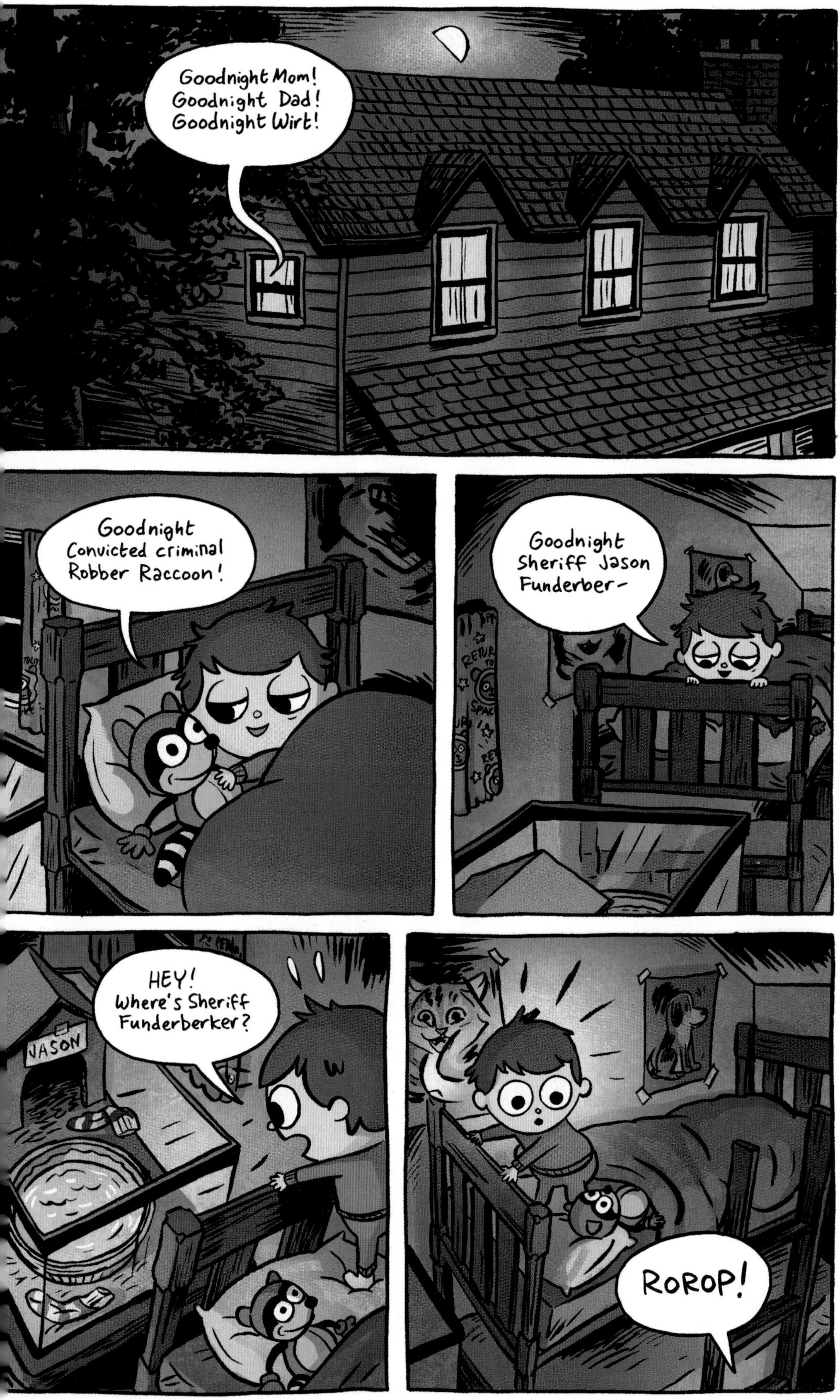
Goodnight Mom! Goodnight Dad! Goodnight Wirt!
Goodnight Convicted criminal Robber Raccoon!
Goodnight Sheriff Jason Funderber-
HEY! Where's Sheriff Funderberker?
JASON
ROROP!

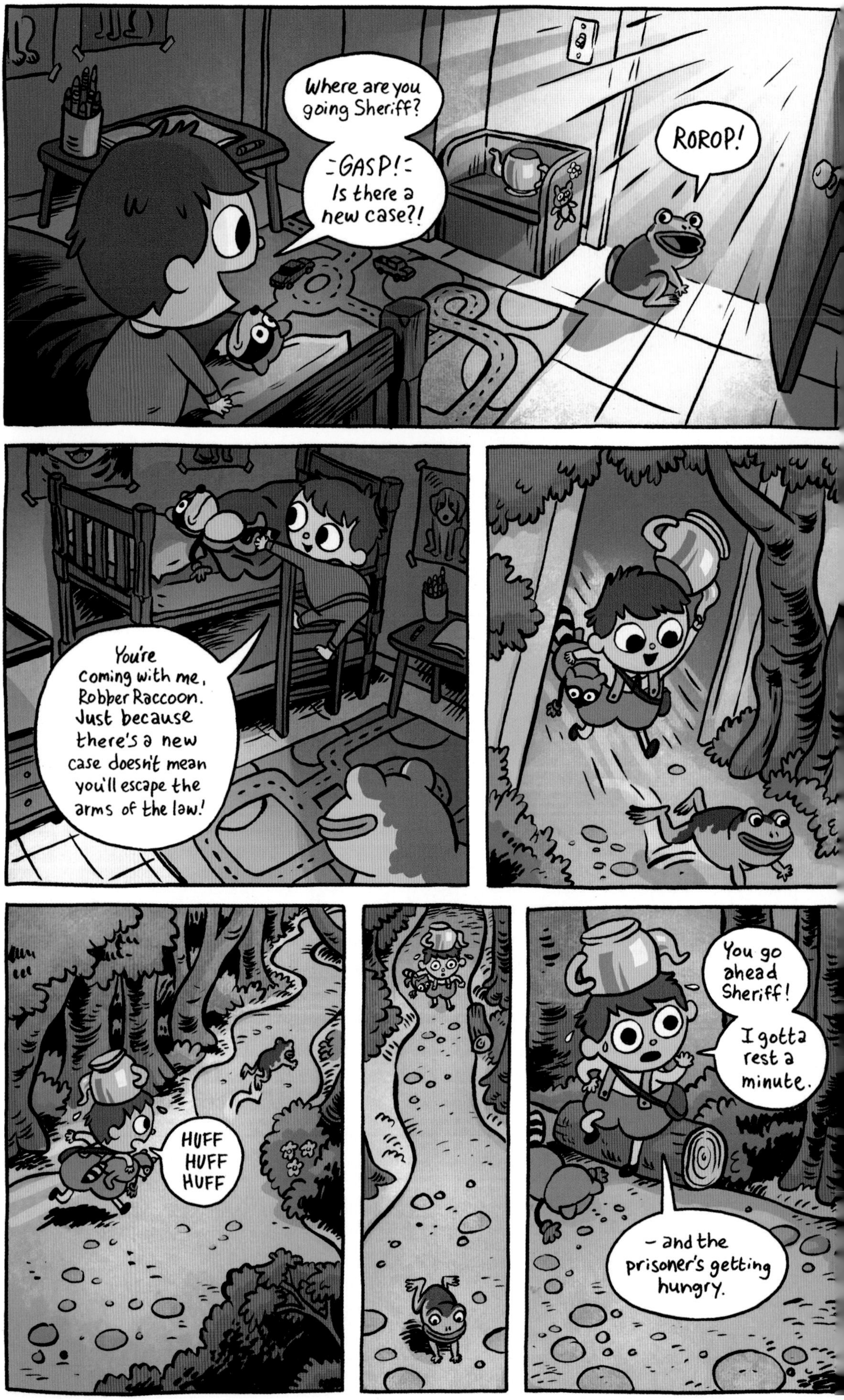
Where are you going Sheriff?
RoROP!
-GASP!- Is there a new case?!
You're coming with me, Robber Raccoon. Just because there's a new case doesn't mean you'll escape the arms of the law!
HUFF HUFF HUFF
You go ahead Sheriff!
I gotta rest a minute.
- and the prisoner's getting hungry.

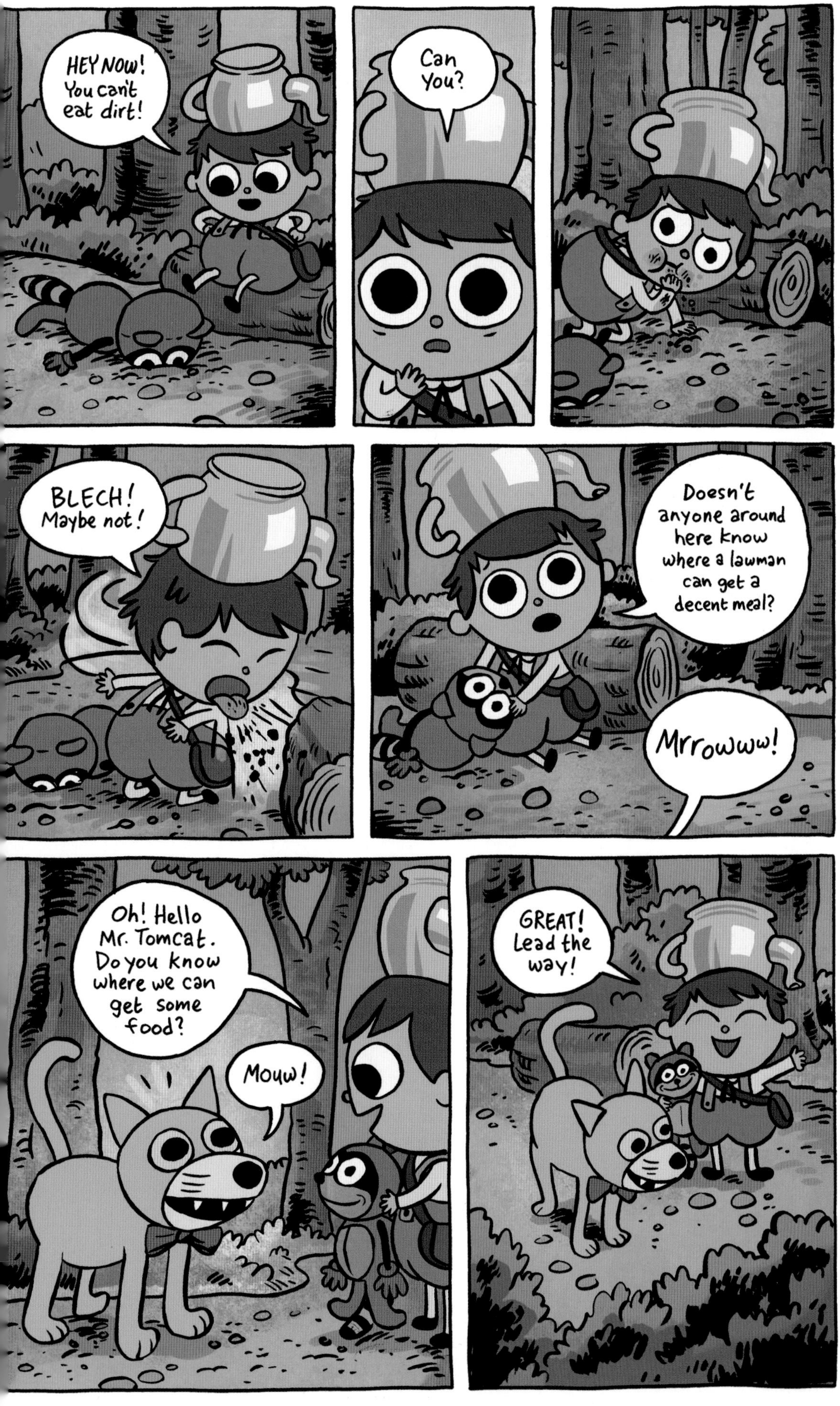

HEY NOW! You can't eat dirt!
Can You?
BLECH! Maybe not!
Doesn't anyone around here know where a lawman can get a decent meal?
Mrrowww!
Oh! Hello Mr. Tomcat. Do you know where we can get some food?
Mouw!
GREAT! Lead the way!

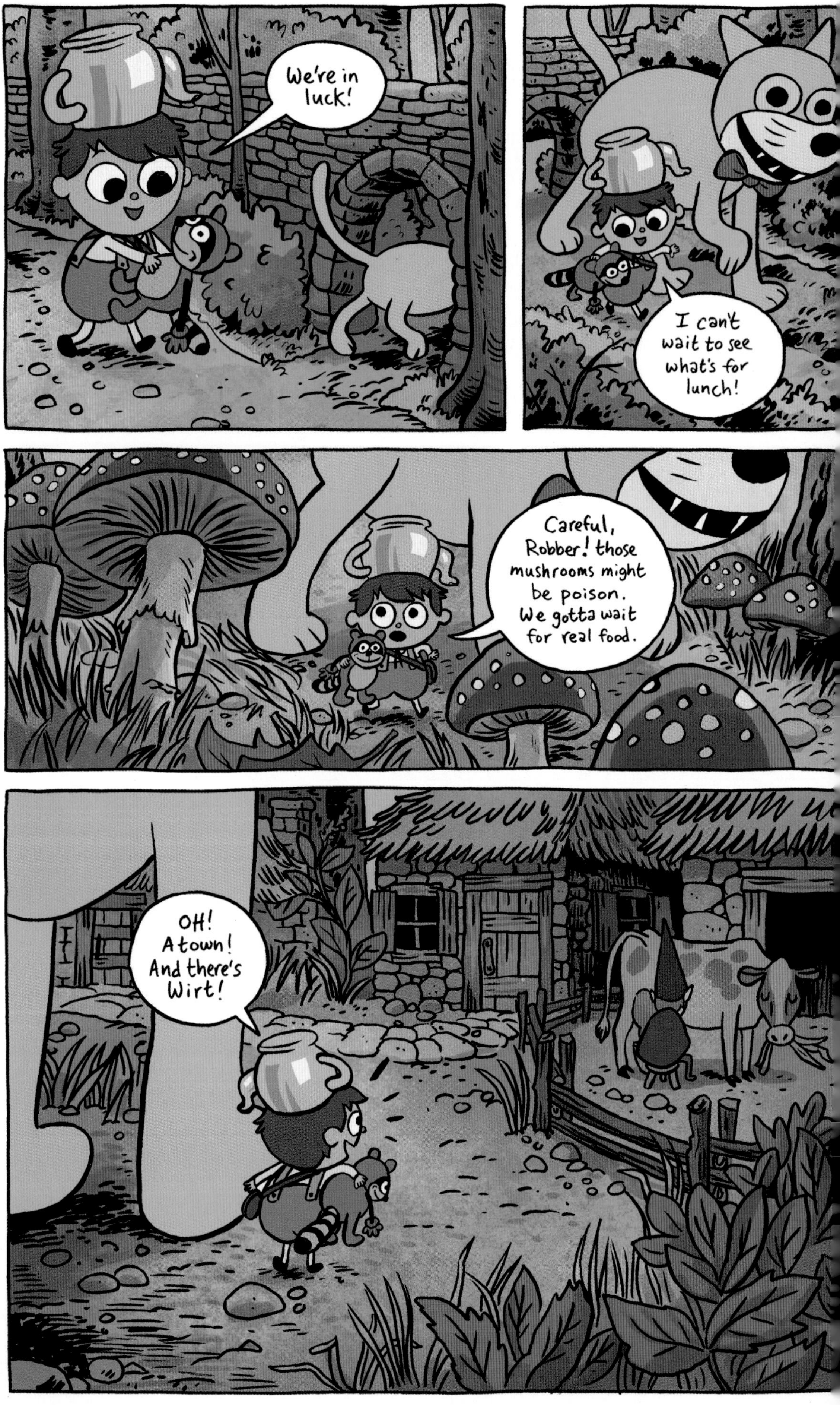
We're in luck!
I can't wait to see what's for lunch!
Careful, Robber! those mushrooms might be poison. We gotta wait for real food.
OH! A town! And there's Wirt!

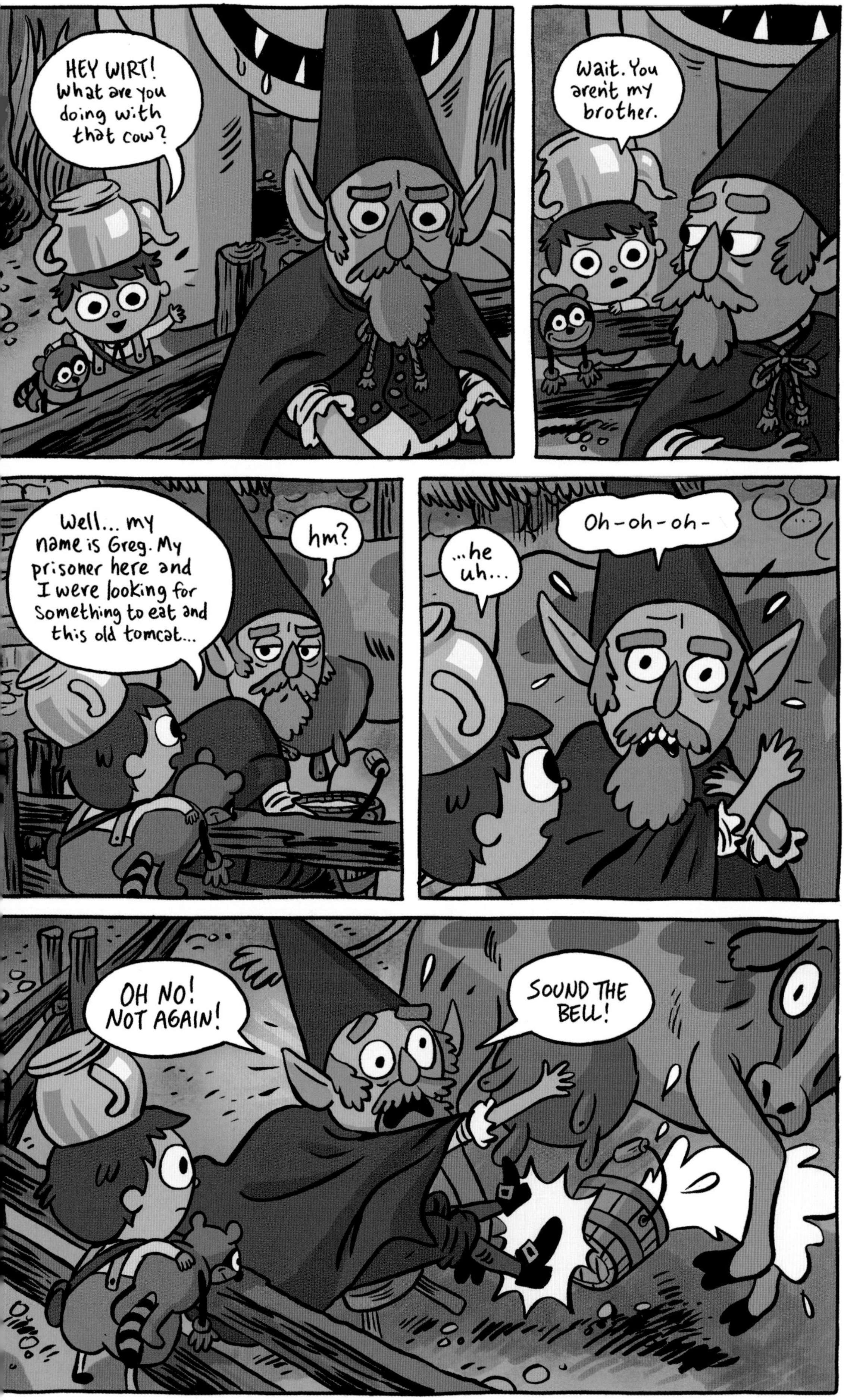
HEY WIRT! What are you doing with that cow?
Wait. You aren't my brother.
Well... my name is Greg. My prisoner here and I were looking for something to eat and this old tomcat...
hm?
...he uh...
Oh-oh-oh-
OH NO! NOT AGAIN!
SOUND THE BELL!

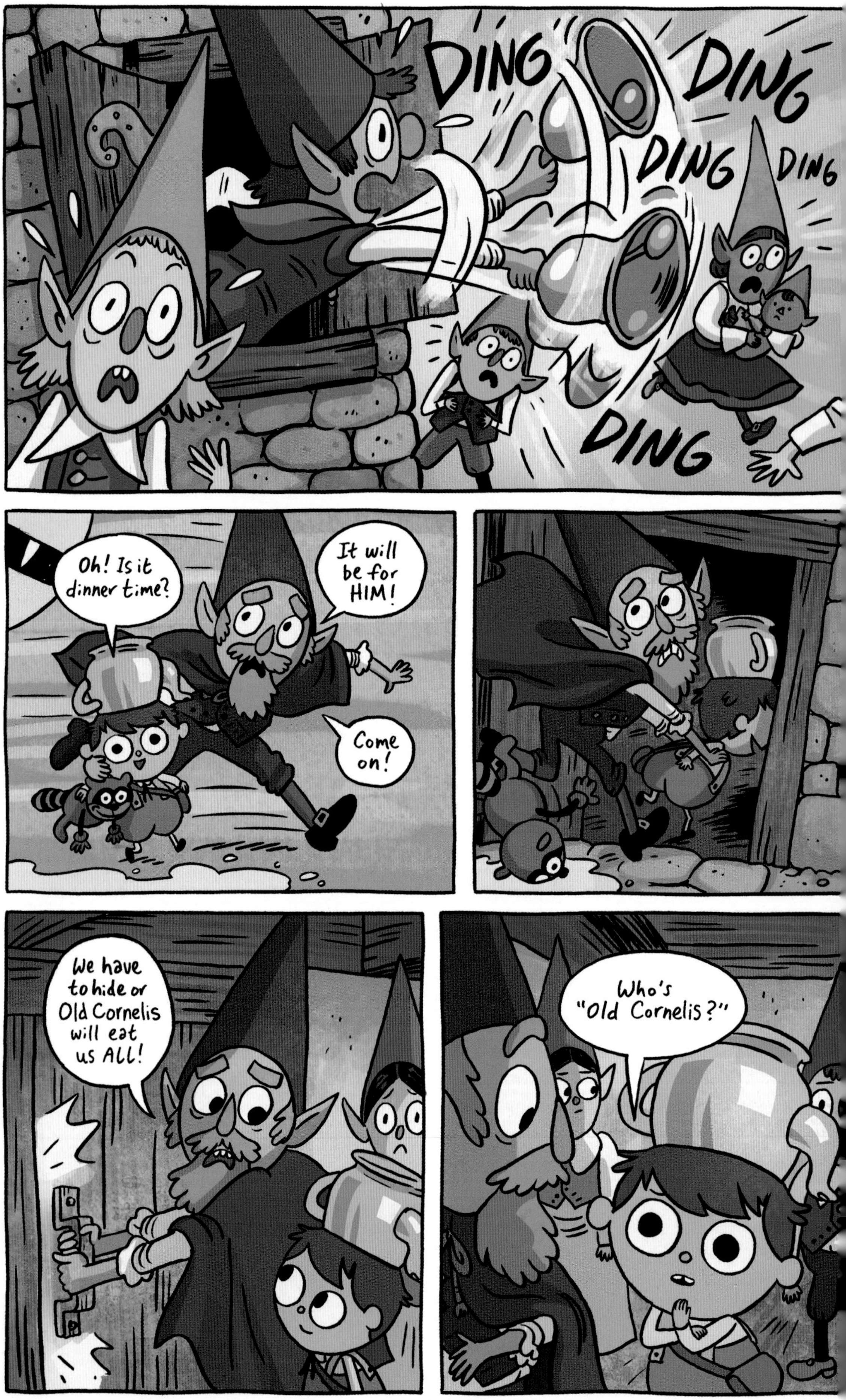
DING
DING
DING
DING
DING
Oh! Is it dinner time?
It will be for HIM!
Come on!
We have to hide or Old Cornelis will eat us ALL!
Who's "Old Cornelis?"

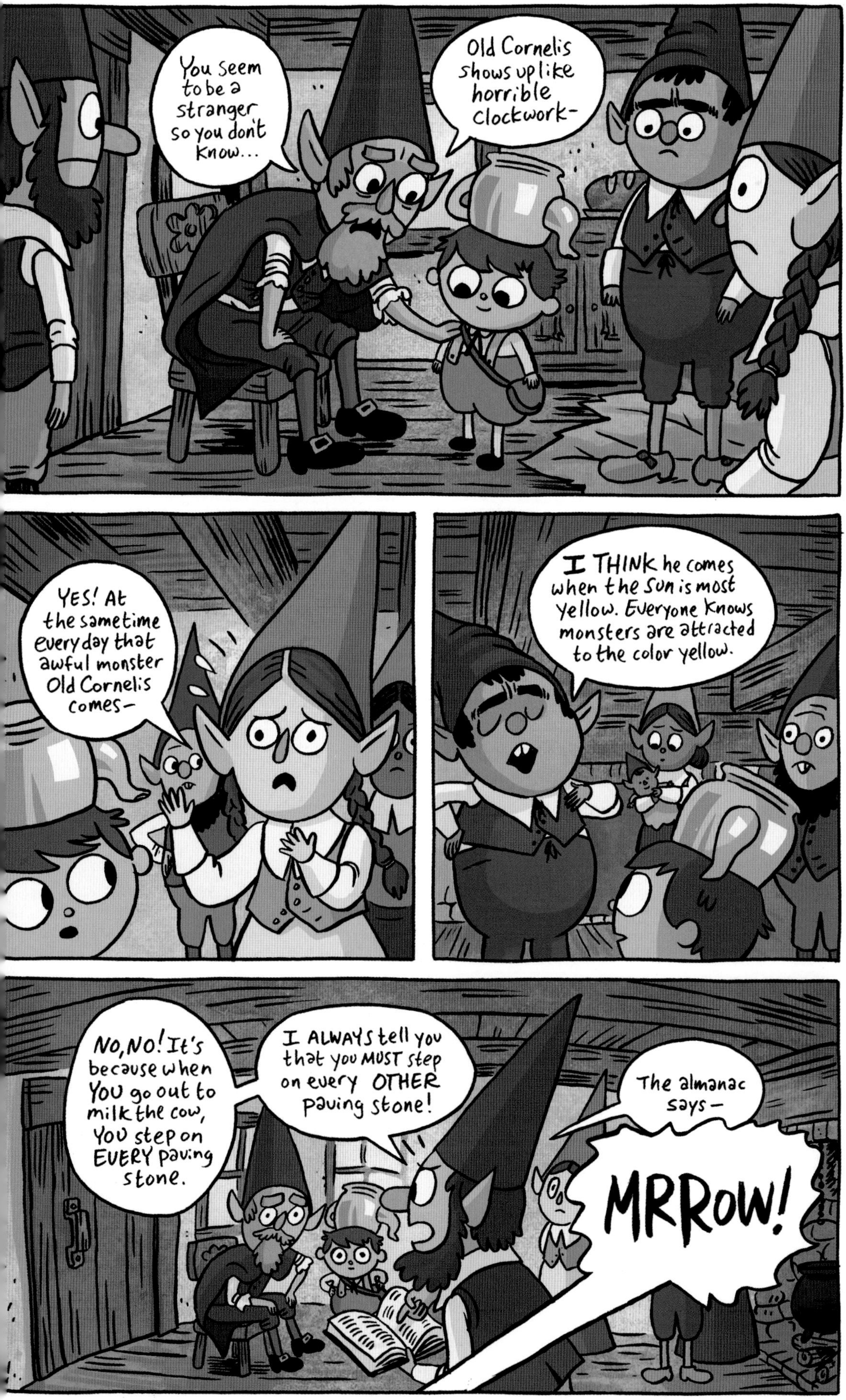

You seem to be a stranger so you don't know...
Old Cornelis shows up like horrible Clockwork-
YES! At the same time every day that awful monster Old Cornelis comes-
I THINK he comes when the Sun is most yellow. Everyone Knows monsters are attracted to the color yellow.
NO, NO! It's because when YOU go out to milk the cow, YOU step on EVERY paving stone.
I ALWAYS tell you that you MUST step on every OTHER paving stone!
The almanac says-
MRROW!

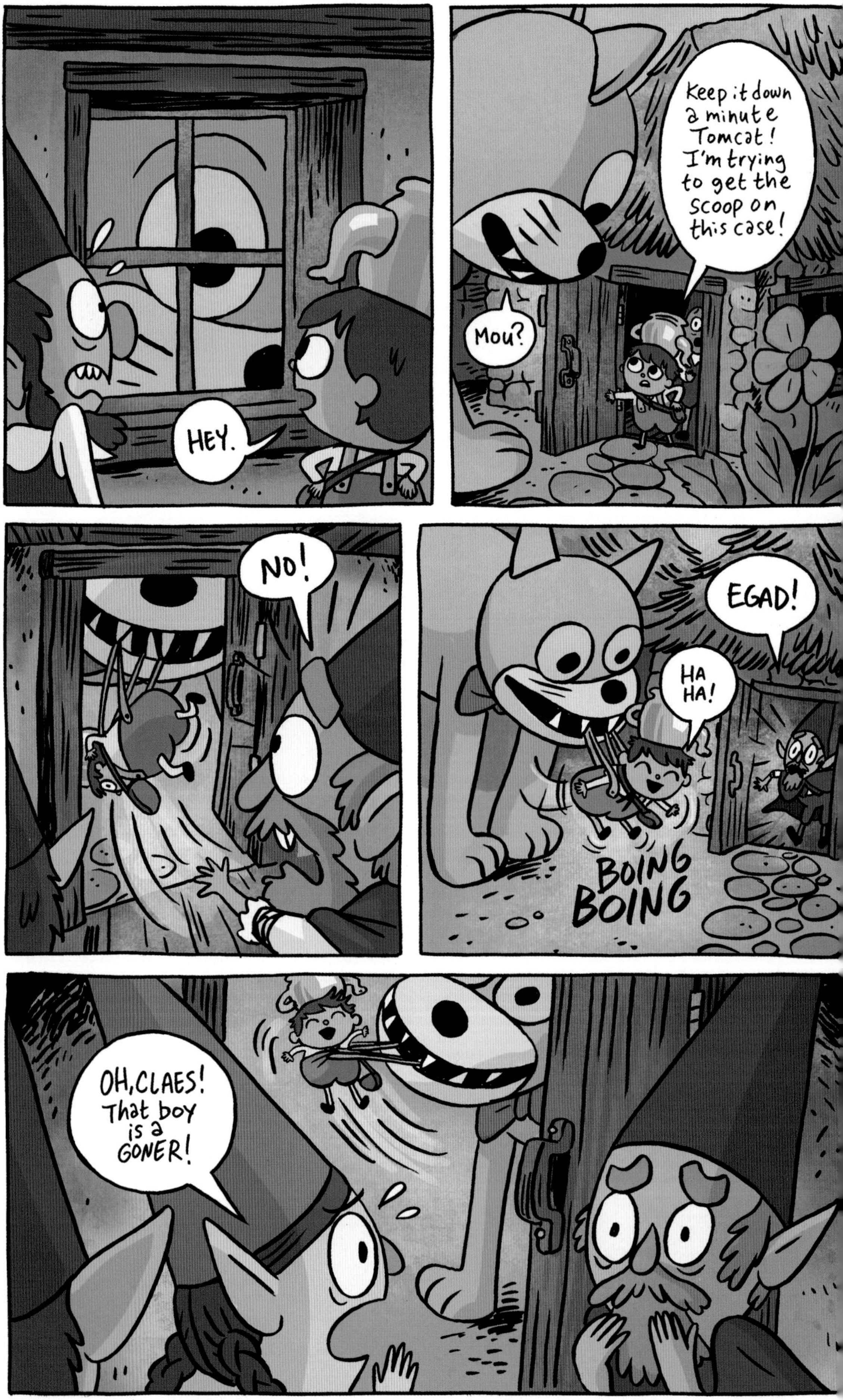
HEY.
Keep it down a minute Tomcat! I'm trying to get the scoop on this case!
Mou?
NO!
EGAD!
HA HA!
BOING BOING
OH, CLAES! That boy is a GONER!

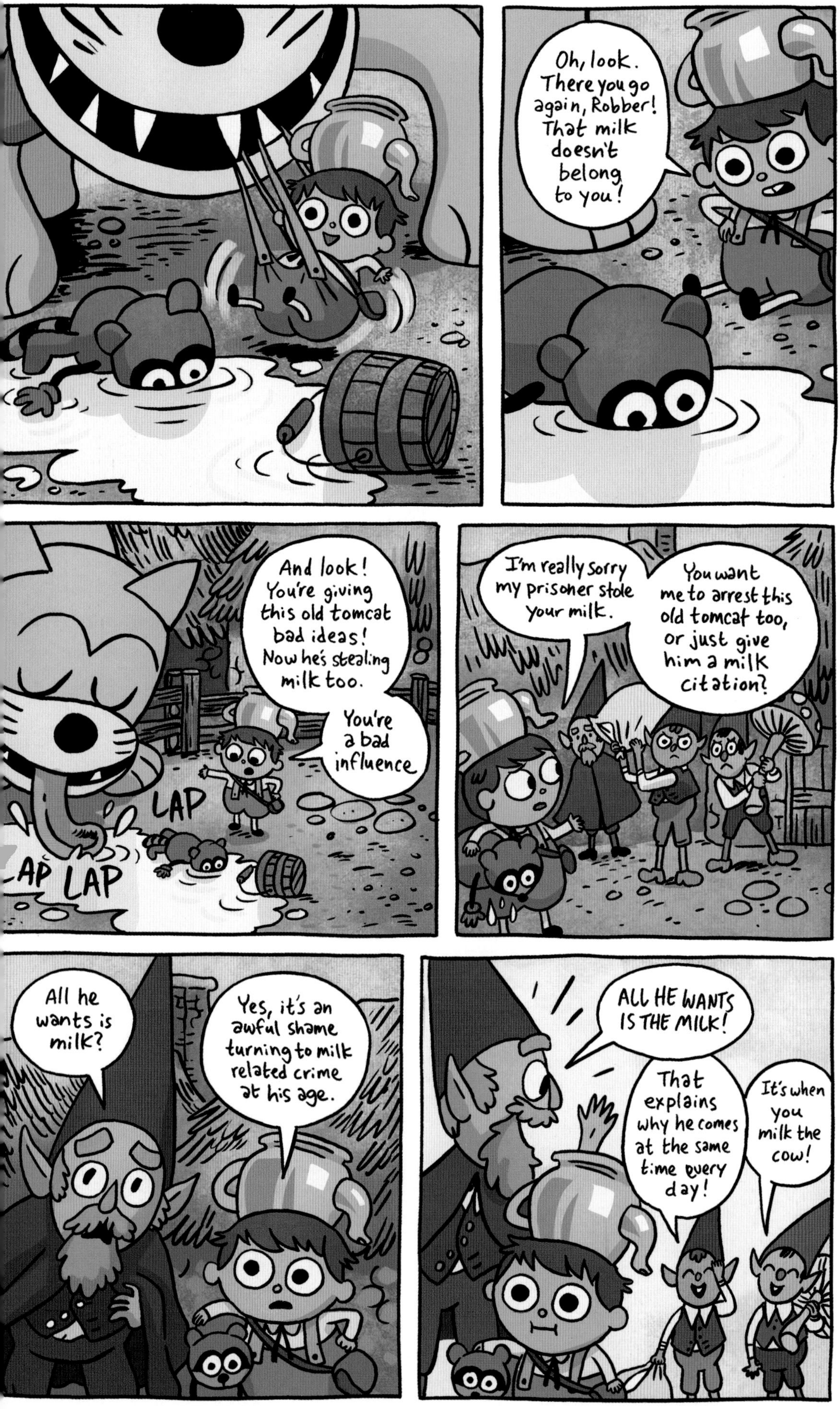
Oh, look. There you go again, Robber! That milk doesn't belong to you!
And look! You're giving this old tomcat bad ideas! Now he's stealing milk too.
You're a bad influence
LAP
LAP LAP
I'm really sorry my prisoner stole your milk.
You want me to arrest this old tomcat too, or just give him a milk citation?
All he wants is milk?
Yes, it's an awful shame turning to milk related crime at his age.
ALL HE WANTS IS THE MILK!
That explains why he comes at the same time every day!
It's when you milk the cow!

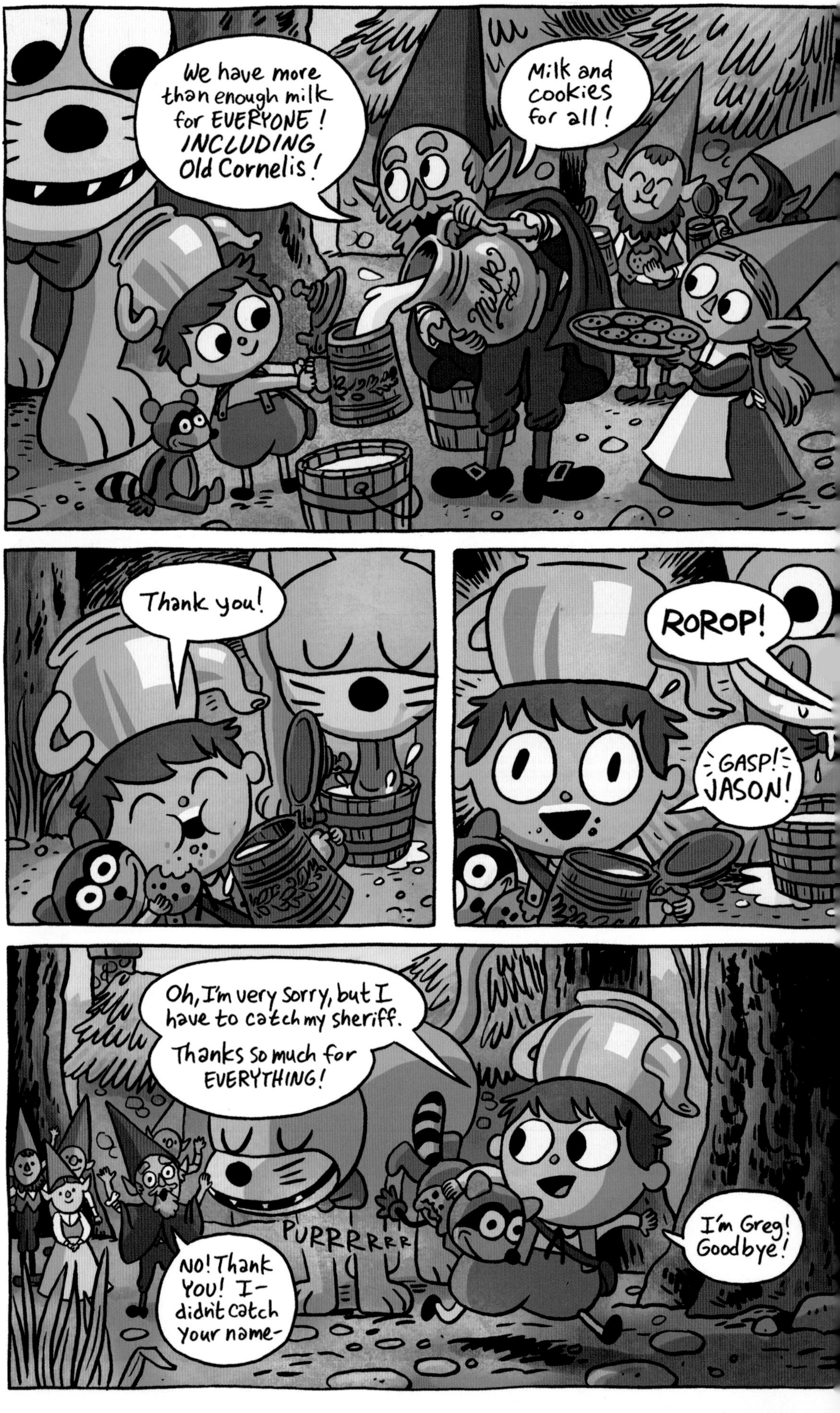
We have more than enough milk for EVERYONE! INCLUDING Old Cornelis!
Milk and cookies for all!
Thank you!
ROROP!
GASP! JASON!
Oh, I'm very sorry, but I have to catch my sheriff.
Thanks so much for EVERYTHING!
PURRRRRRR
No! Thank You! I- didn't catch Your name-
I'm Greg! Goodbye!

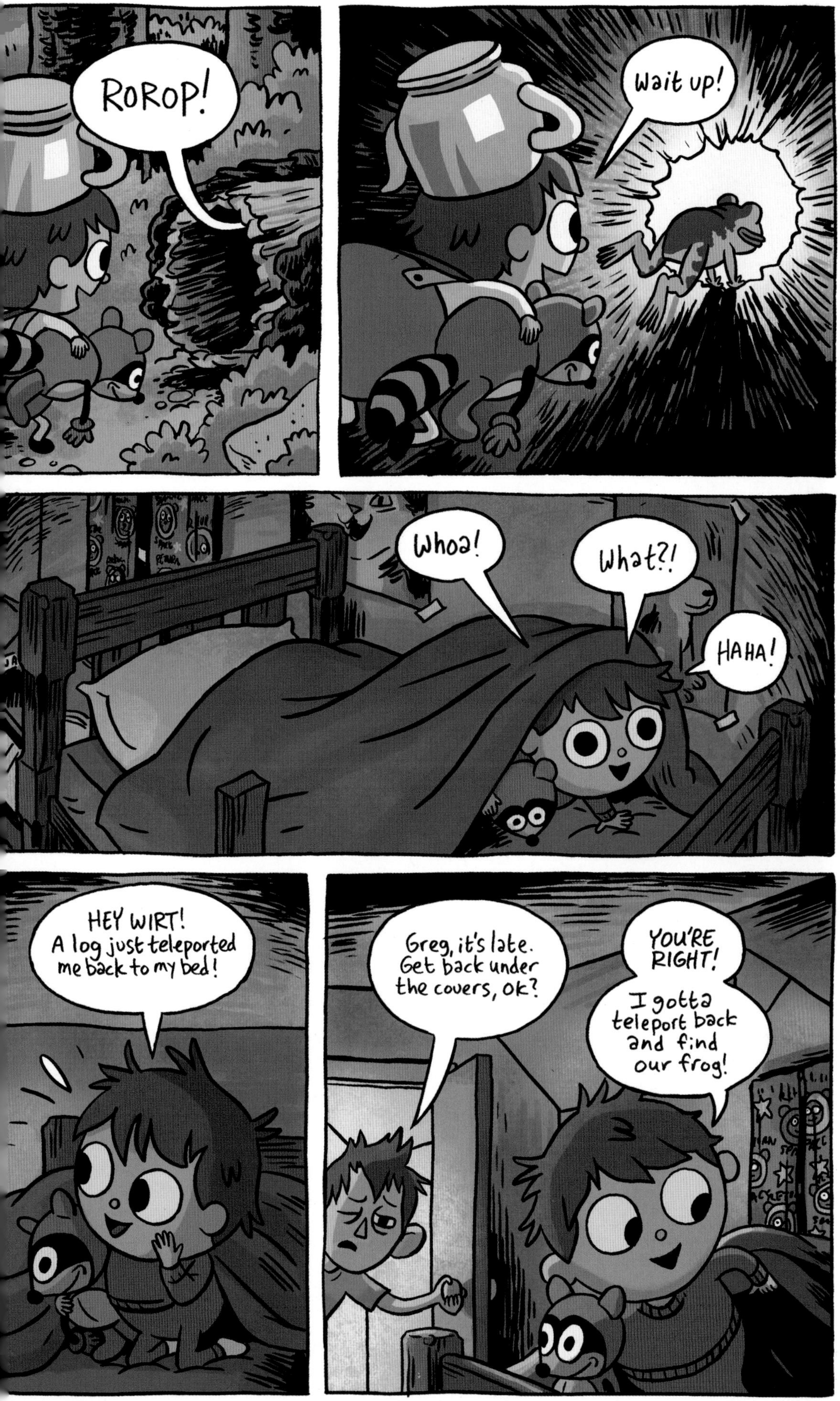

ROROP!
Wait up!
Whoa!
What?!
HAHA!
HEY WIRT! A log just teleported me back to my bed!
Greg, it's late. Get back under the covers, ok?
YOU'RE RIGHT!
I gotta teleport back and find our frog!

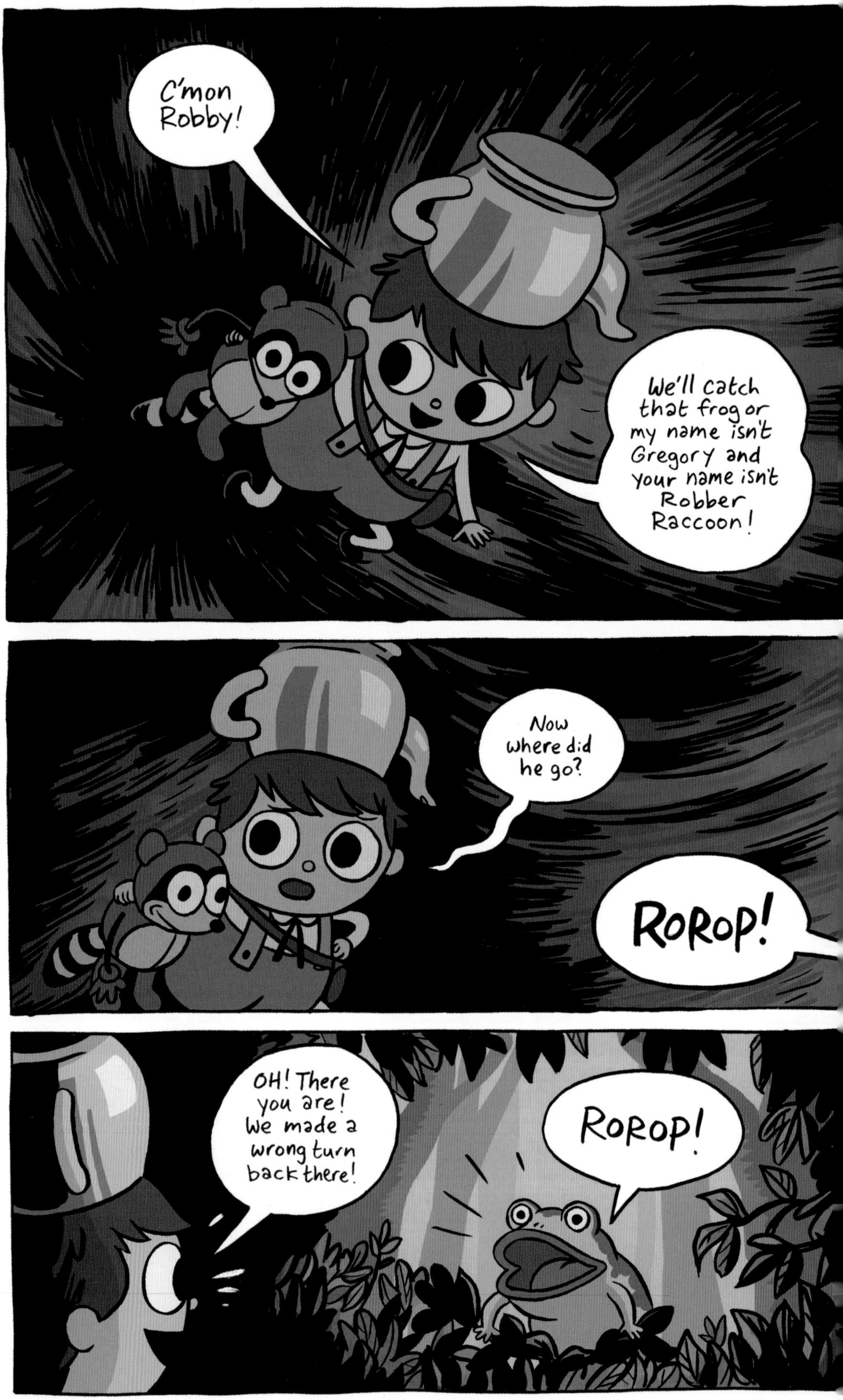
C'mon Robby!
We'll catch that frog or my name isn't Gregory and your name isn't Robber Raccoon!
Now where did he go?
ROROP!
OH! There you are! We made a wrong turn back there!
ROROP!

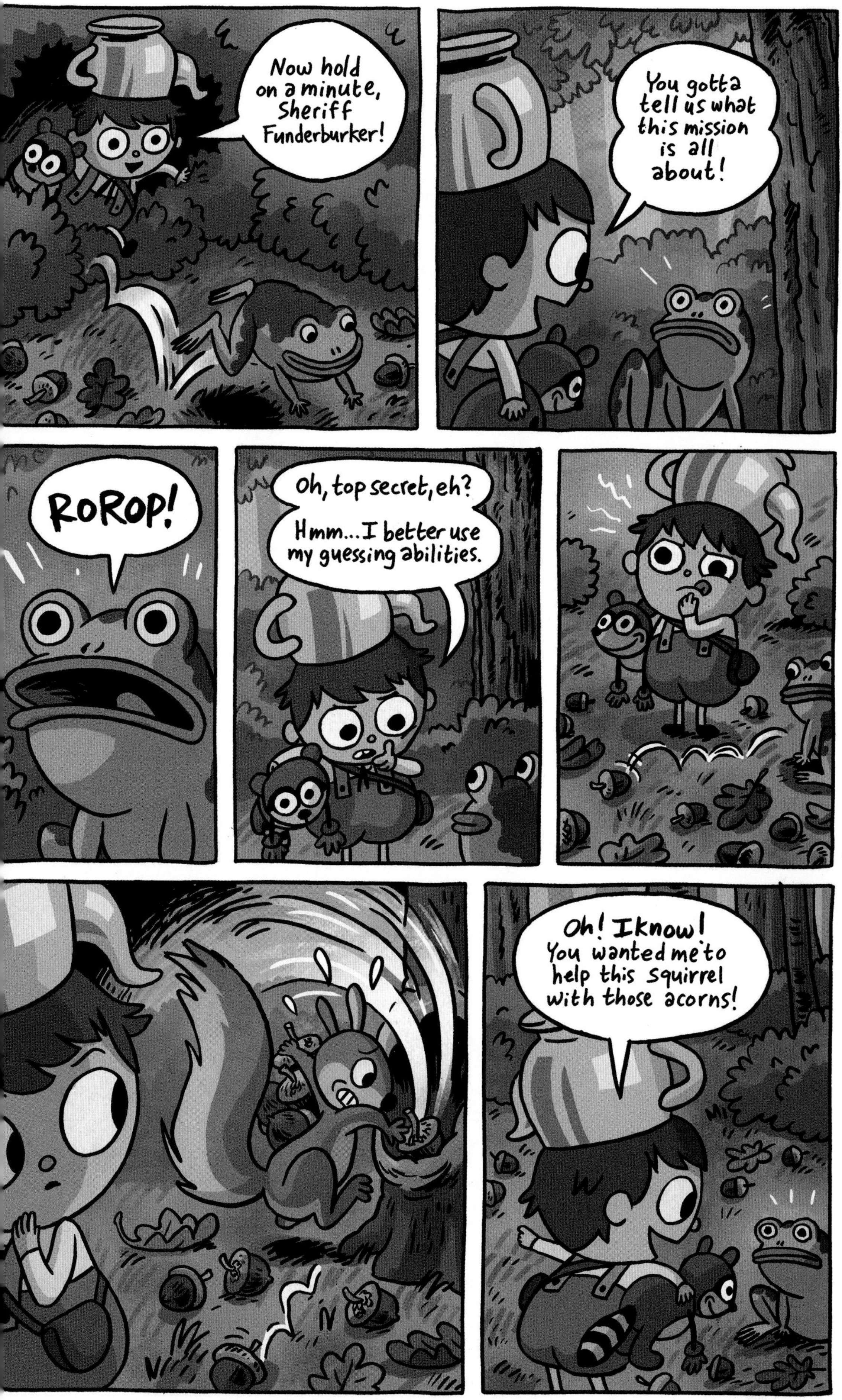
Now hold on a minute, Sheriff Funderburker!
You gotta tell us what this mission is all about!
ROROP!
Oh, top secret, eh?
Hmm... I better use my guessing abilities.
Oh! I know! You wanted me to help this squirrel with those acorns!

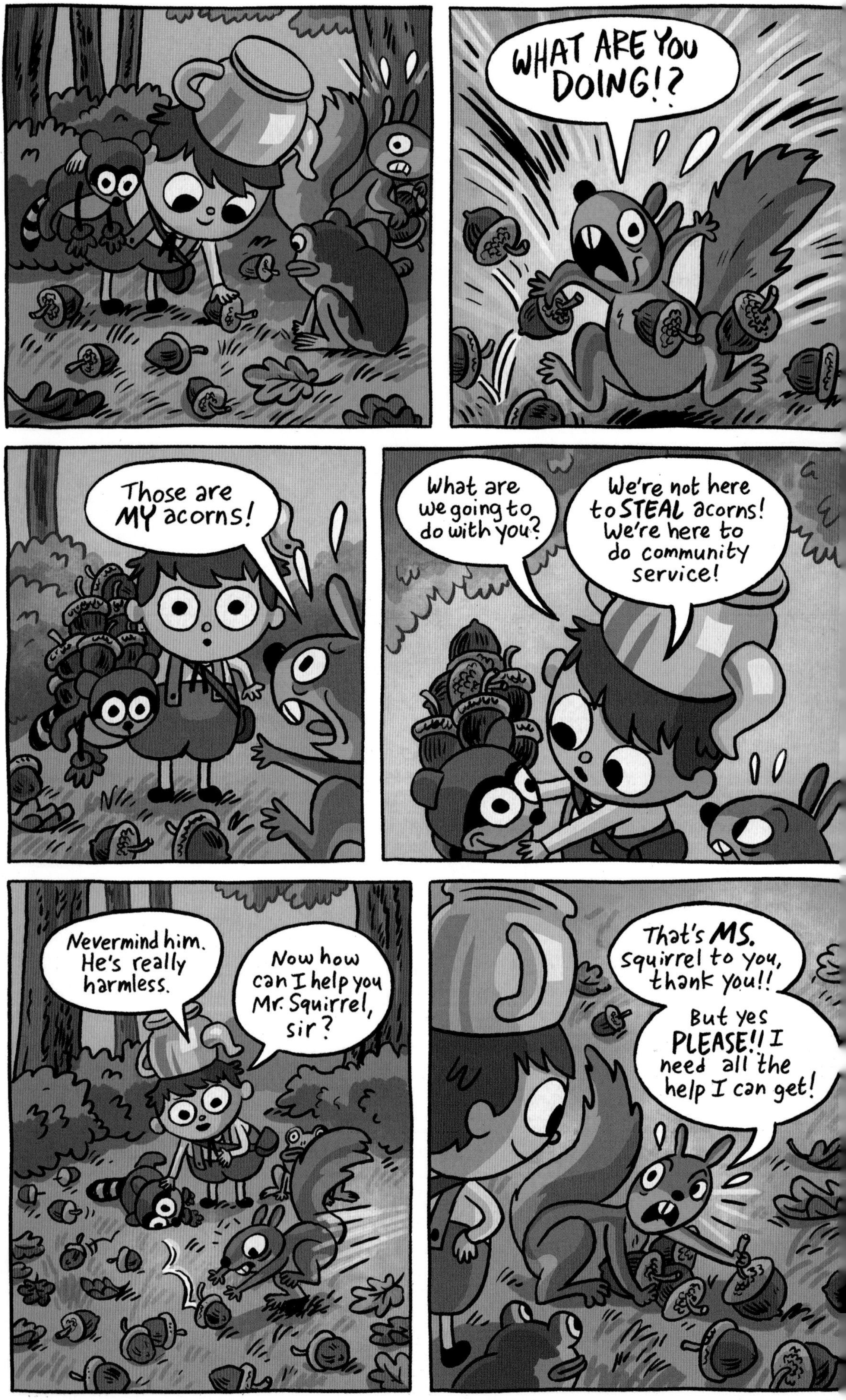
WHAT ARE YOU DOING!?
Those are MY acorns!
What are we going to do with you?
We're not here to STEAL acorns! We're here to do community service!
Nevermind him. He's really harmless.
Now how can I help you Mr. Squirrel, sir?
That's MS. squirrel to you, thank you!!
But yes PLEASE!! I need all the help I can get!

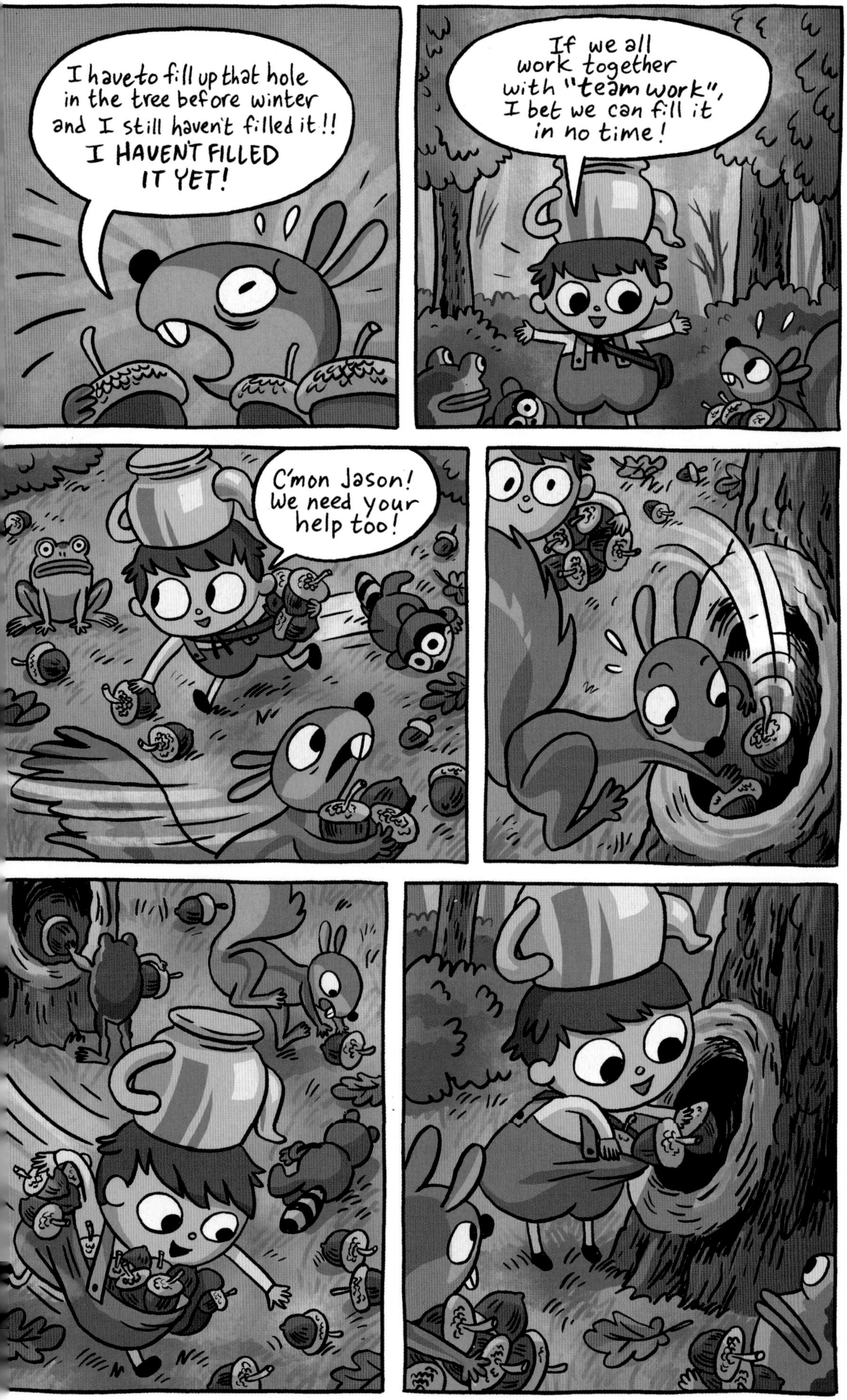
I have to fill up that hole in the tree before winter and I still haven't filled it!!
I HAVEN'T FILLED IT YET!
If we all work together with "team work", I bet we can fill it in no time!
C'mon Jason! We need your help too!

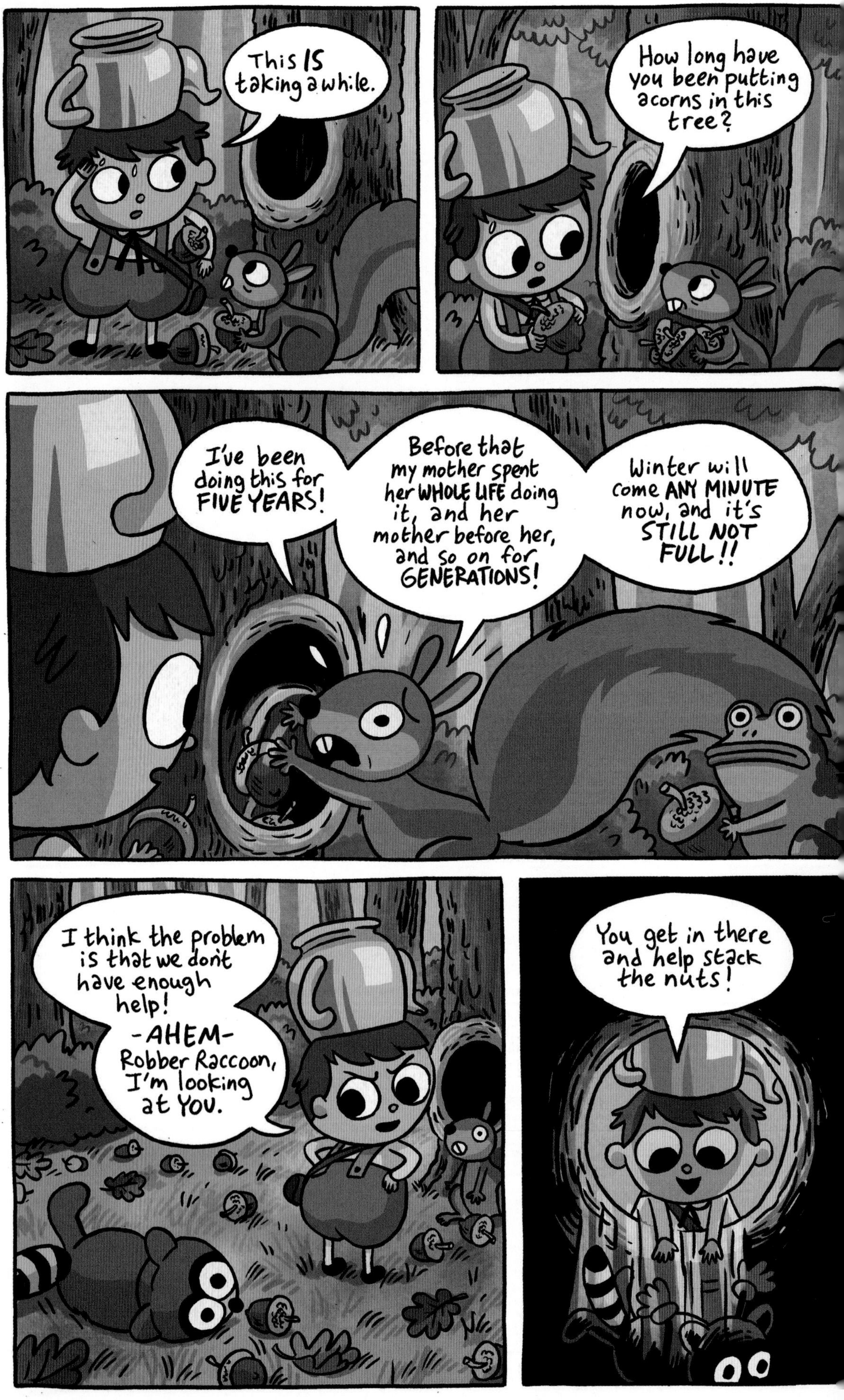
This IS taking a while.
How long have you been putting acorns in this tree?
I've been doing this for FIVE YEARS!
Before that my mother spent her WHOLE LIFE doing it, and her mother before her, and so on for GENERATIONS!
Winter will come ANY MINUTE now, and it's STILL NOT FULL!!
I think the problem is that we don't have enough help!
-AHEM-
Robber Raccoon, I'm looking at YOU.
You get in there and help stack the nuts!

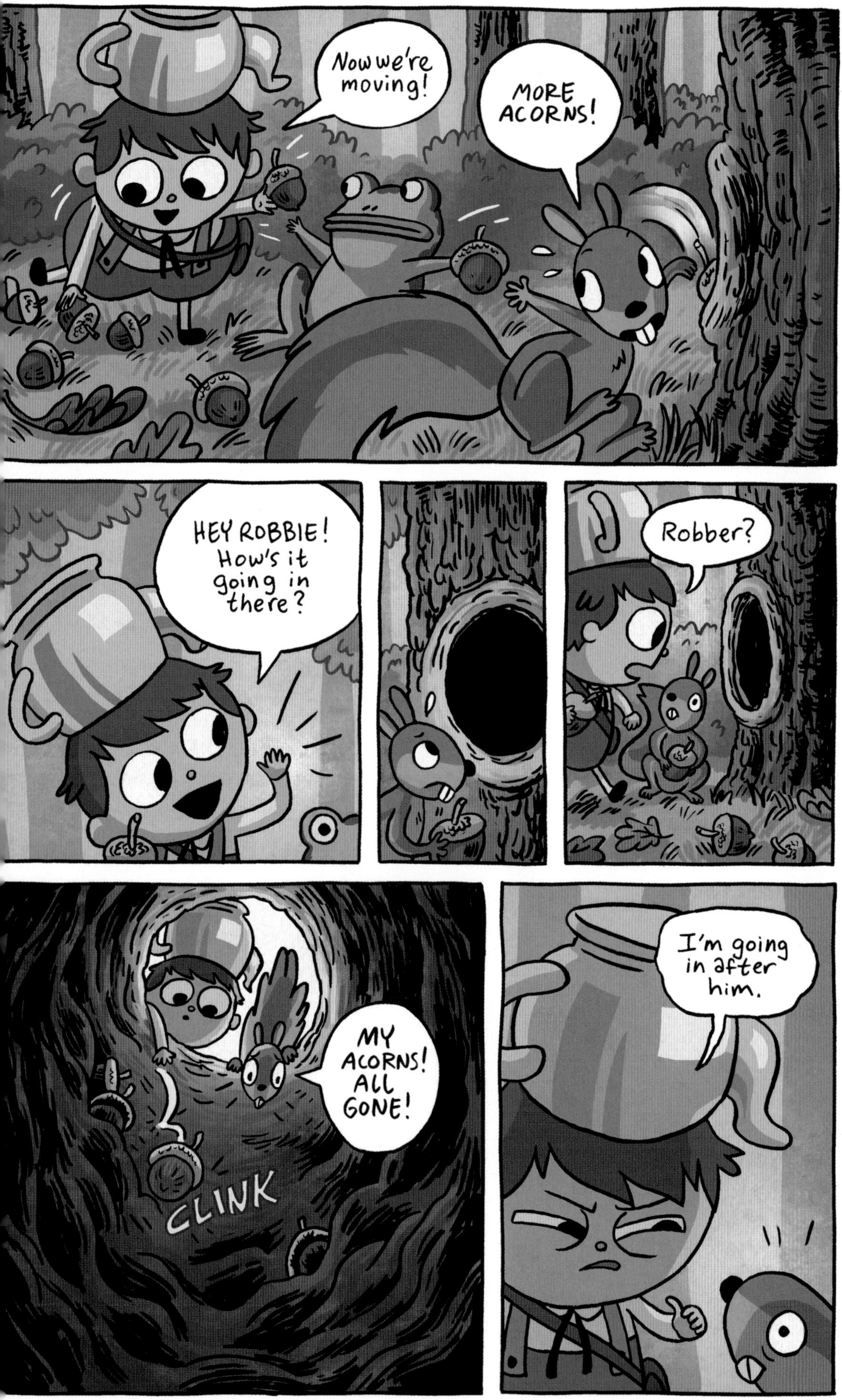
Now we're moving!
MORE ACORNS!
HEY ROBBIE! How's it going in there?
Robber?
MY ACORNS! ALL GONE!
CLINK
I'm going in after him.

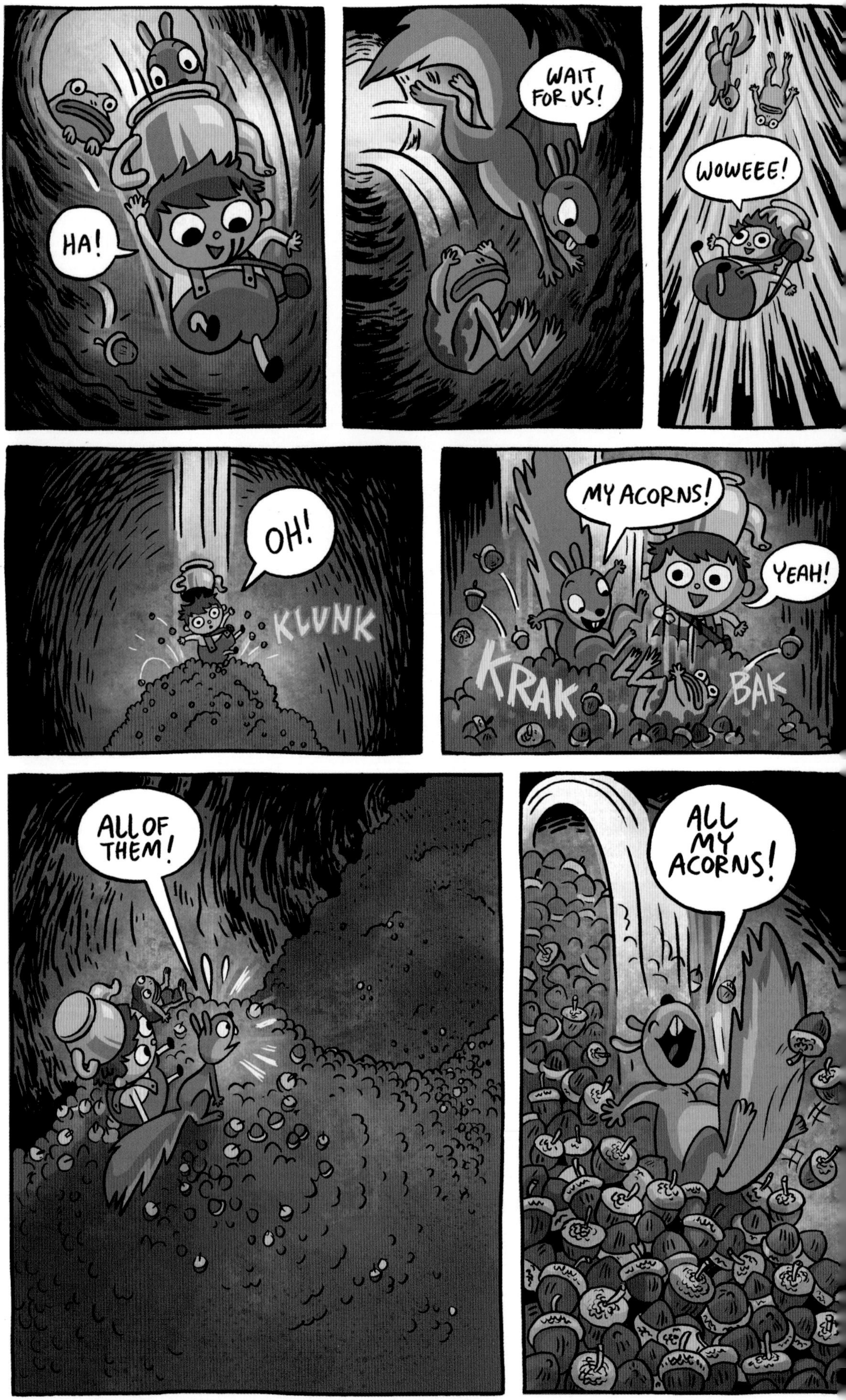
HA!
WAIT FOR US!
WOWEEE!
OH!
KLUNK
MY ACORNS!
YEAH!
KRAK
BAK
ALL OF THEM!
ALL MY ACORNS!

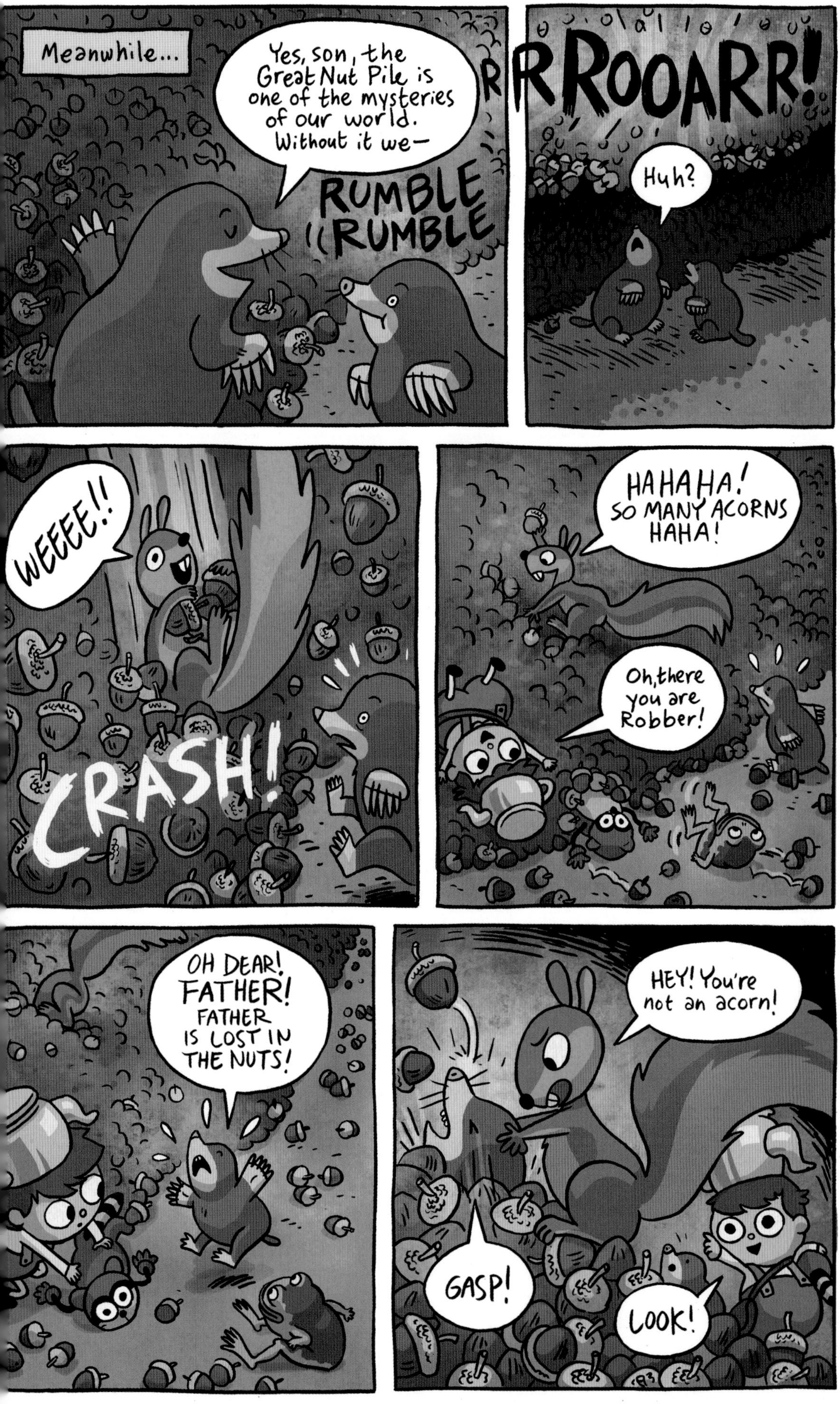
Meanwhile...
Yes, son, the Great Nut Pile is one of the mysteries of our world. Without it we—
RUMBLE RUMBLE
RRROOARR!
Huh?
WEEEE!!
CRASH!
HAHAHA! SO MANY ACORNS HAHA!
Oh, there you are Robber!
OH DEAR! FATHER! FATHER IS LOST IN THE NUTS!
HEY! You're not an acorn!
GASP!
LOOK!

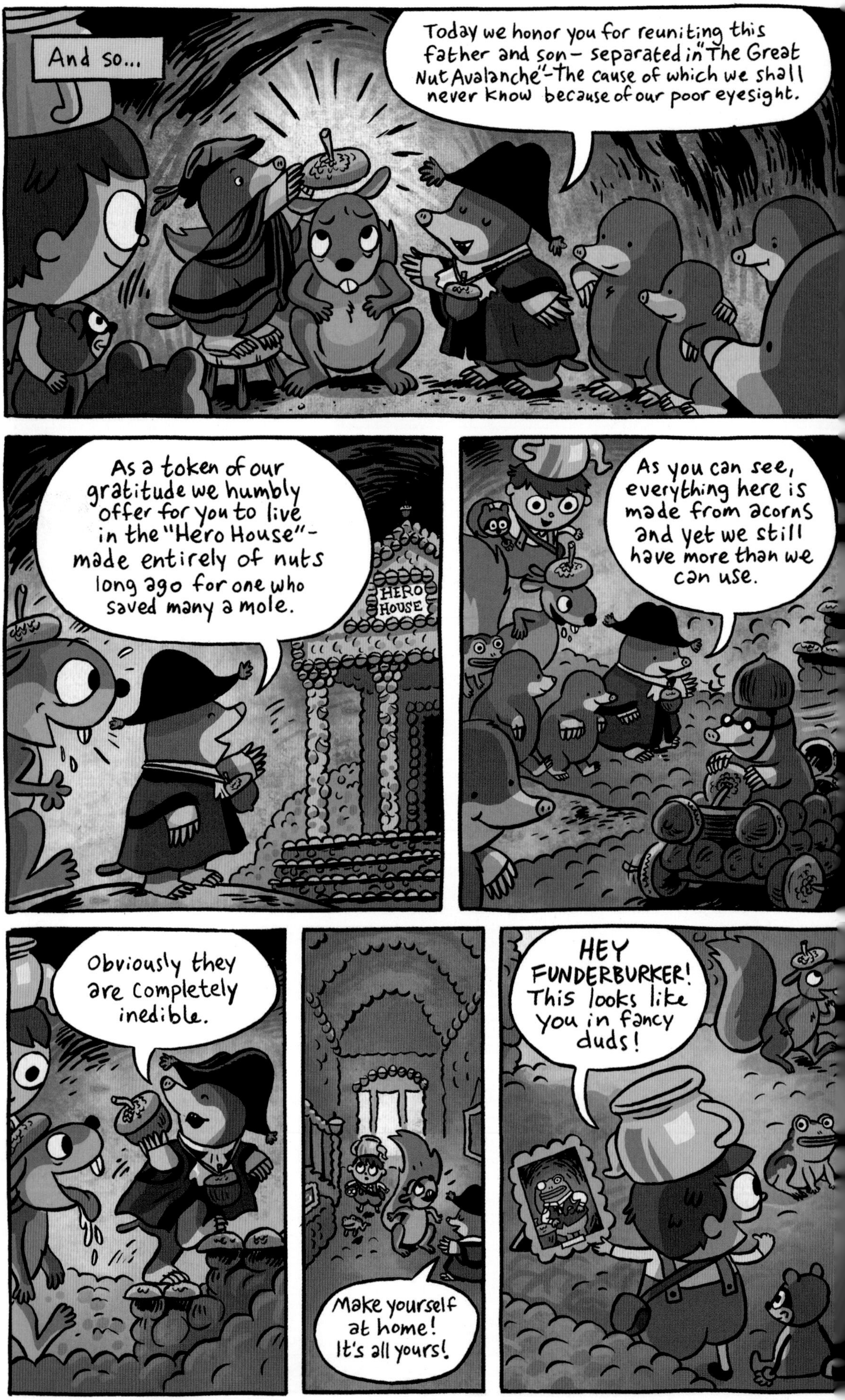
And so...
Today we honor you for reuniting this father and son – separated in "The Great Nut Avalanche" – the cause of which we shall never know because of our poor eyesight.
As a token of our gratitude we humbly offer for you to live in the "Hero House" – made entirely of nuts long ago for one who saved many a mole.
HERO HOUSE
As you can see, everything here is made from acorns and yet we still have more than we can use.
Obviously they are completely inedible.
Make yourself at home! It's all yours!
HEY FUNDERBURKER! This looks like you in fancy duds!

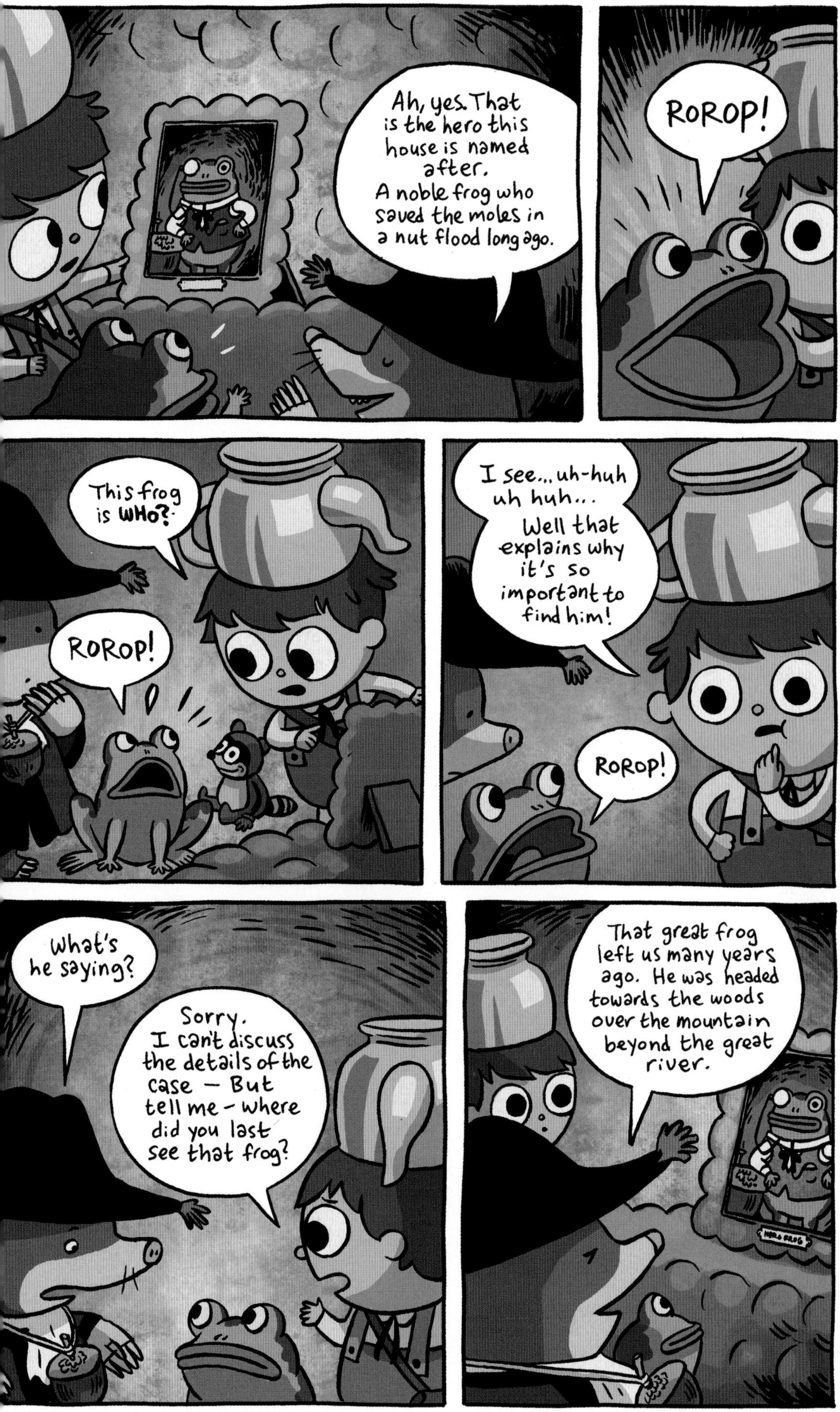
Ah, yes. That is the hero this house is named after. A noble frog who saved the moles in a nut flood long ago.
ROROP!
This frog is WHO?
ROROP!
I see... uh-huh uh huh... Well that explains why it's so important to find him!
ROROP!
What's he saying?
Sorry. I can't discuss the details of the case — But tell me — where did you last see that frog?
That great frog left us many years ago. He was headed towards the woods over the mountain beyond the great river.

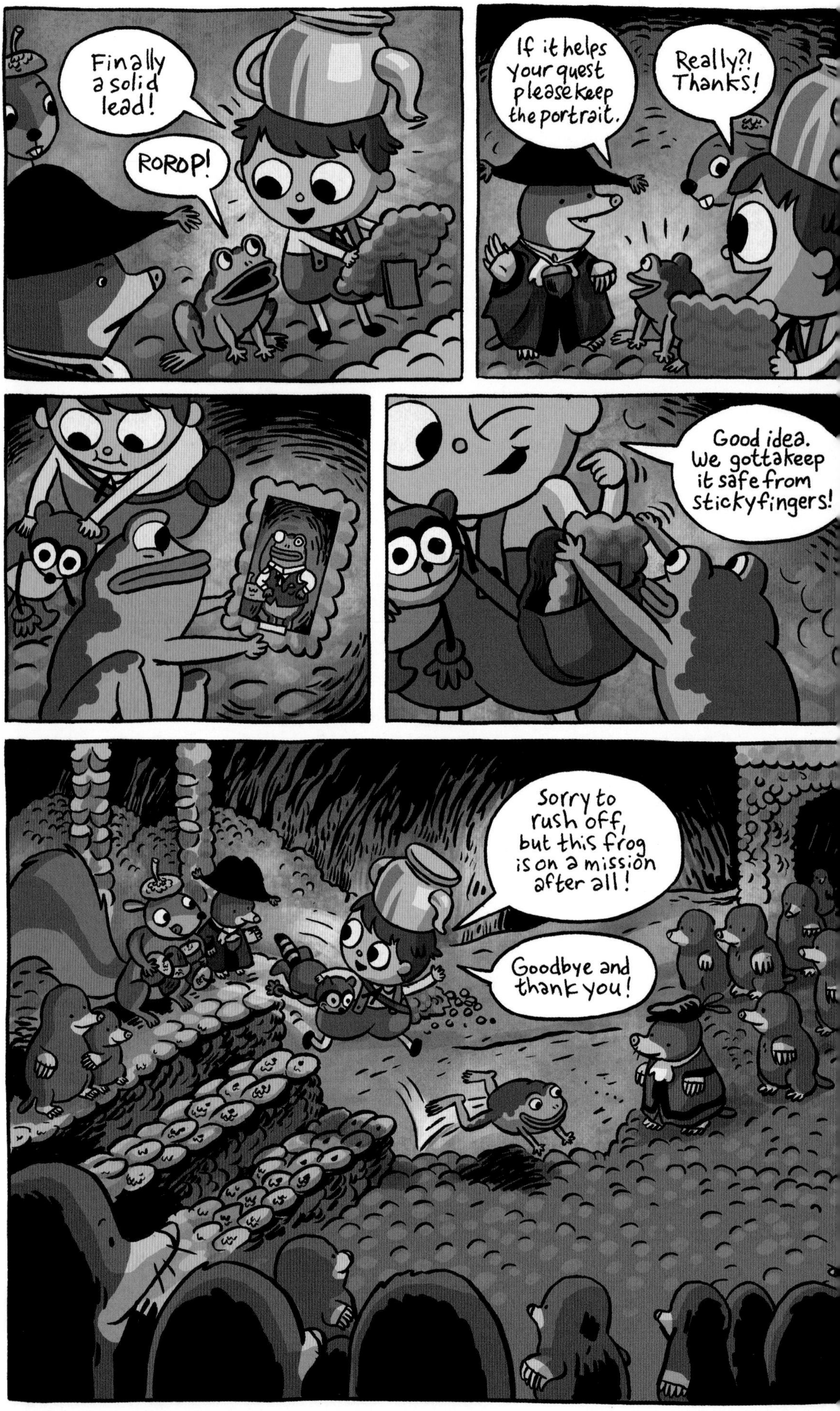
Finally a solid lead!
ROROP!
If it helps your quest please keep the portrait.
Really?! Thanks!
Good idea. We gotta keep it safe from sticky fingers!
Sorry to rush off, but this frog is on a mission after all!
Goodbye and thank you!

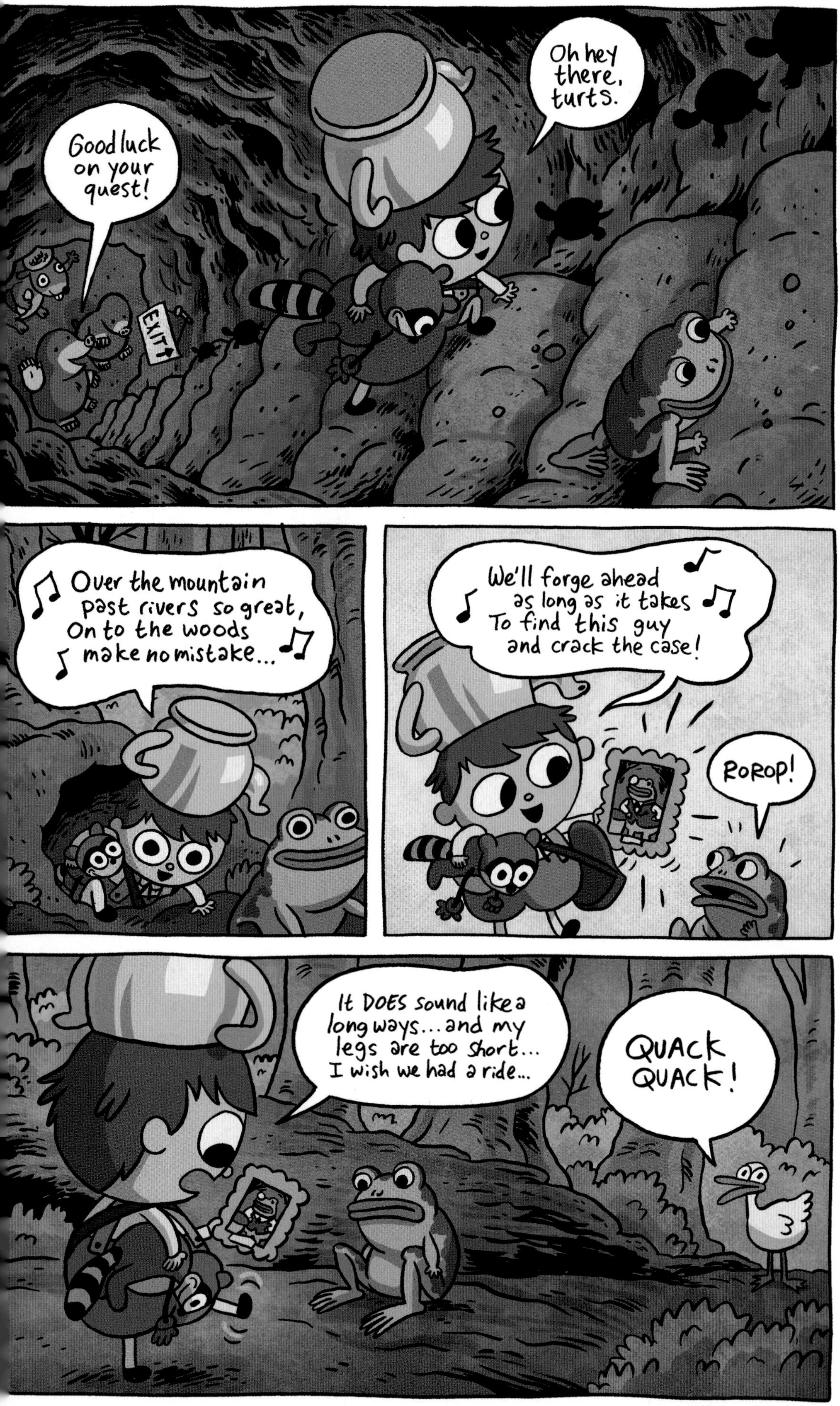
Good luck on your quest!
EXIT
Oh hey there, turts.
Over the mountain past rivers so great, On to the woods make no mistake...
We'll forge ahead as long as it takes To find this guy and crack the case!
ROROP!
It DOES sound like a long ways... and my legs are too short... I wish we had a ride...
QUACK QUACK!

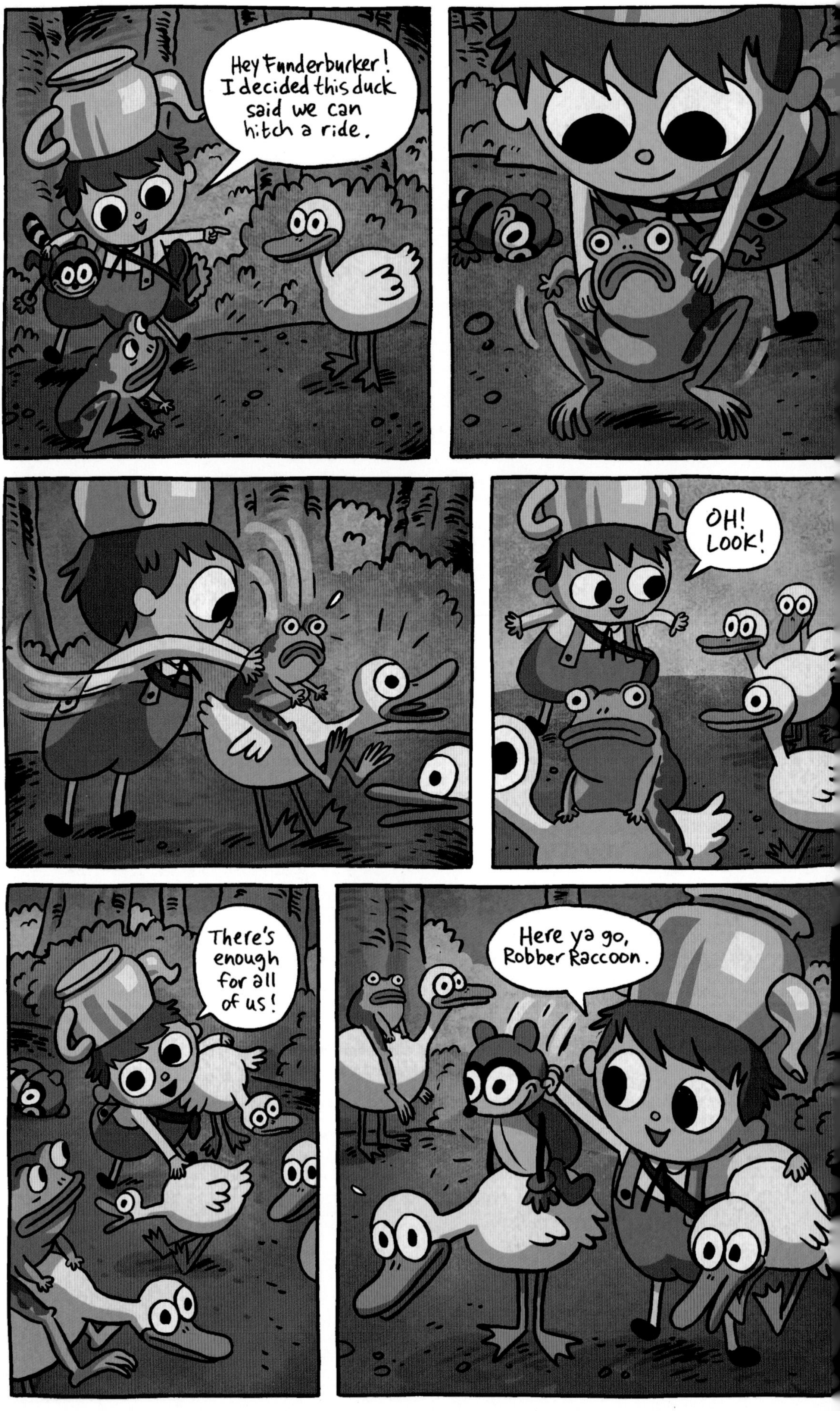

Hey Funderburker! I decided this duck said we can hitch a ride.
OH! LOOK!
There's enough for all of us!
Here ya go, Robber Raccoon.

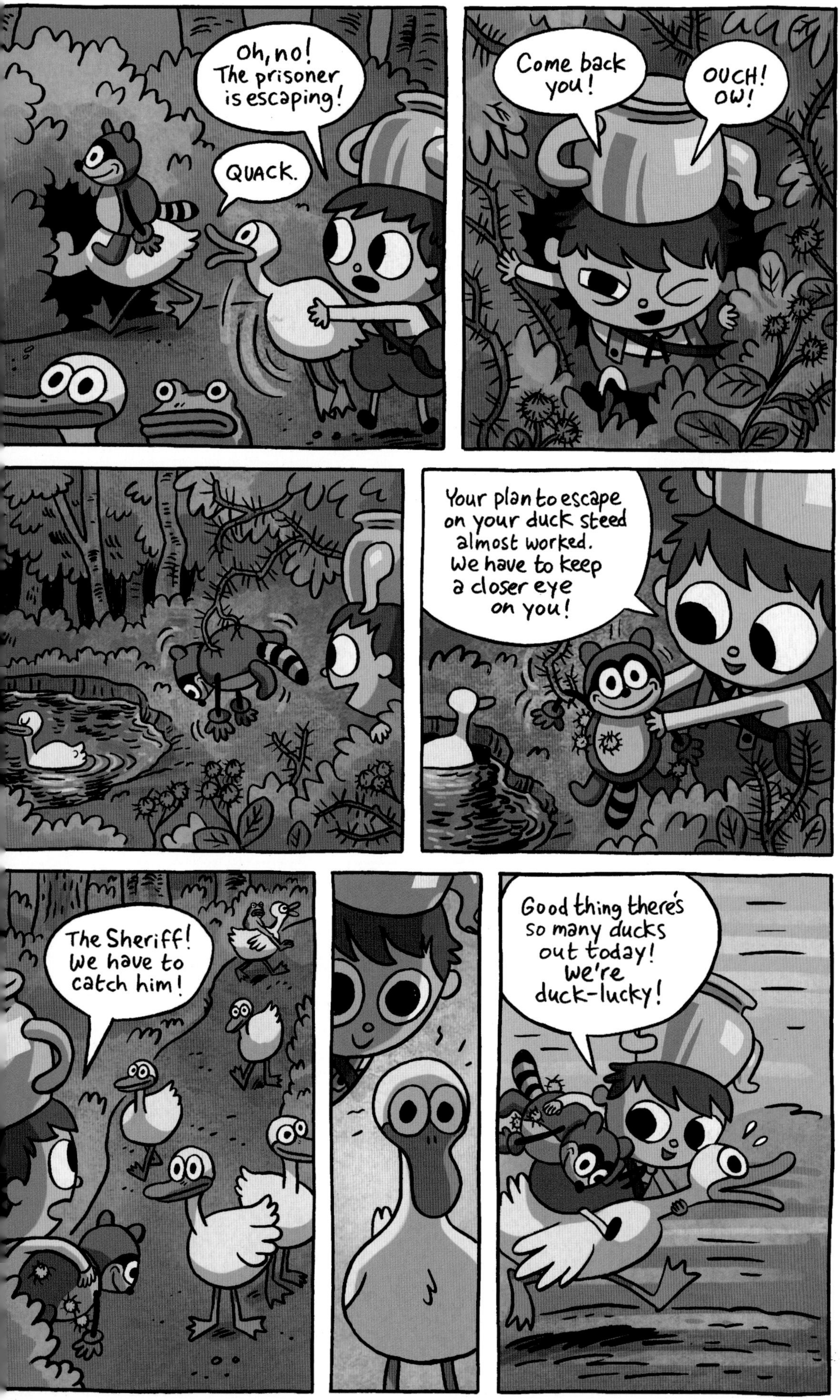
Oh, no! The prisoner is escaping!
QUACK.
Come back you!
OUCH! OW!
Your plan to escape on your duck steed almost worked. We have to keep a closer eye on you!
The Sheriff! We have to catch him!
Good thing there's so many ducks out today! We're duck-lucky!

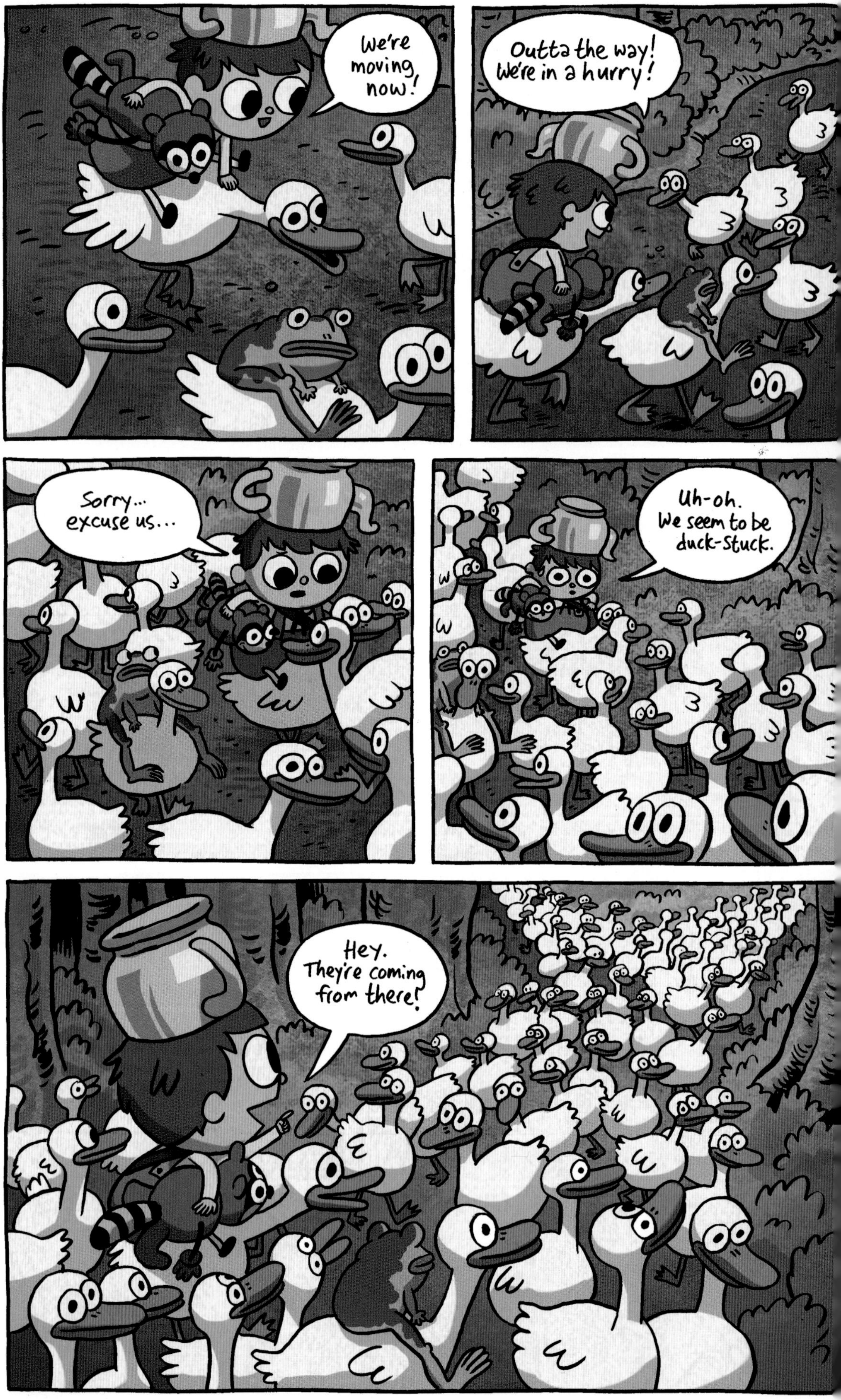
We're moving now!
Outta the way! We're in a hurry!
Sorry... excuse us...
Uh-oh. We seem to be duck-stuck.
Hey. They're coming from there!

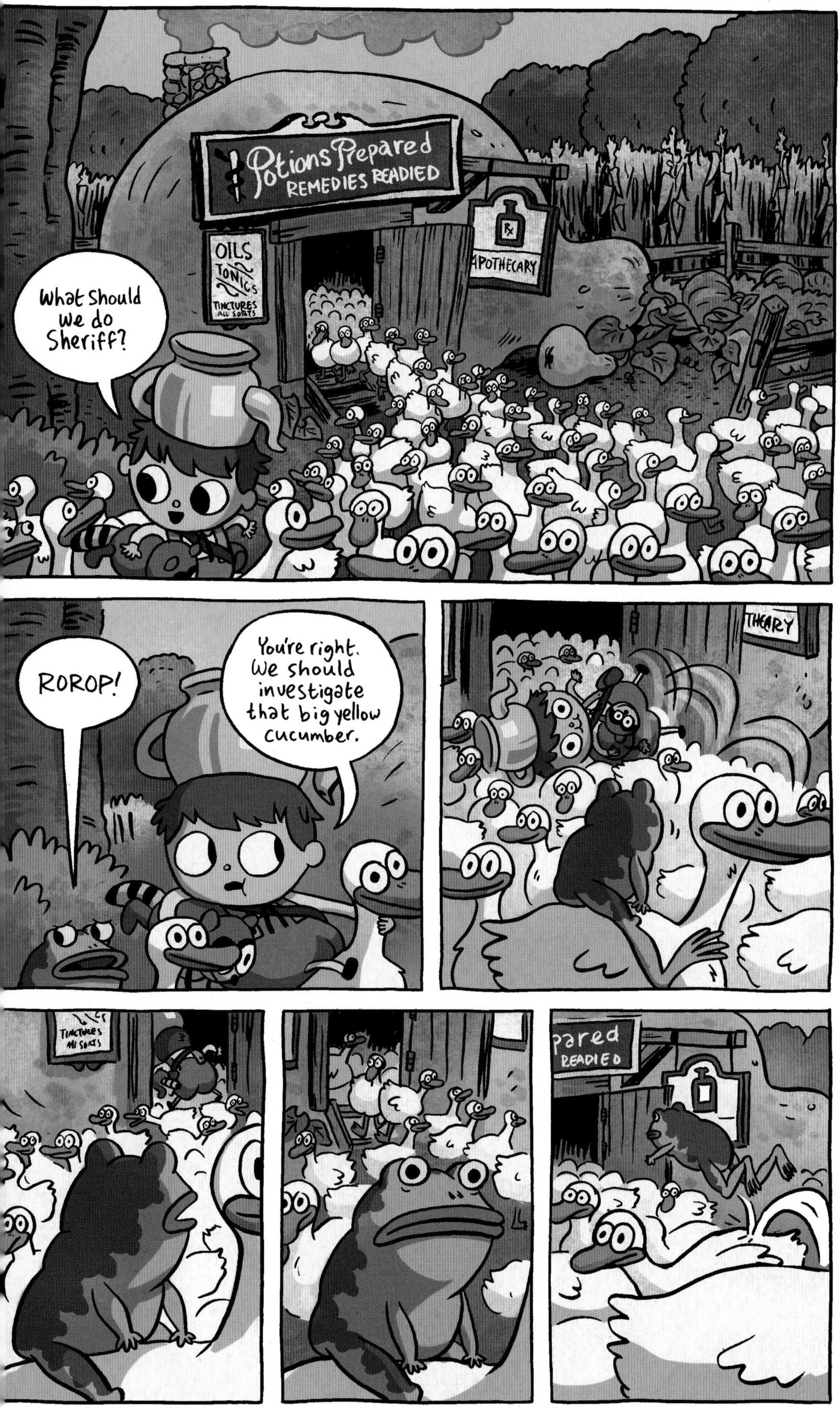
Potions Prepared
REMEDIES READIED
OILS
TONICS
TINCTURES ALL SORTS
APOTHECARY
What Should we do Sheriff?
ROROP!
You're right. We should investigate that big yellow cucumber.
THECARY
TINCTURES ALL SORTS
pared
READIED

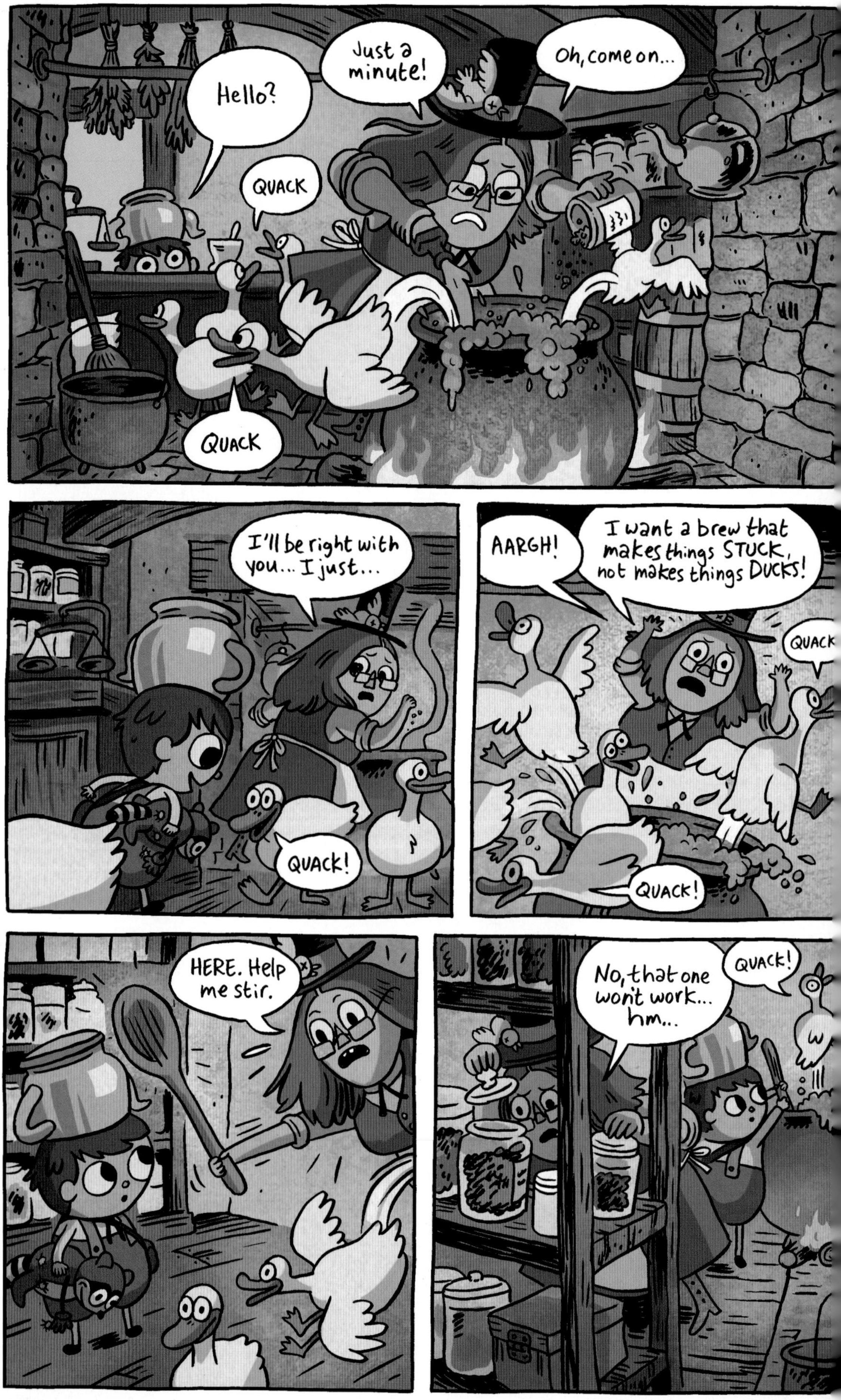
Hello?
Just a minute!
Oh, come on...
QUACK
QUACK
I'll be right with you... I just...
QUACK!
AARGH!
I want a brew that makes things STUCK, not makes things DUCKS!
QUACK
QUACK!
HERE. Help me stir.
No, that one won't work... hm...
QUACK!

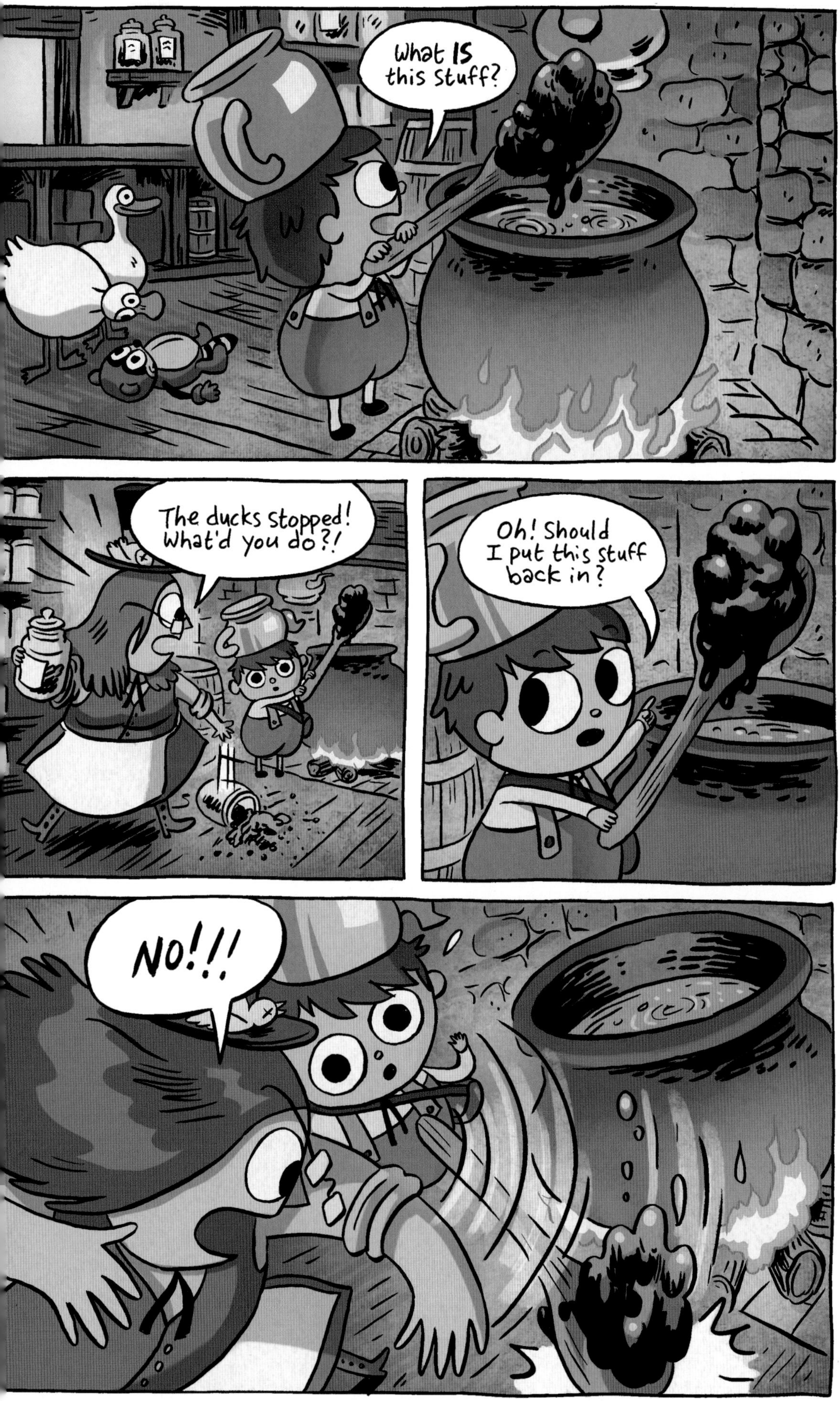
What IS this stuff?
The ducks stopped! What'd you do?!
Oh! Should I put this stuff back in?
NO!!!

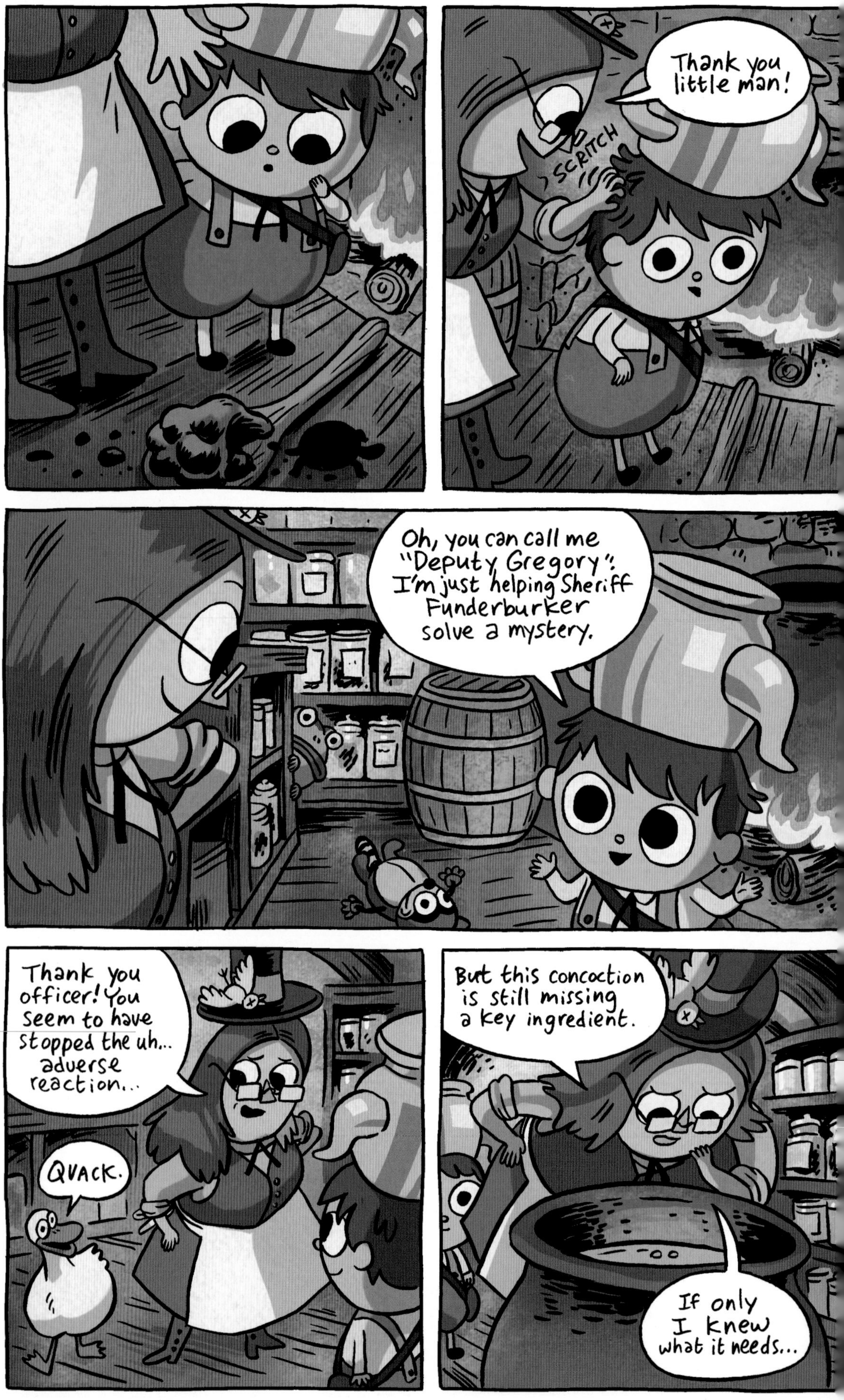
Thank you little man!
SCRITCH
Oh, you can call me "Deputy Gregory". I'm just helping Sheriff Funderburker solve a mystery.
Thank you officer! You seem to have stopped the uh... adverse reaction...
QUACK.
But this concoction is still missing a key ingredient.
If only I knew what it needs...

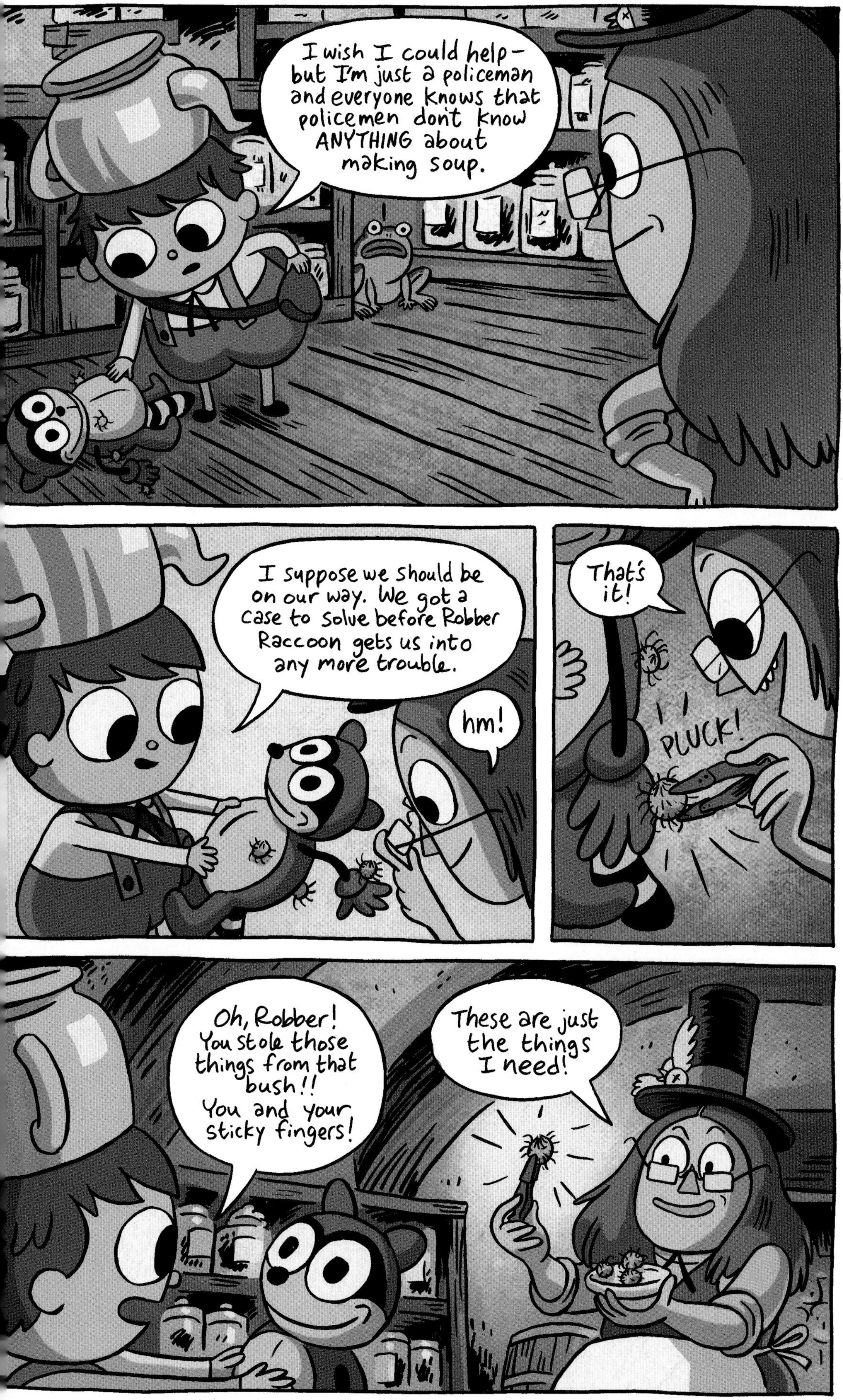
I wish I could help- but I'm just a policeman and everyone knows that policemen don't know ANYTHING about making soup.
I suppose we should be on our way. We got a case to solve before Robber Raccoon gets us into any more trouble.
hm!
That's it!
PLUCK!
Oh, Robber! You stole those things from that bush!! You and your sticky fingers!
These are just the things I need!

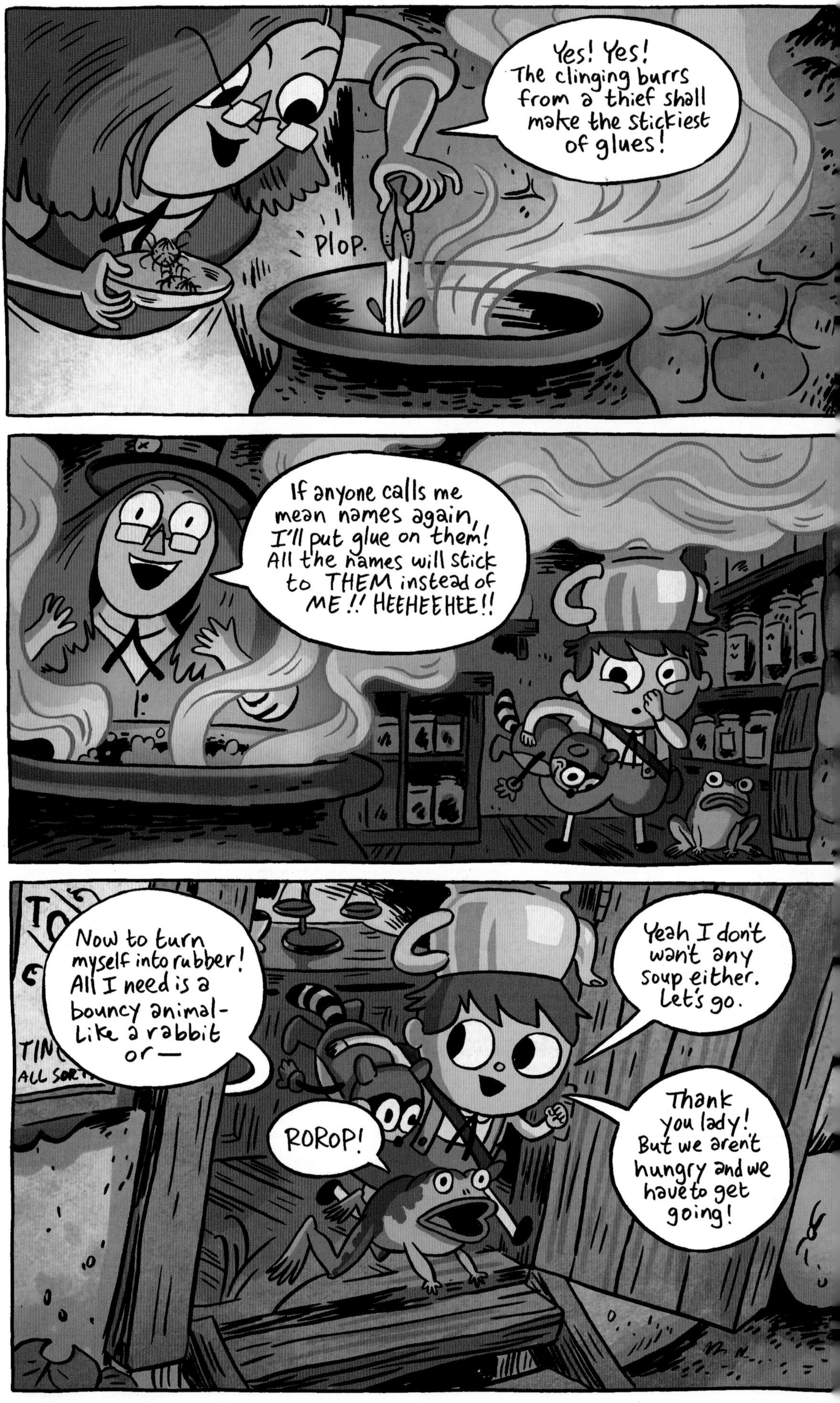
Yes! Yes! The clinging burrs from a thief shall make the stickiest of glues!
PLOP.
If anyone calls me mean names again, I'll put glue on them! All the names will stick to THEM instead of ME!! HEEHEEHEE!!
Now to turn myself into rubber! All I need is a bouncy animal- Like a rabbit or—
Yeah I don't want any soup either. Let's go.
RoROP!
Thank you lady! But we aren't hungry and we have to get going!

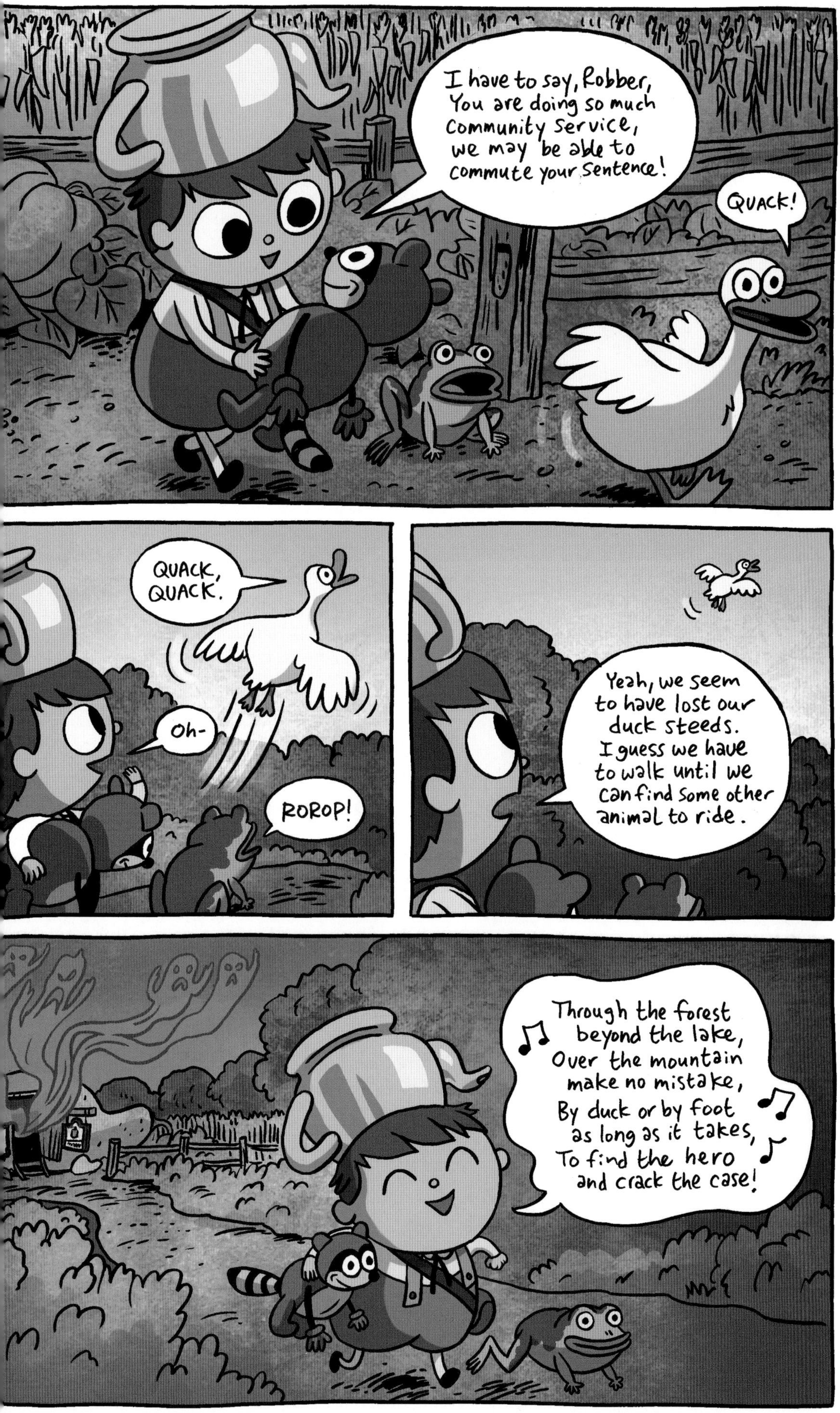
I have to say, Robber,
You are doing so much
Community Service,
we may be able to
commute your Sentence!
QUACK!
QUACK, QUACK.
Oh-
ROROP!
Yeah, we seem to have lost our duck steeds. I guess we have to walk until we can find some other animal to ride.
Through the forest beyond the lake,
Over the mountain make no mistake,
By duck or by foot as long as it takes,
To find the hero and crack the case!

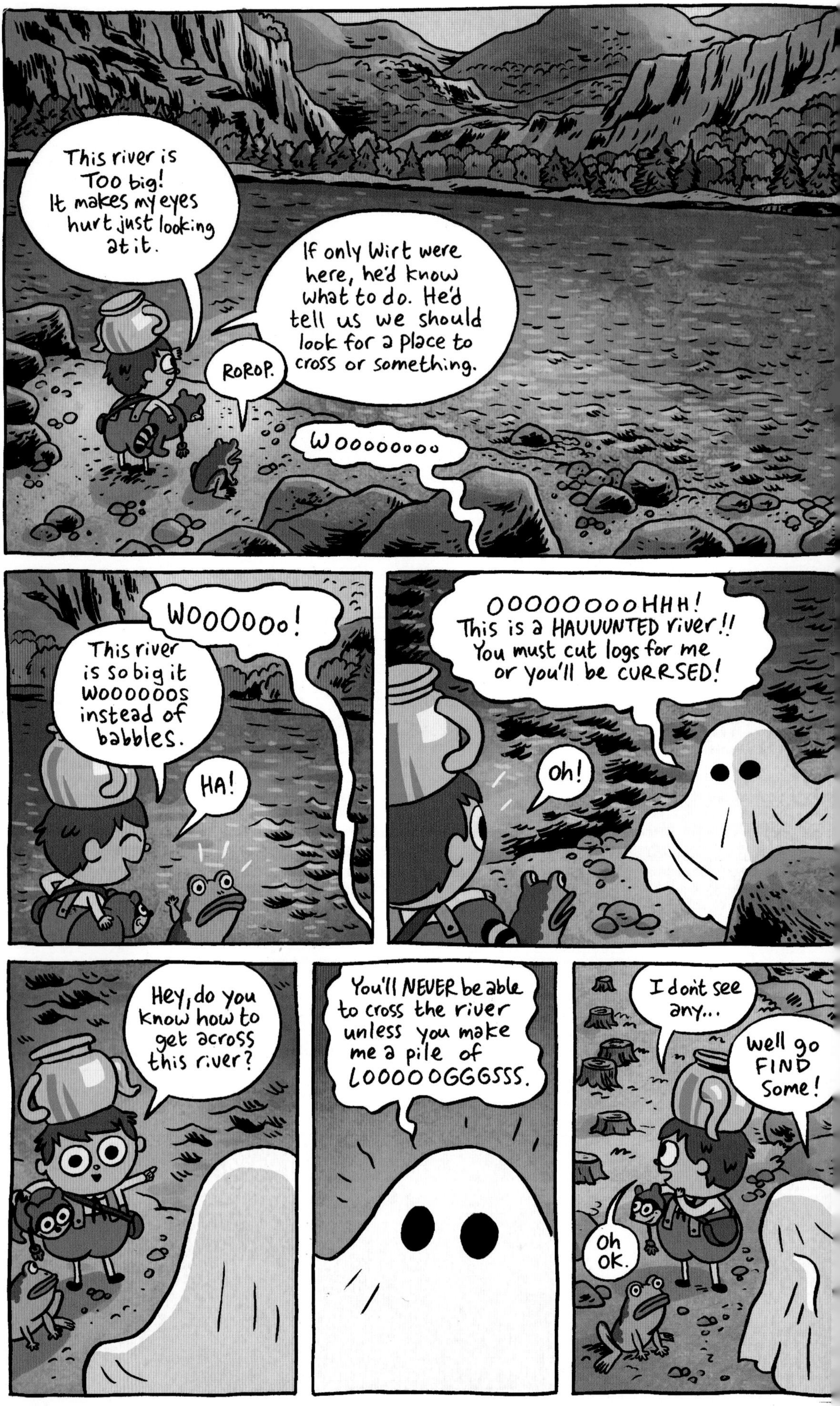
This river is TOO big! It makes my eyes hurt just looking at it.
If only Wirt were here, he'd know what to do. He'd tell us we should look for a place to cross or something.
ROROP.
Wooooooooo
WOOOOOo!
This river is so big it WOOOOOOS instead of babbles.
HA!
OOOOOOOOHHH! This is a HAUUUNTED river!! You must cut logs for me or you'll be CURRSED!
Oh!
Hey, do you know how to get across this river?
You'll NEVER be able to cross the river unless you make me a pile of LOOOOOGGGSSS.
I don't see any...
Well go FIND Some!
Oh OK.

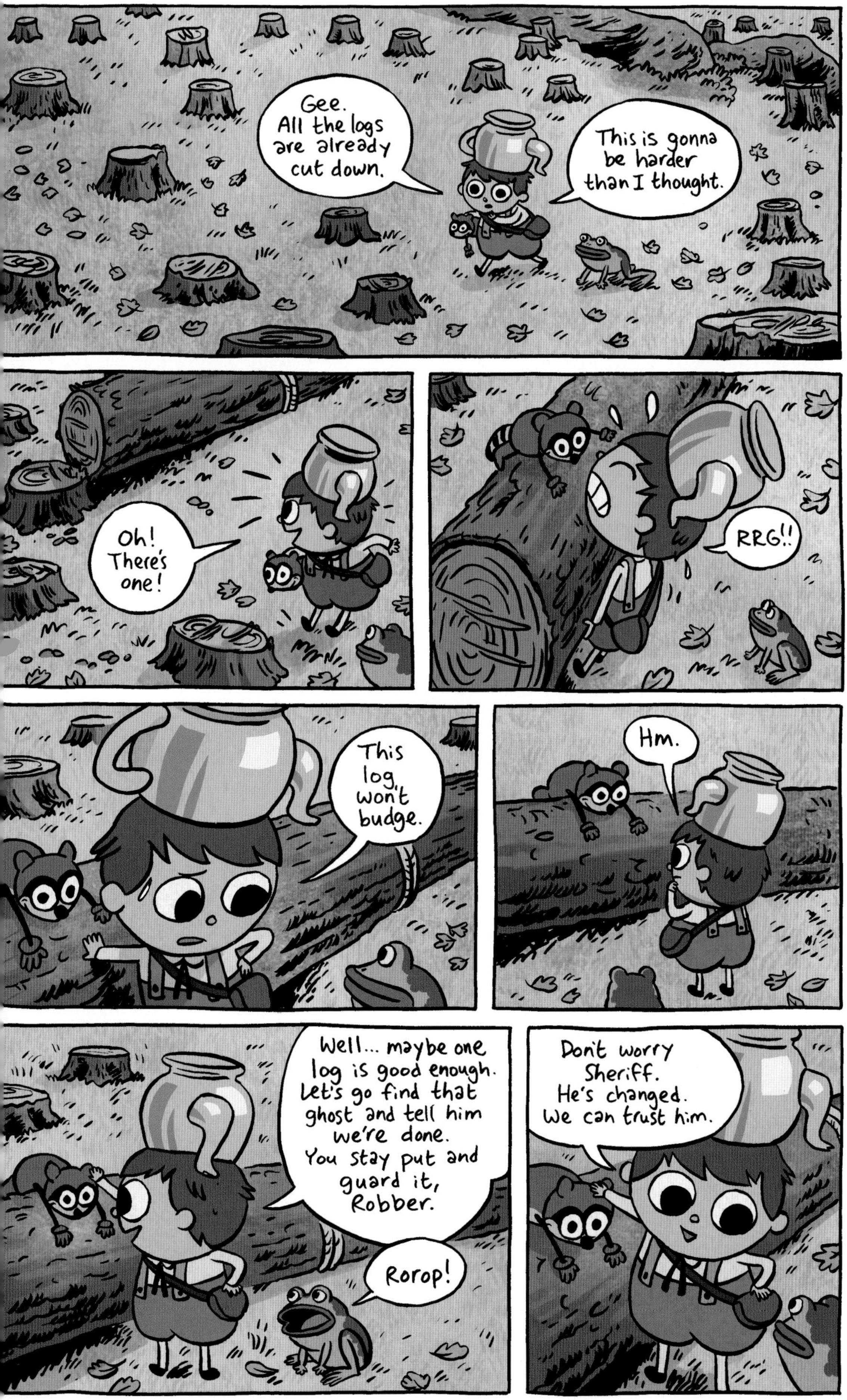
Gee.
All the logs are already cut down.
This is gonna be harder than I thought.
Oh! There's one!
RRG!!
This log won't budge.
Hm.
Well... maybe one log is good enough. Let's go find that ghost and tell him we're done. You stay put and guard it, Robber.
Rorop!
Don't worry Sheriff. He's changed. We can trust him.

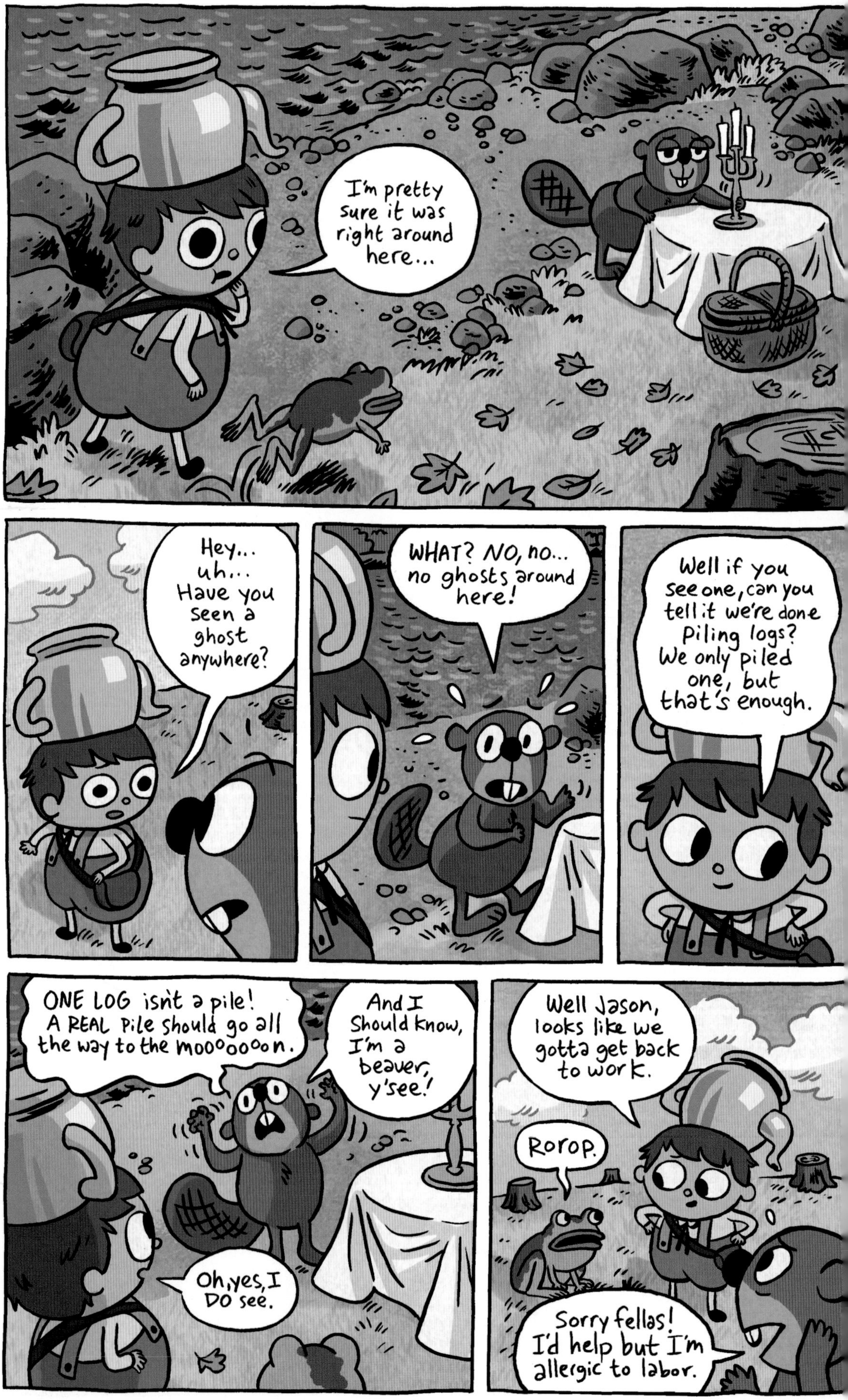
I'm pretty sure it was right around here...
Hey... uh... Have you seen a ghost anywhere?
WHAT? NO, no... no ghosts around here!
Well if you see one, can you tell it we're done piling logs? We only piled one, but that's enough.
ONE LOG isn't a pile! A REAL pile should go all the way to the moooooooon.
And I should know, I'm a beaver, y'see!
Oh, yes, I DO see.
Well Jason, looks like we gotta get back to work.
Rorop.
Sorry fellas! I'd help but I'm allergic to labor.

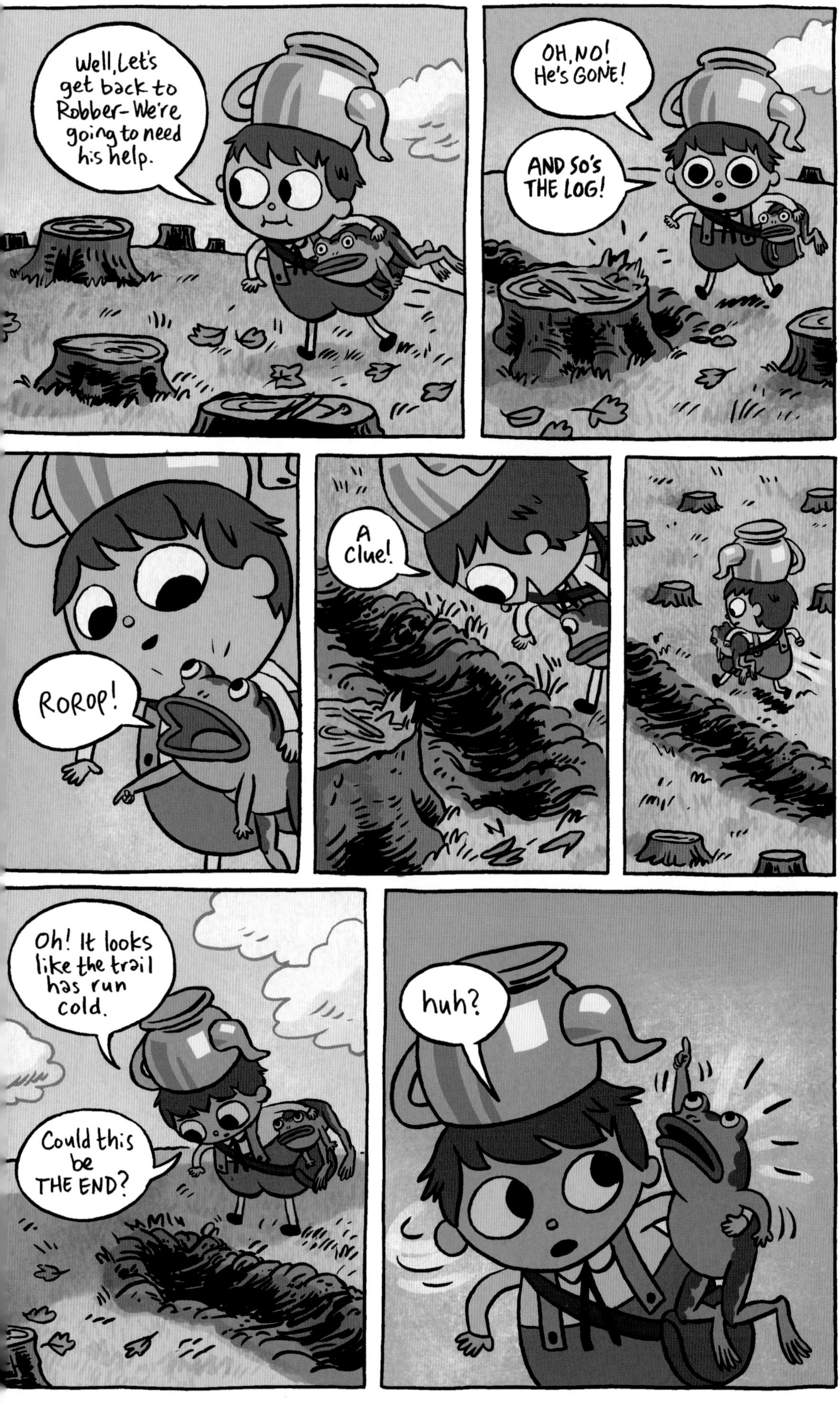
Well, Let's get back to Robber- We're going to need his help.
OH, NO! He's GONE!
AND SO's THE LOG!
ROROP!
A Clue!
Oh! It looks like the trail has run cold.
Could this be THE END?
huh?

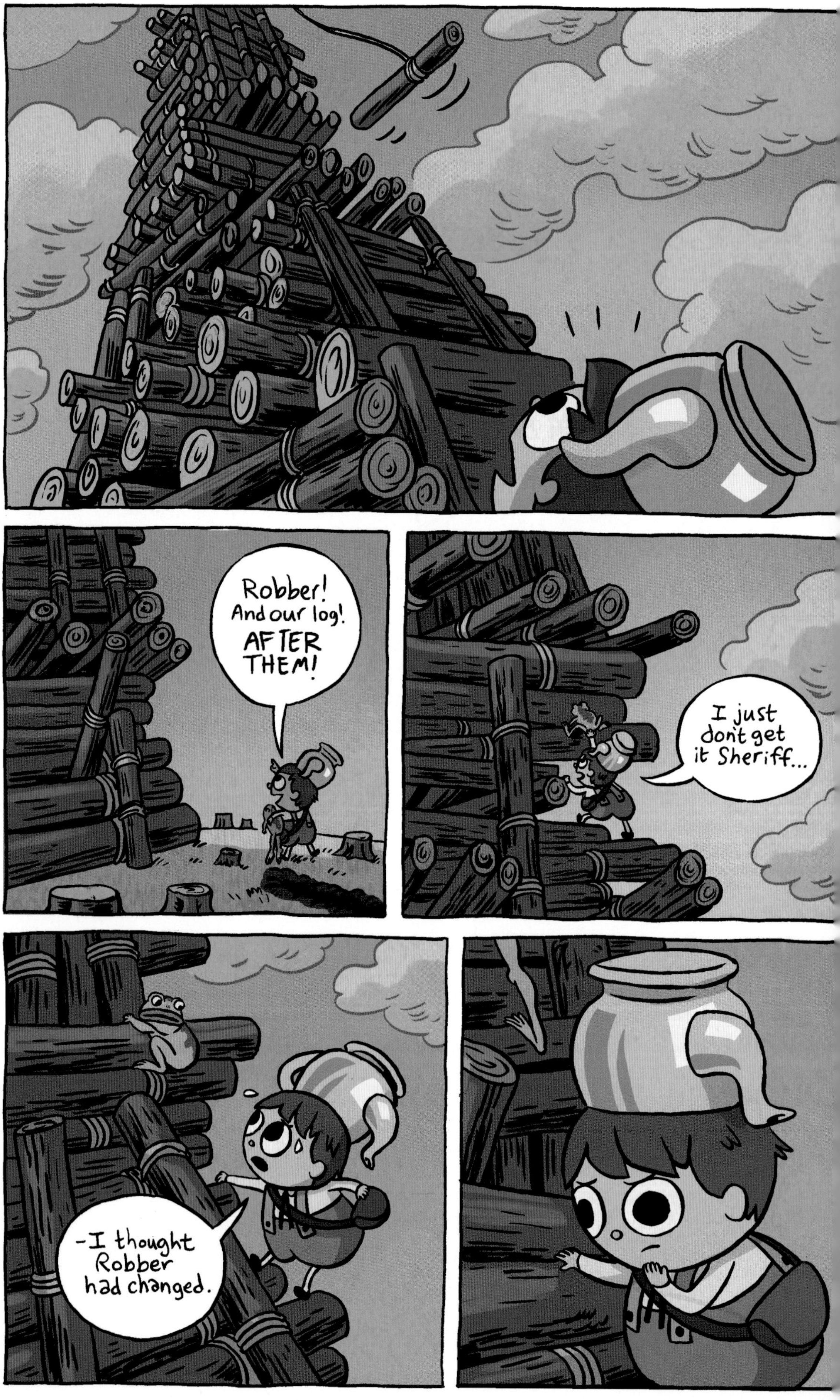
Robber! And our log! AFTER THEM!
I just don't get it Sheriff...
-I thought Robber had changed.

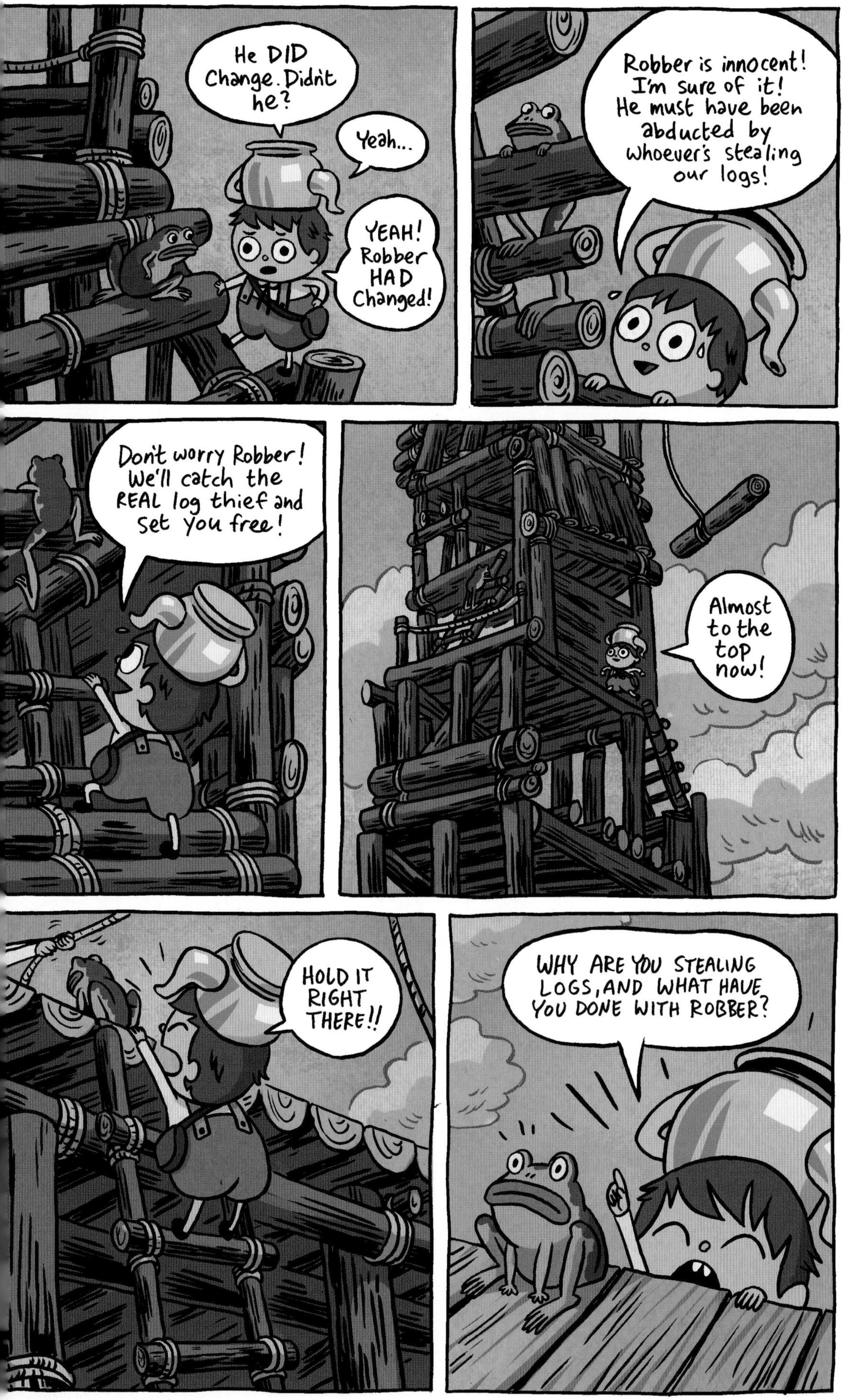
He DID Change. Didn't he?
Yeah...
YEAH! Robber HAD Changed!
Robber is innocent! I'm sure of it! He must have been abducted by whoever's stealing our logs!
Don't worry Robber! We'll catch the REAL log thief and set you free!
Almost to the top now!
HOLD IT RIGHT THERE!!
WHY ARE YOU STEALING LOGS, AND WHAT HAVE YOU DONE WITH ROBBER?

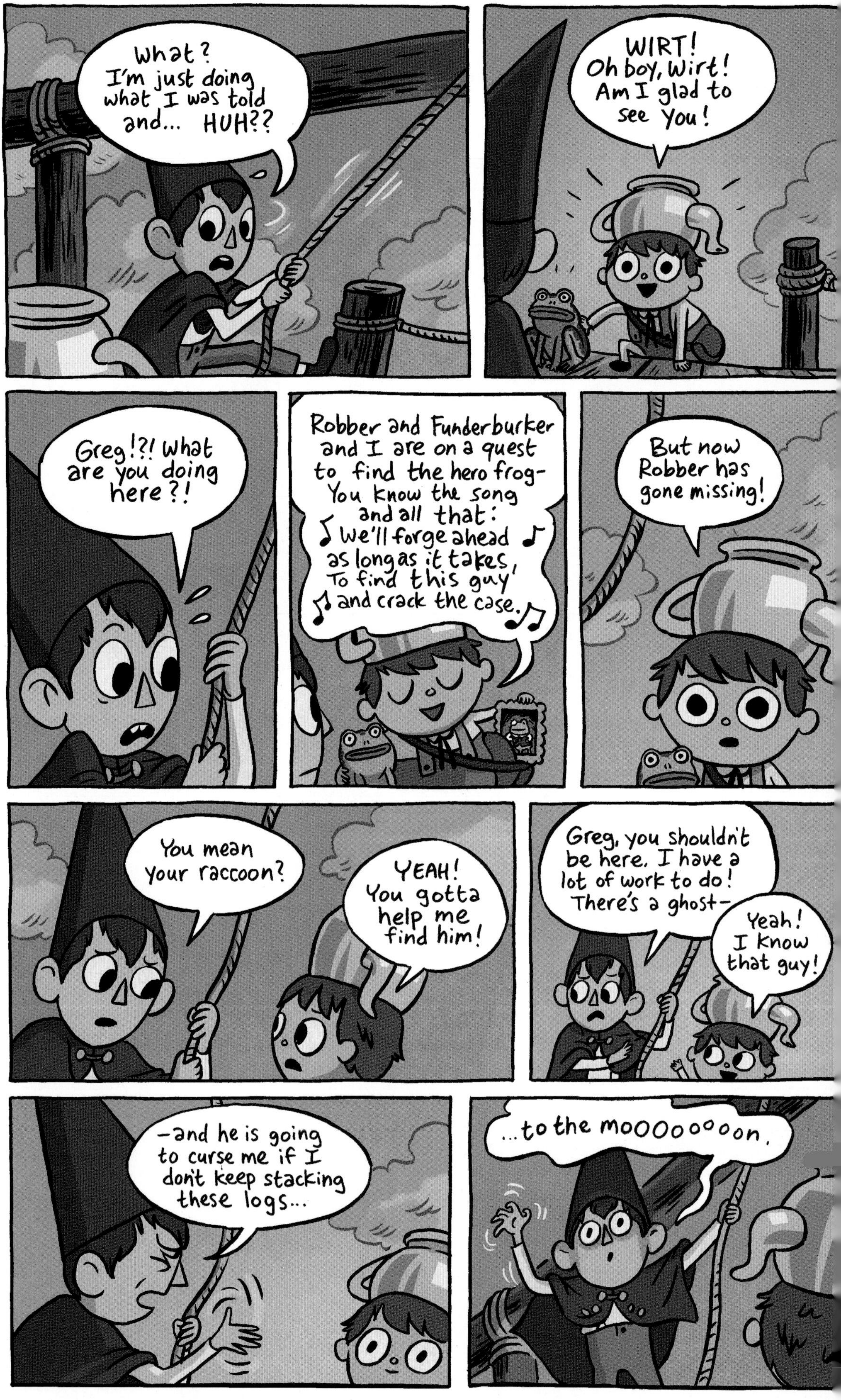
What? I'm just doing what I was told and... HUH??
WIRT! Oh boy, Wirt! Am I glad to see you!
Greg!?! What are you doing here?!
Robber and Funderburker and I are on a quest to find the hero frog- You know the song and all that: ♩We'll forge ahead ♪ as long as it takes, To find this guy ♫ and crack the case.♫
But now Robber has gone missing!
You mean your raccoon?
YEAH! You gotta help me find him!
Greg, you shouldn't be here. I have a lot of work to do! There's a ghost-
Yeah! I know that guy!
-and he is going to curse me if I don't keep stacking these logs...
...to the mooOoooooon.

"To the mooooooooon"?

Yeah, "to the mooooon". - I cant do a good ghost accent.

hmm...

Funderburker, I think I may have cracked the case.

C'mon Wirt! Trust me! We have to get back to the river.

Look Greg - I don't know how curses work - I just try to avoid them. I'd love to help but - I must forever build this obelisk to the heavens; this wooden shrine commemorating the pointlessness of our own existence...

Darn thing is still stuck.

Wirt, I didn't trust a friend and now I've lost him forever...

You gotta trust me! I know what to do! We just have to get back to the river.

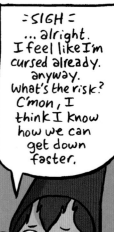

=SIGH=
...alright. I feel like I'm cursed already. anyway. What's the risk? C'mon, I think I know how we can get down faster.

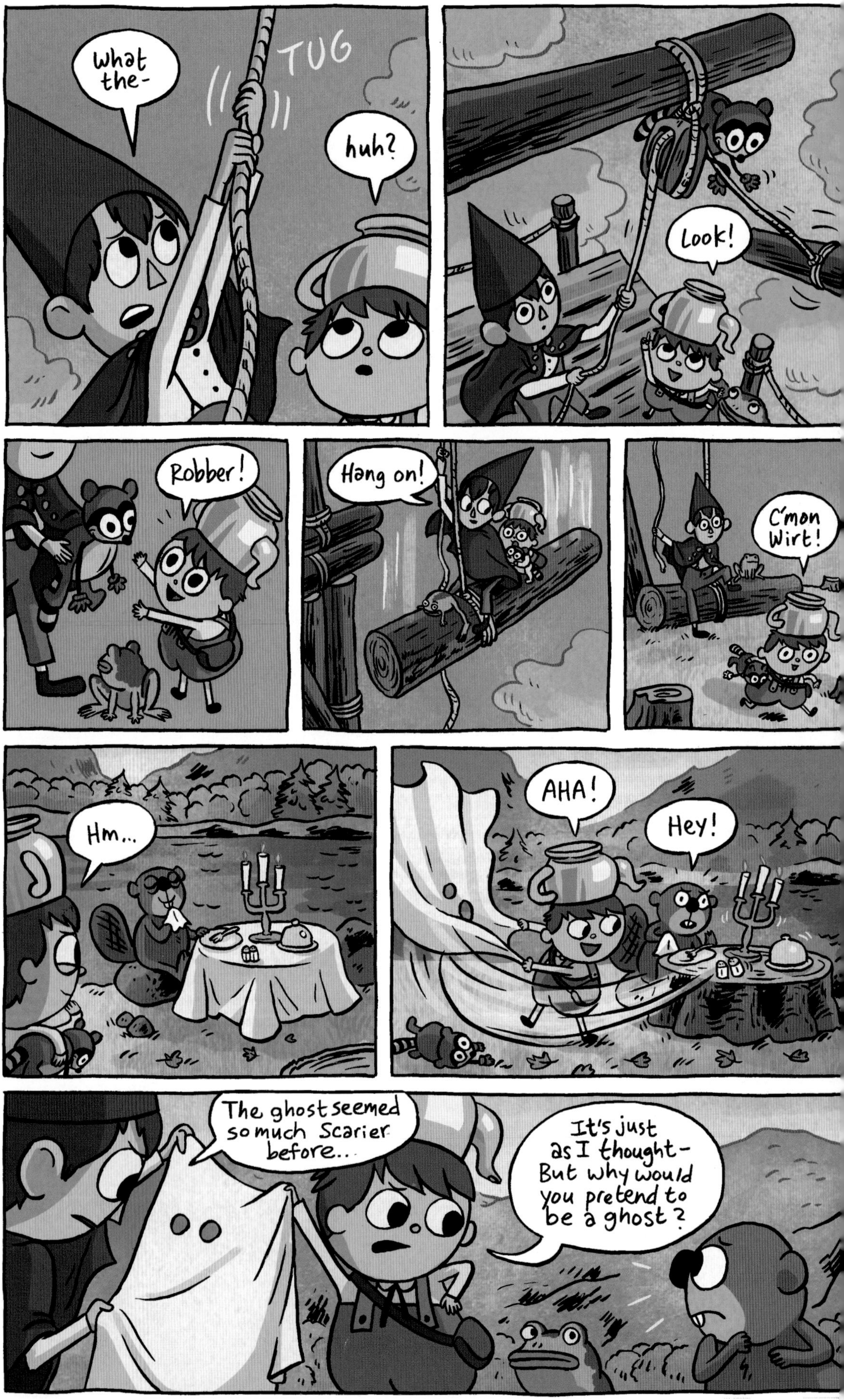
what the-
TUG
huh?
Look!
Robber!
Hang on!
C'mon Wirt!
Hm...
AHA!
Hey!
The ghost seemed so much Scarier before...
It's just as I thought- But why would you pretend to be a ghost?

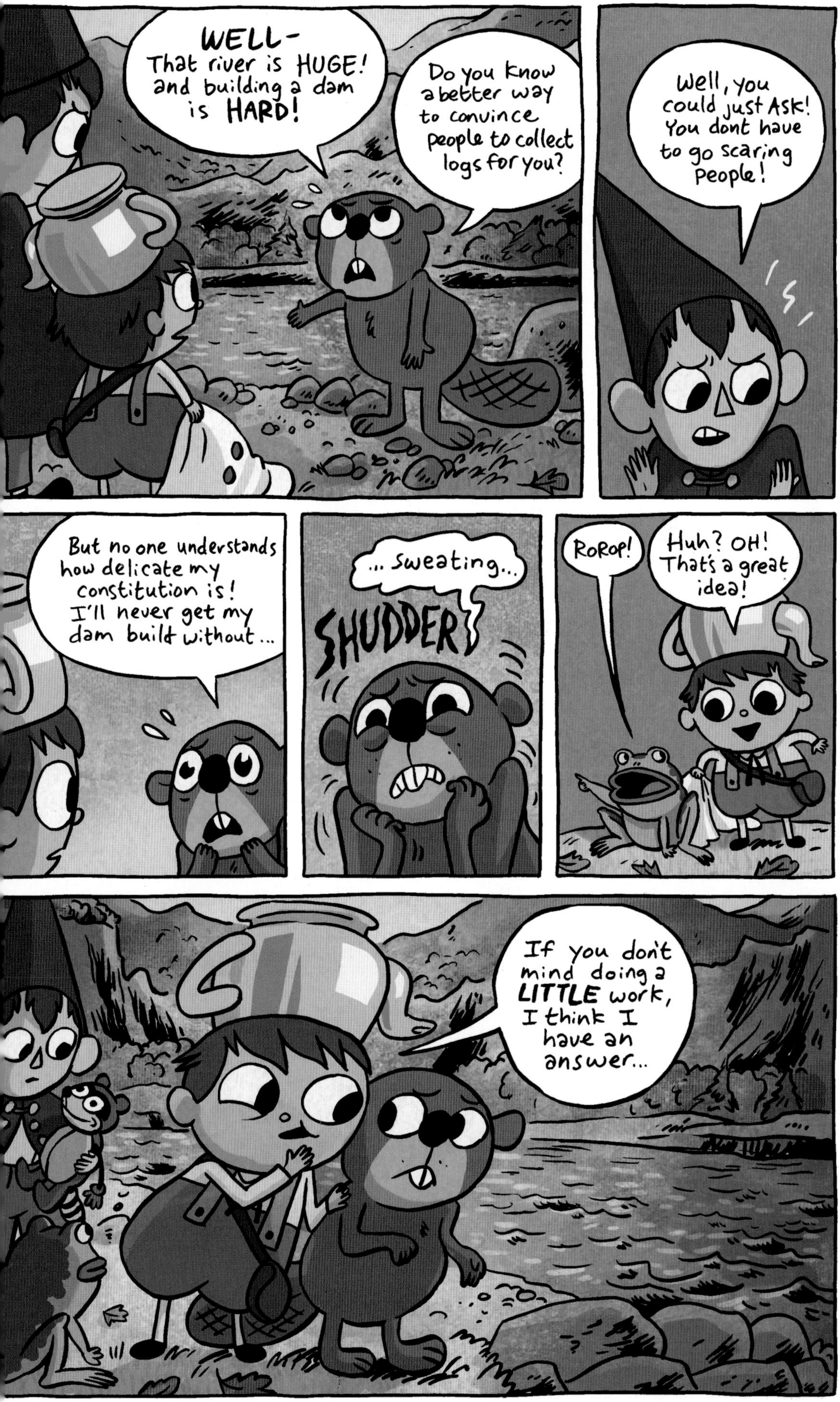
WELL-
That river is HUGE! and building a dam is HARD!
Do you know a better way to convince people to collect logs for you?
Well, you could just ASK! You dont have to go scaring people!
But no one understands how delicate my constitution is! I'll never get my dam built without...
... sweating...
SHUDDER
RoRop!
Huh? OH! That's a great idea!
If you don't mind doing a LITTLE work, I think I have an answer...

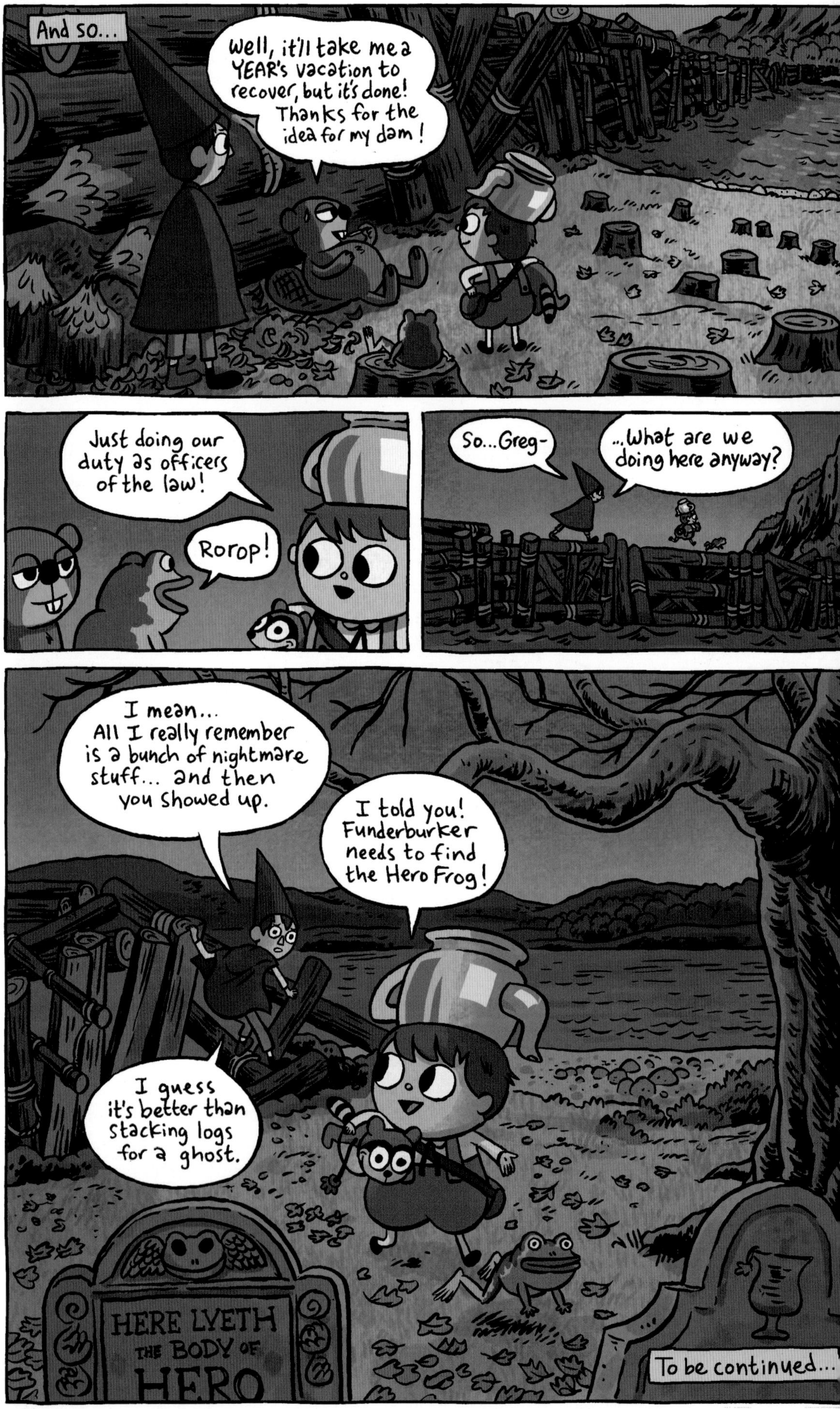
And so...
Well, it'll take me a YEAR's vacation to recover, but it's done! Thanks for the idea for my dam!
Just doing our duty as officers of the law!
Rorop!
So...Greg-
...What are we doing here anyway?
I mean... All I really remember is a bunch of nightmare stuff... and then you showed up.
I told you! Funderburker needs to find the Hero Frog!
I guess it's better than stacking logs for a ghost.
HERE LYETH THE BODY OF HERO
To be continued...

HOMELAND

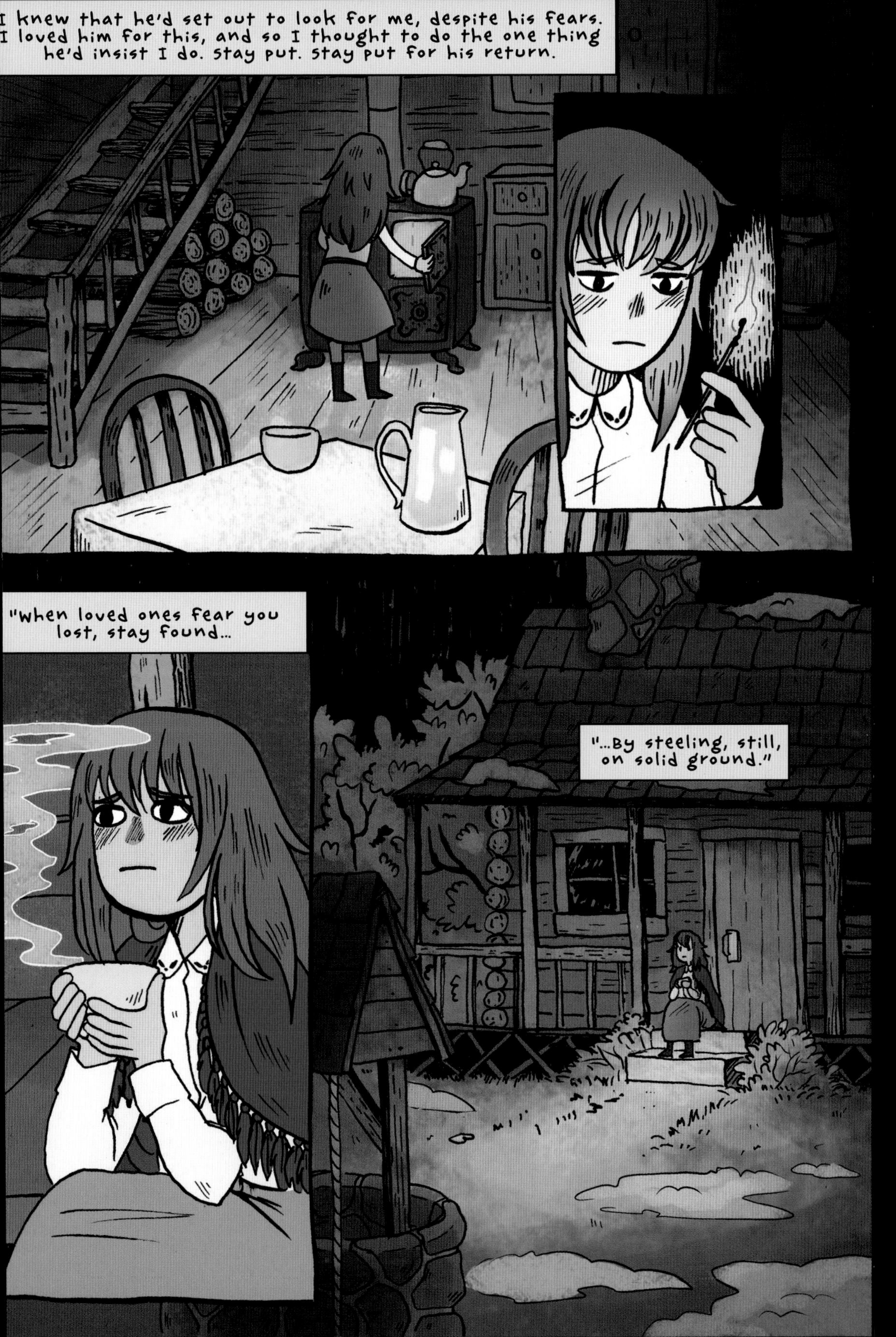
I knew that he'd set out to look for me, despite his fears. I loved him for this, and so I thought to do the one thing he'd insist I do. Stay put. Stay put for his return.
"When loved ones fear you lost, stay found...
"...By steeling, still, on solid ground."

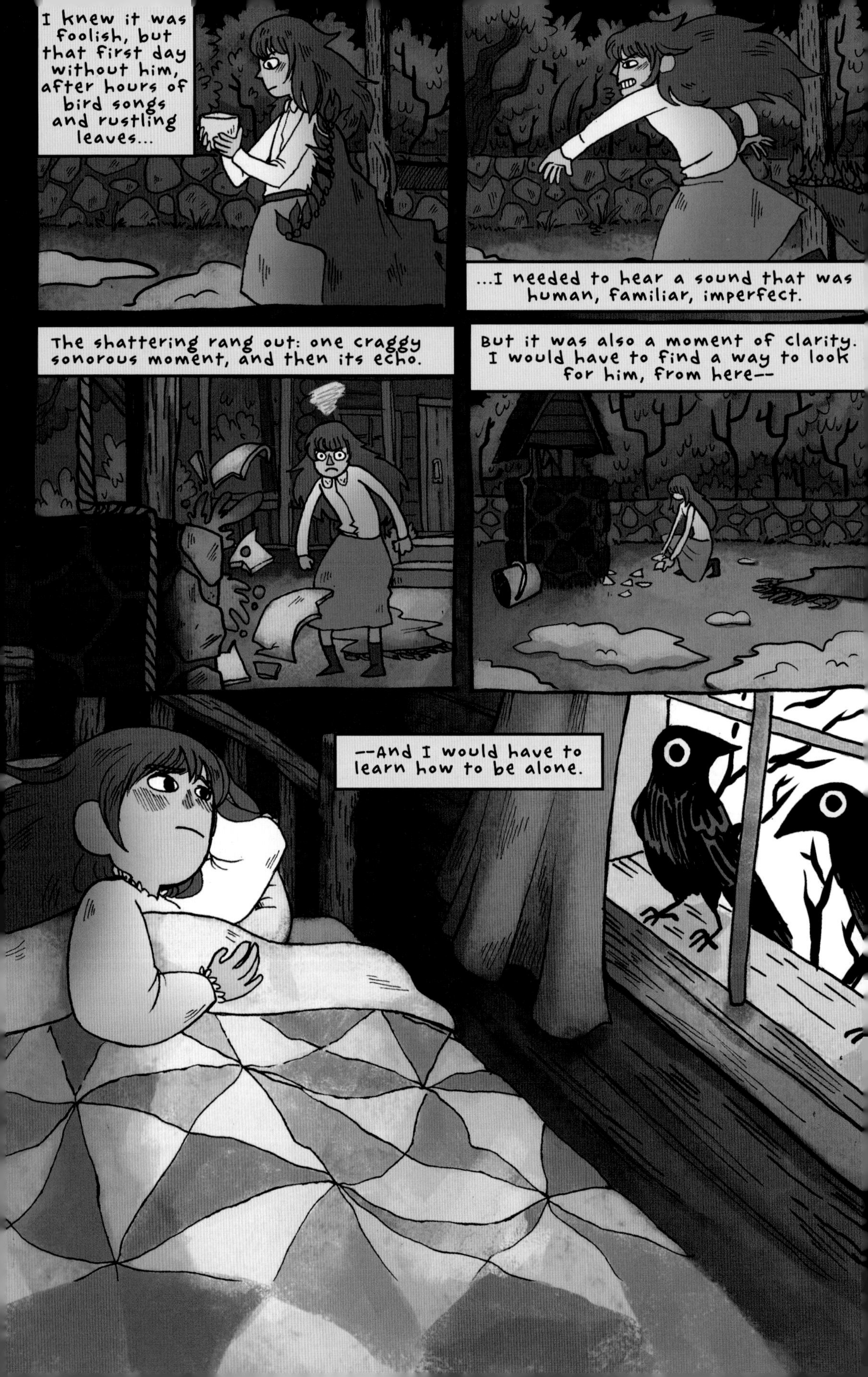
I knew it was foolish, but that first day without him, after hours of bird songs and rustling leaves...
...I needed to hear a sound that was human, familiar, imperfect.
The shattering rang out: one craggy sonorous moment, and then its echo.
But it was also a moment of clarity. I would have to find a way to look for him, from here--
--And I would have to learn how to be alone.

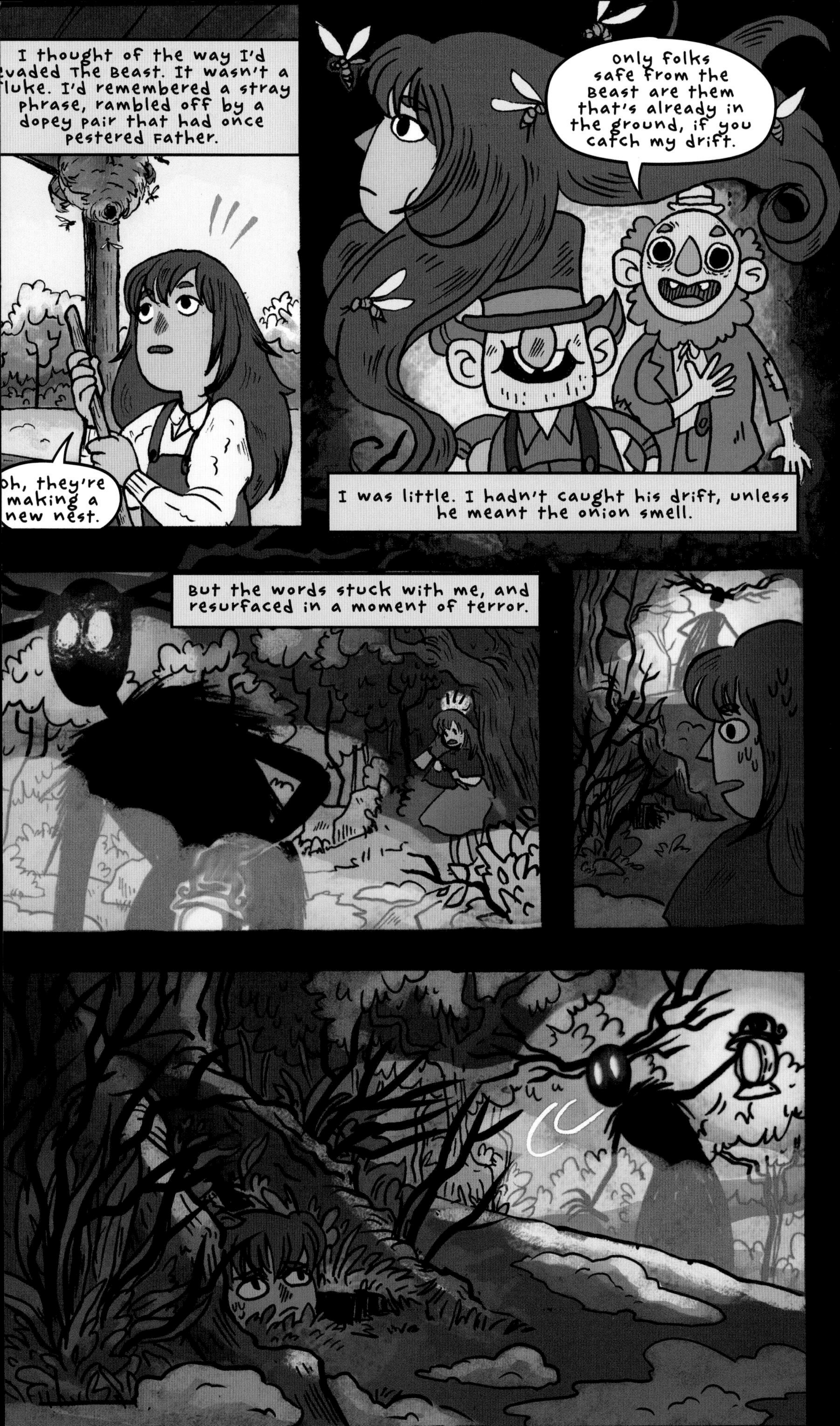
I thought of the way I'd evaded The Beast. It wasn't a fluke. I'd remembered a stray phrase, rambled off by a dopey pair that had once pestered Father.
Oh, they're making a new nest.
Only folks safe from the Beast are them that's already in the ground, if you catch my drift.
I was little. I hadn't caught his drift, unless he meant the onion smell.
But the words stuck with me, and resurfaced in a moment of terror.

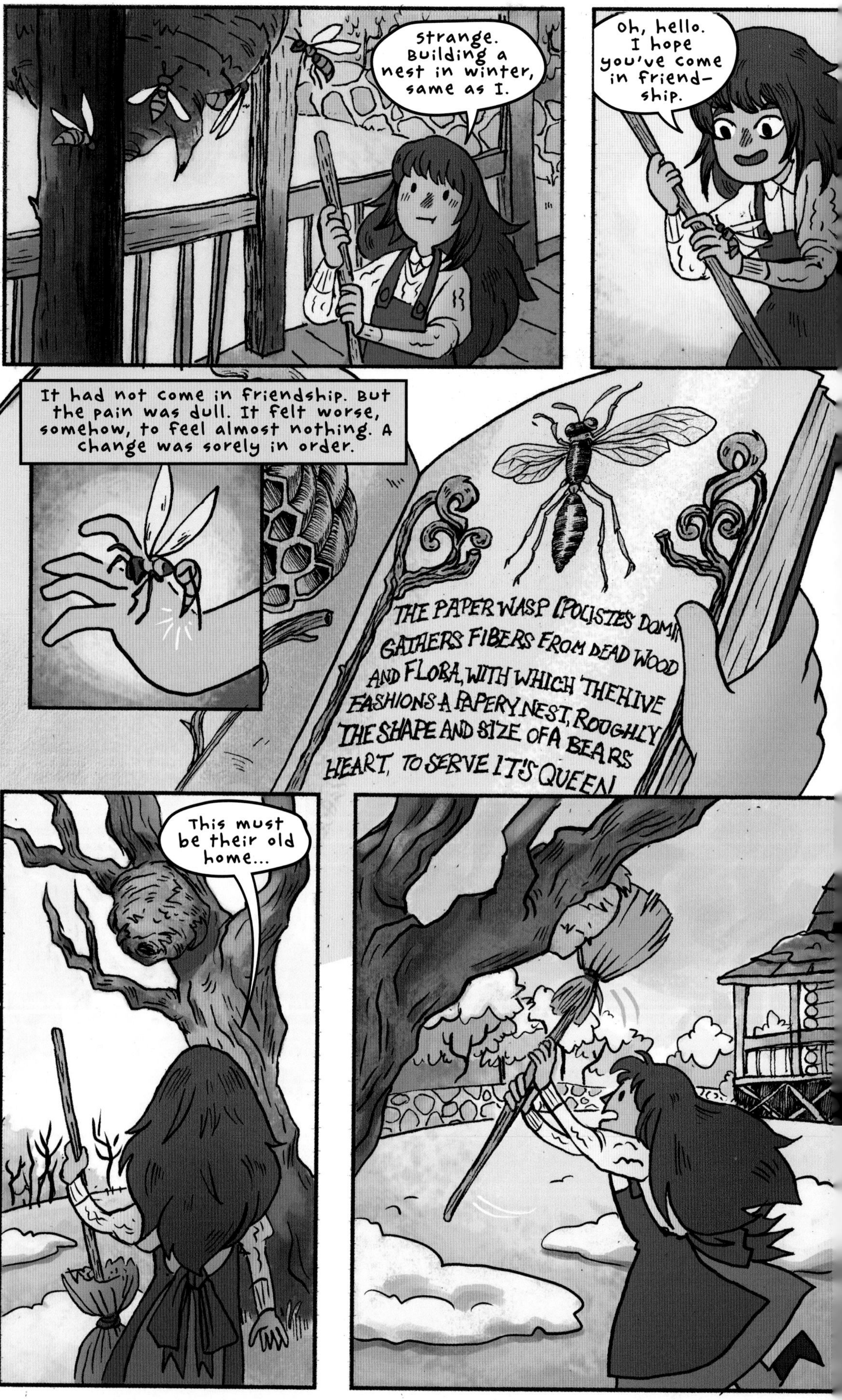
Strange. Building a nest in winter, same as I.
Oh, hello. I hope you've come in friendship.
It had not come in friendship. But the pain was dull. It felt worse, somehow, to feel almost nothing. A change was sorely in order.
THE PAPER WASP [POLISTES DOMI
GATHERS FIBERS FROM DEAD WOOD
AND FLORA, WITH WHICH THE HIVE
FASHIONS A PAPERY NEST, ROUGHLY
THE SHAPE AND SIZE OF A BEARS
HEART, TO SERVE IT'S QUEEN
This must be their old home...

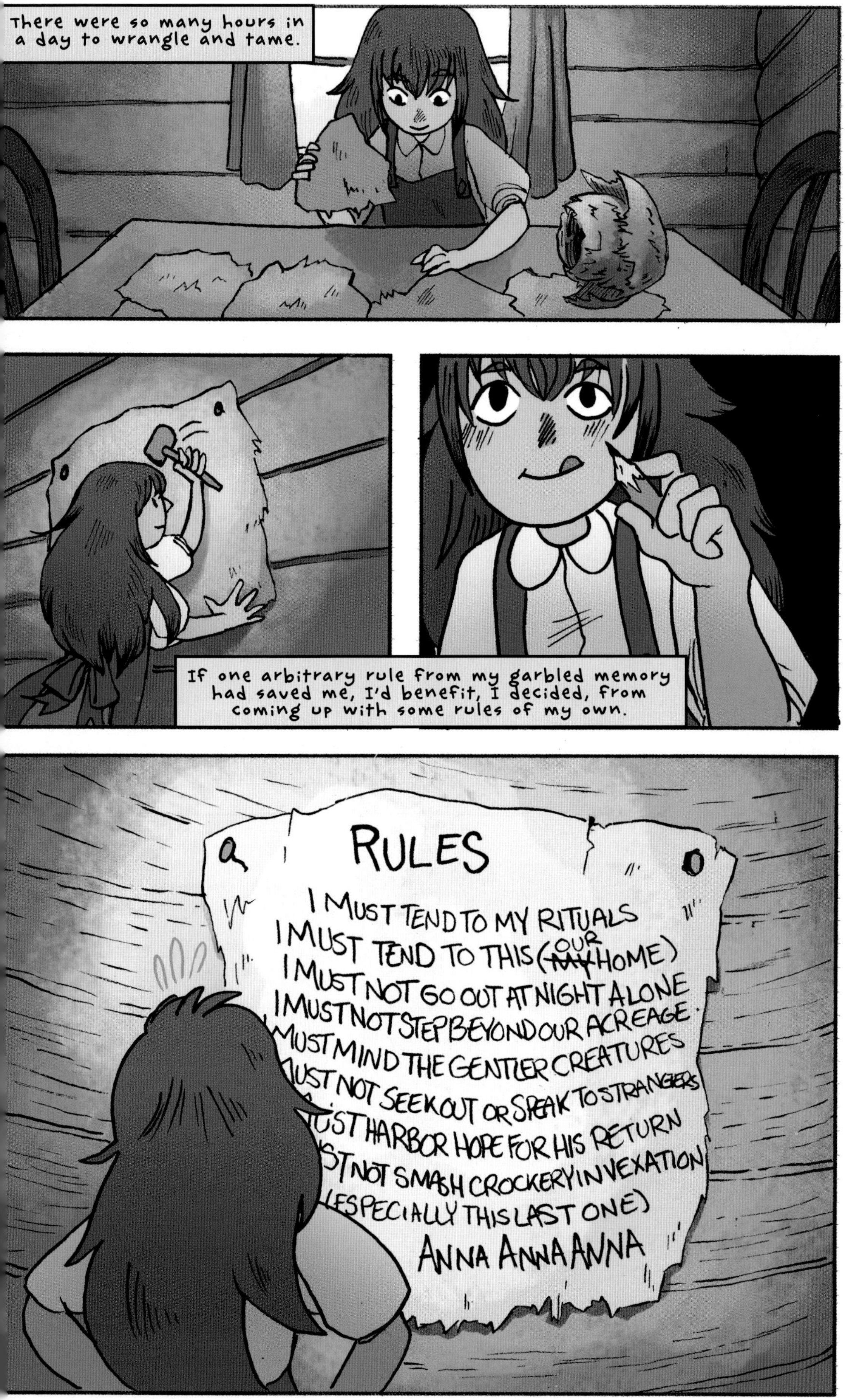
There were so many hours in a day to wrangle and tame.
If one arbitrary rule from my garbled memory had saved me, I'd benefit, I decided, from coming up with some rules of my own.
RULES
I MUST TEND TO MY RITUALS
I MUST TEND TO THIS (~~MY~~ OUR HOME)
I MUST NOT GO OUT AT NIGHT ALONE
I MUST NOT STEP BEYOND OUR ACREAGE.
MUST MIND THE GENTLER CREATURES
UST NOT SEEK OUT OR SPEAK TO STRANGERS
UST HARBOR HOPE FOR HIS RETURN
ST NOT SMASH CROCKERY IN VEXATION
(ESPECIALLY THIS LAST ONE)
ANNA ANNA ANNA

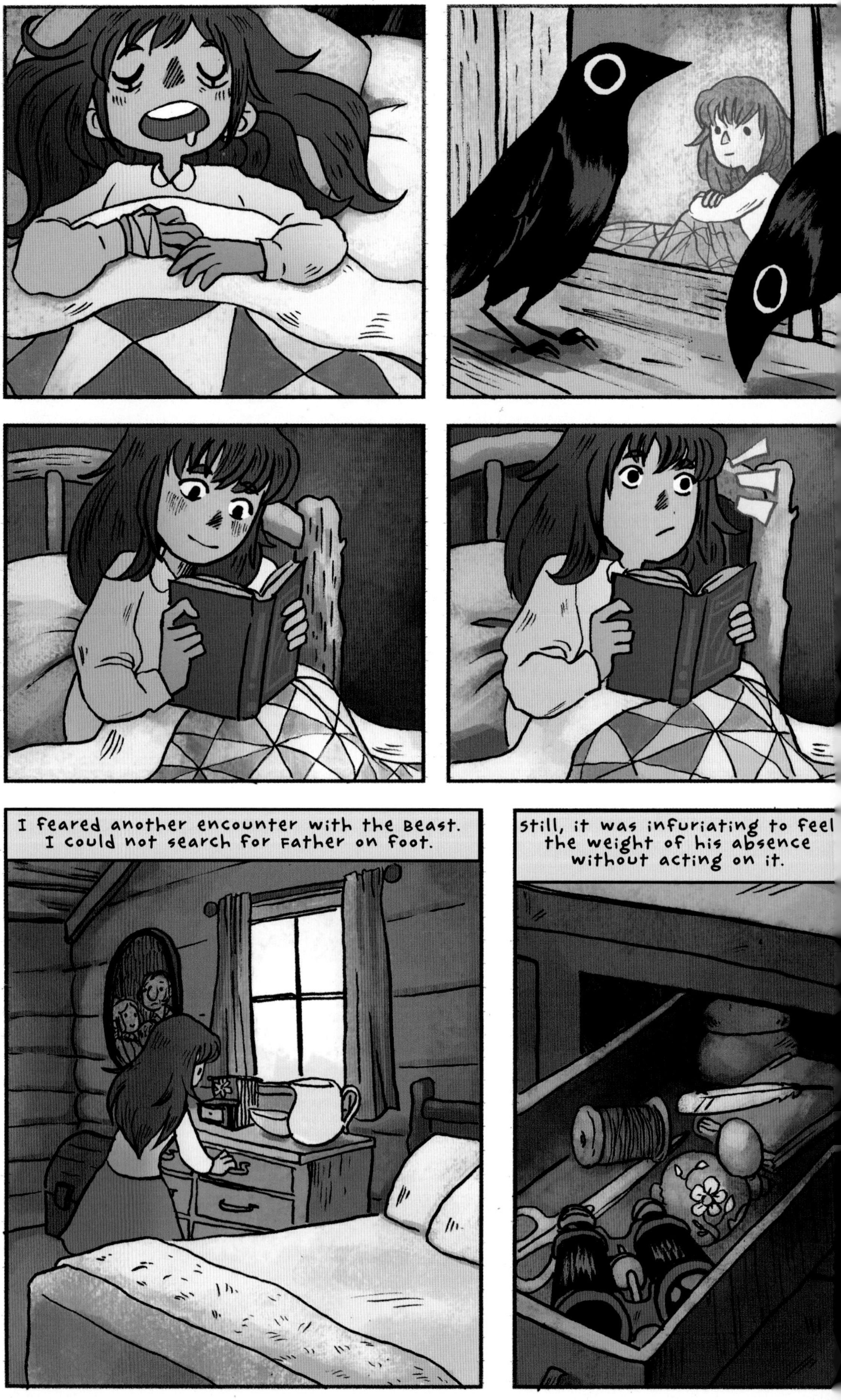
I feared another encounter with the Beast.
I could not search for Father on foot.
Still, it was infuriating to feel the weight of his absence without acting on it.

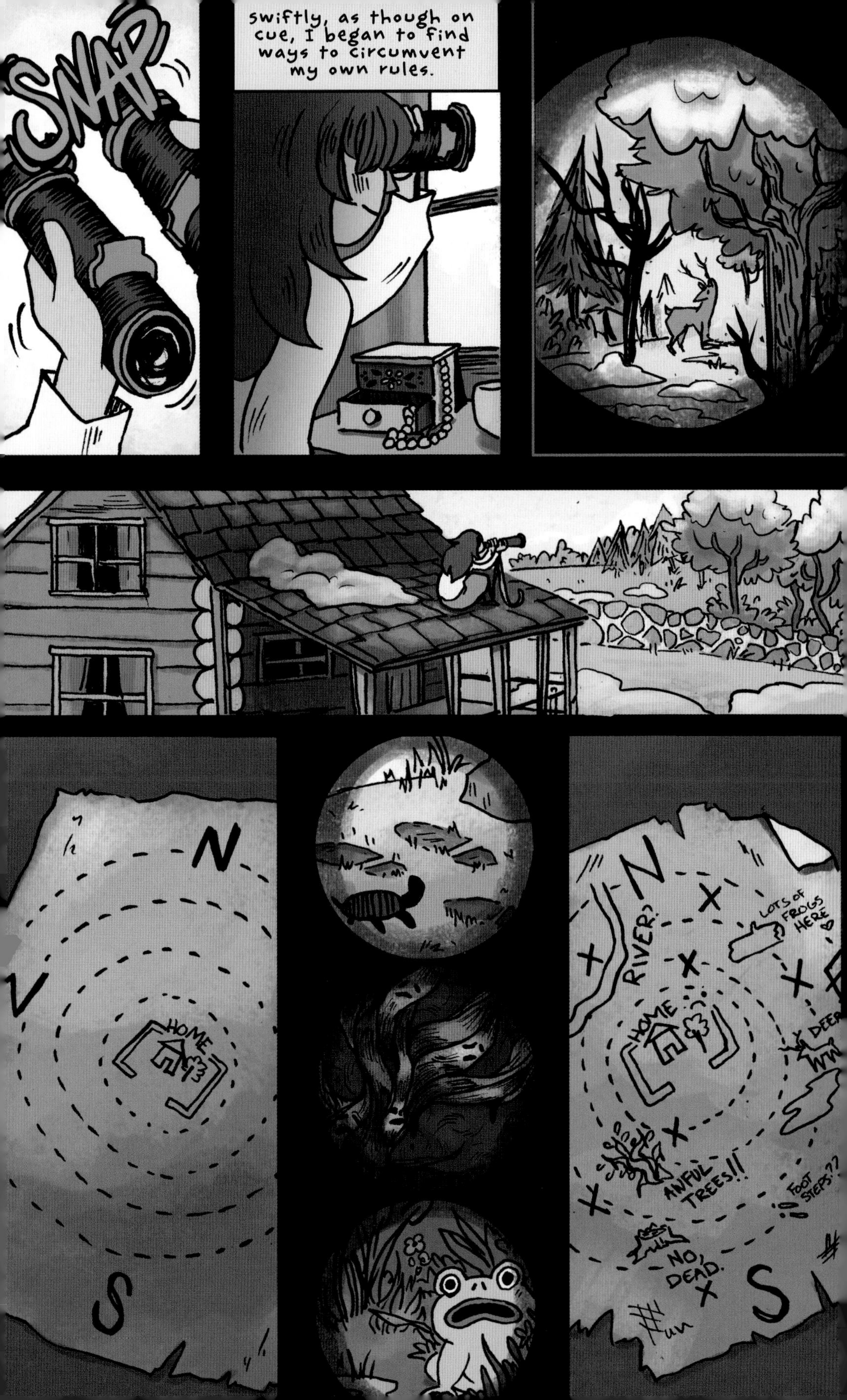
SNAP
swiftly, as though on cue, I began to find ways to circumvent my own rules.
N
HOME
S
N
RIVER?
LOTS OF FROGS HERE
HOME
DEER
AWFUL TREES!!
FOOT STEPS??
NO, DEAD.
S

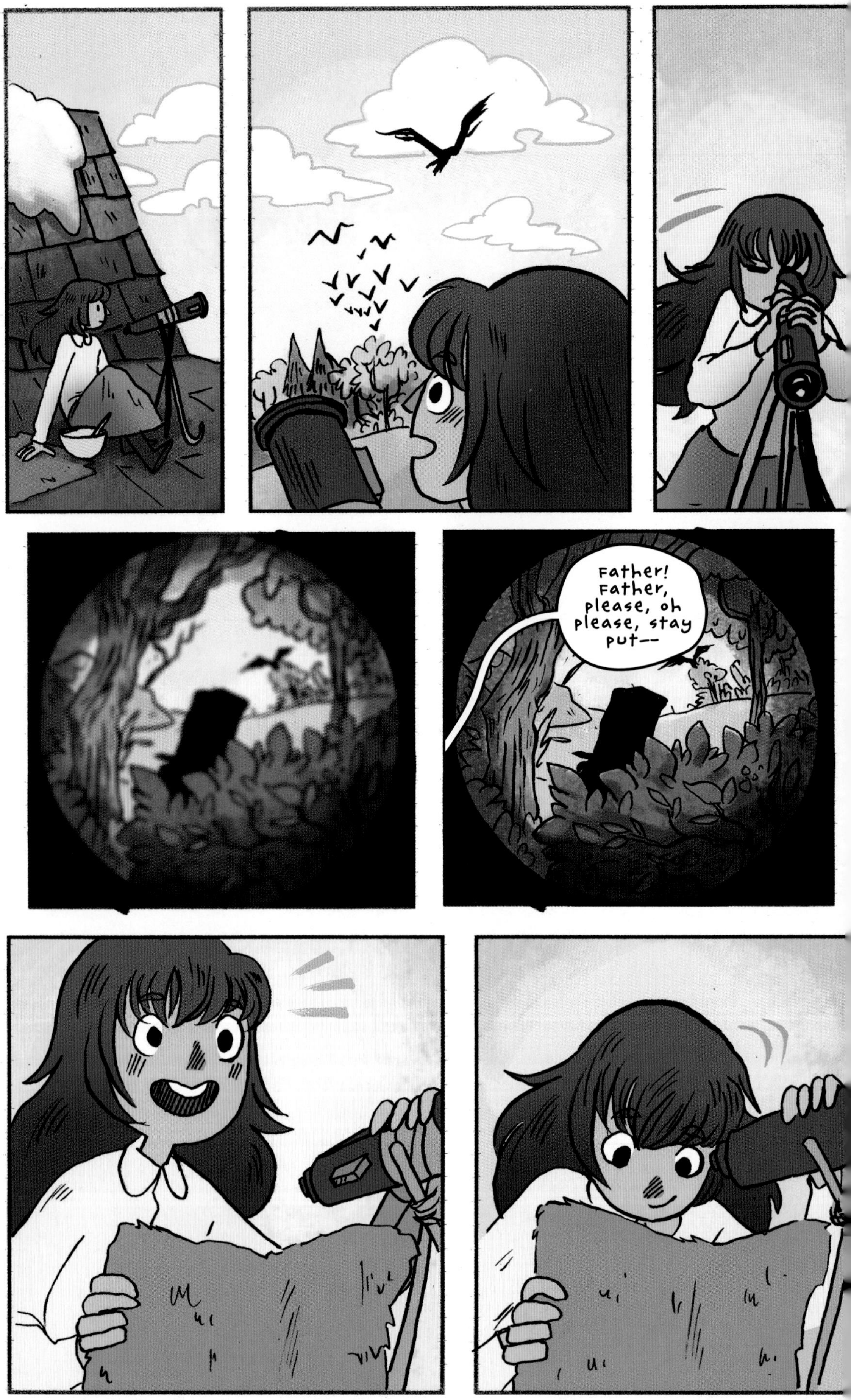
Father! Father, please, oh please, stay put--

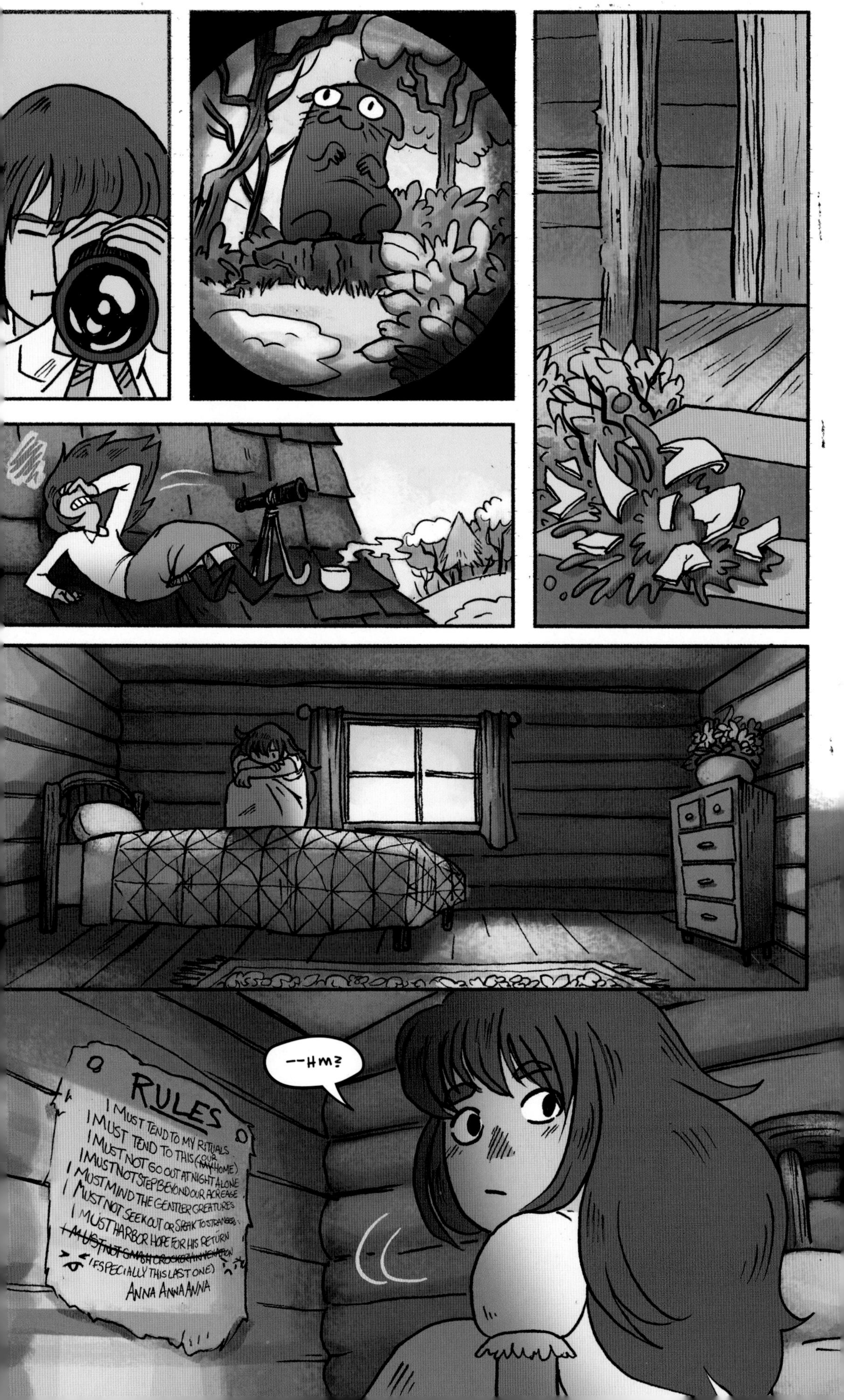

--HM?
RULES
I MUST TEND TO MY RITUALS
I MUST TEND TO THIS (~~MY~~ OUR HOME)
I MUST NOT GO OUT AT NIGHT ALONE
I MUST NOT STEP BEYOND OUR ACREAGE
I MUST MIND THE GENTLER CREATURES
I MUST NOT SEEK OUT OR SPEAK TO STRANGERS
I MUST HARBOR HOPE FOR HIS RETURN
~~I MUST NOT SMASH CROCKERY IN VEXATION~~
(ESPECIALLY THIS LAST ONE)
ANNA ANNA ANNA

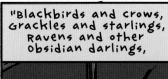

"Blackbirds and crows,
Grackles and starlings,
Ravens and other
Obsidian darlings,

"When flocks circle
upward, Dear Daughter,
take heed, quell all
trepidation. And follow
their lead."

I couldn't part with caution in that moment—not yet. But the forest echoed some faraway hymn...

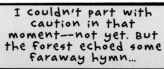

...and I thought of how distance can be bridged by something so simple.

--but it could have clamored like a cyclone of ornery squirrels, and I would have been just as taken with the sound. What mattered was its purpose. I'd made a beacon for Father to hear.

The wind through the chimes rang out like bells, lovely and loud--

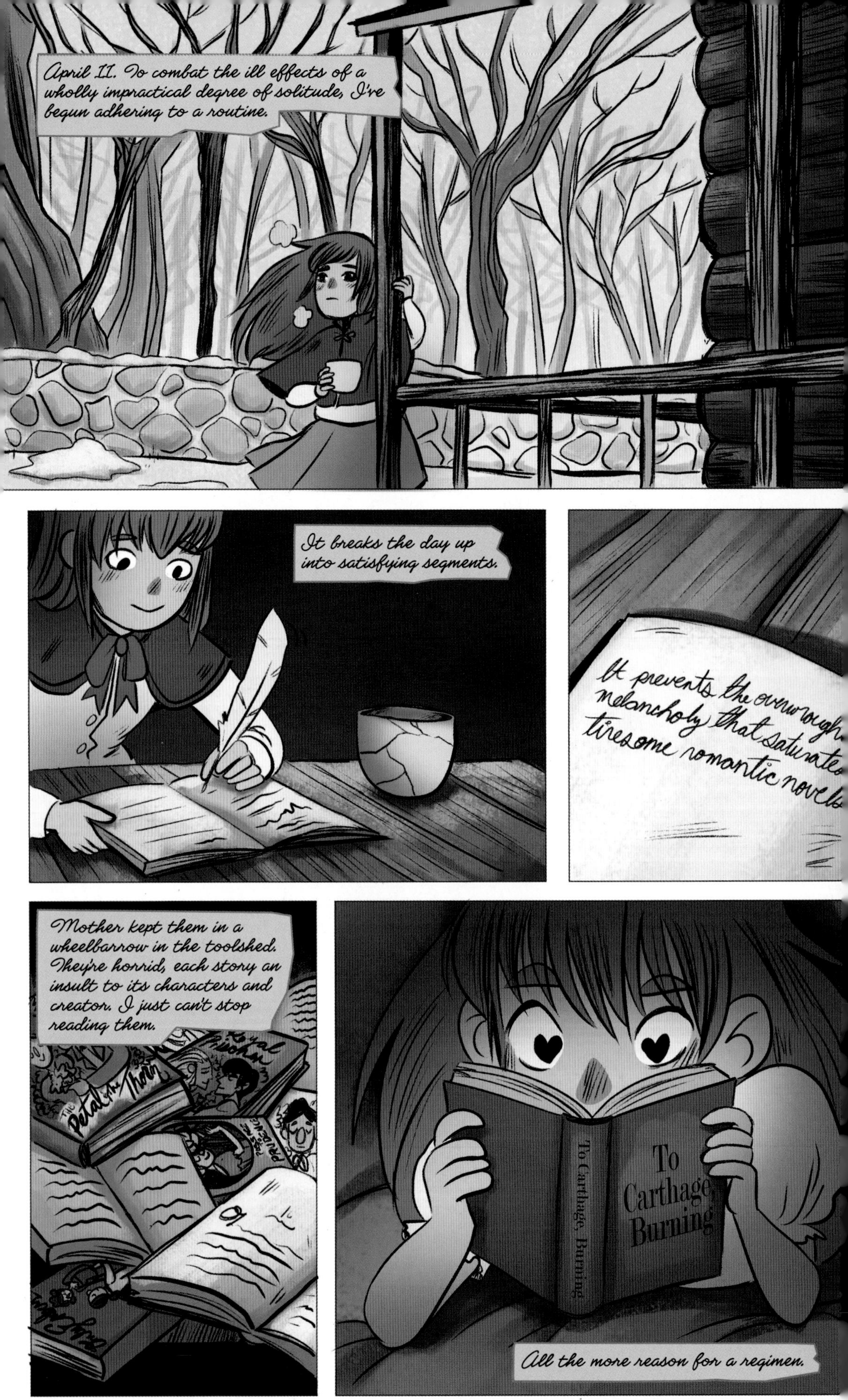
April 11. To combat the ill effects of a wholly impractical degree of solitude, I've begun adhering to a routine.
It breaks the day up into satisfying segments.
It prevents the overwrough
melancholy that saturates
tiresome romantic novels
Mother kept them in a wheelbarrow in the toolshed. They're horrid, each story an insult to its characters and creator. I just can't stop reading them.
Royal Prisoner
The Petal and the Thorn
To Carthage, Burning
To Carthage, Burning
All the more reason for a regimen.

Mornings I do my best to allow the homestead to sustain itself. I say "allow" because I suspect that my presence isn't necessary.

...it rains, the sun resurfaces, things grow.

Not to undercut my efforts, which left me sore for weeks before my bones settled into the daily rhythm, and which deposit dirt into my fingernails like a demented Lady-in-Waiting.

All I mean is that when I complete my tasks to the letter, it feels just like winding up a clock at daybreak that ticks steadily until the next day.

First I tend to the geese, then the goats.

I have a favorite one: a kid with a lame front leg that sometimes rests his head on my lap like a dog.

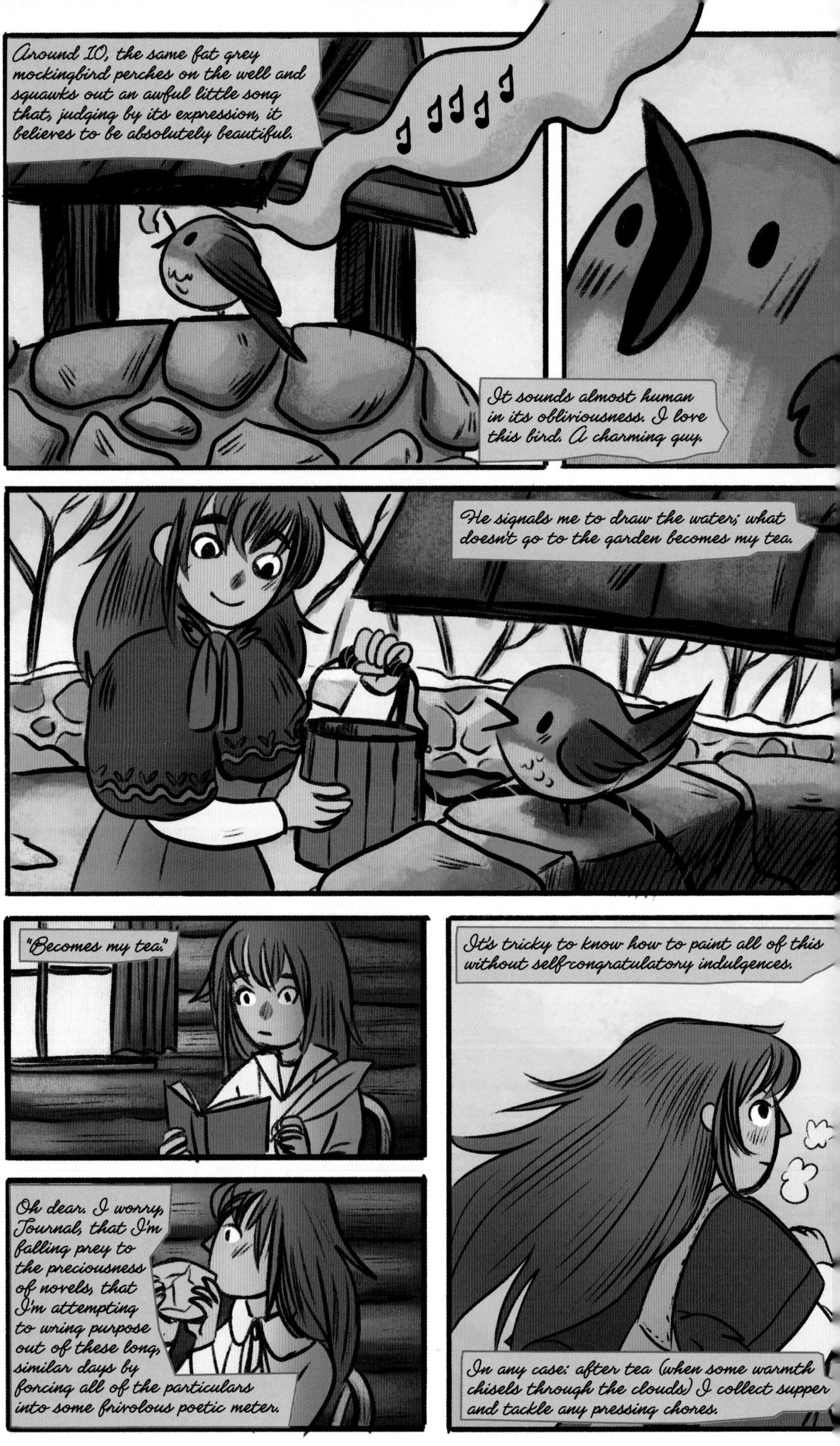
Around 10, the same fat grey mockingbird perches on the well and squawks out an awful little song that, judging by its expression, it believes to be absolutely beautiful.
It sounds almost human in its obliviousness. I love this bird. A charming guy.
He signals me to draw the water; what doesn't go to the garden becomes my tea.
"Becomes my tea."
Oh dear. I worry, Journal, that I'm falling prey to the preciousness of novels, that I'm attempting to wring purpose out of these long, similar days by forcing all of the particulars into some frivolous poetic meter.
It's tricky to know how to paint all of this without self-congratulatory indulgences.
In any case: after tea (when some warmth chisels through the clouds) I collect supper and tackle any pressing chores.

Then I take a walk for as long as it takes to sweep the spiders from my brain. Not literally, Journal. I clear my head, that's all.

Then there's "lessons time" which is where I use Mother and Father's books to pretend that a proper education can be attained without instruction. I've improved in arithmetic and cartography. I wish I knew how to train my own voice.

Then supper. Then I head to the roof, where the search for Father resumes.

I've managed to cover a great deal of the woods. I scan as much as I can until sundown, always searching in concentric circles.

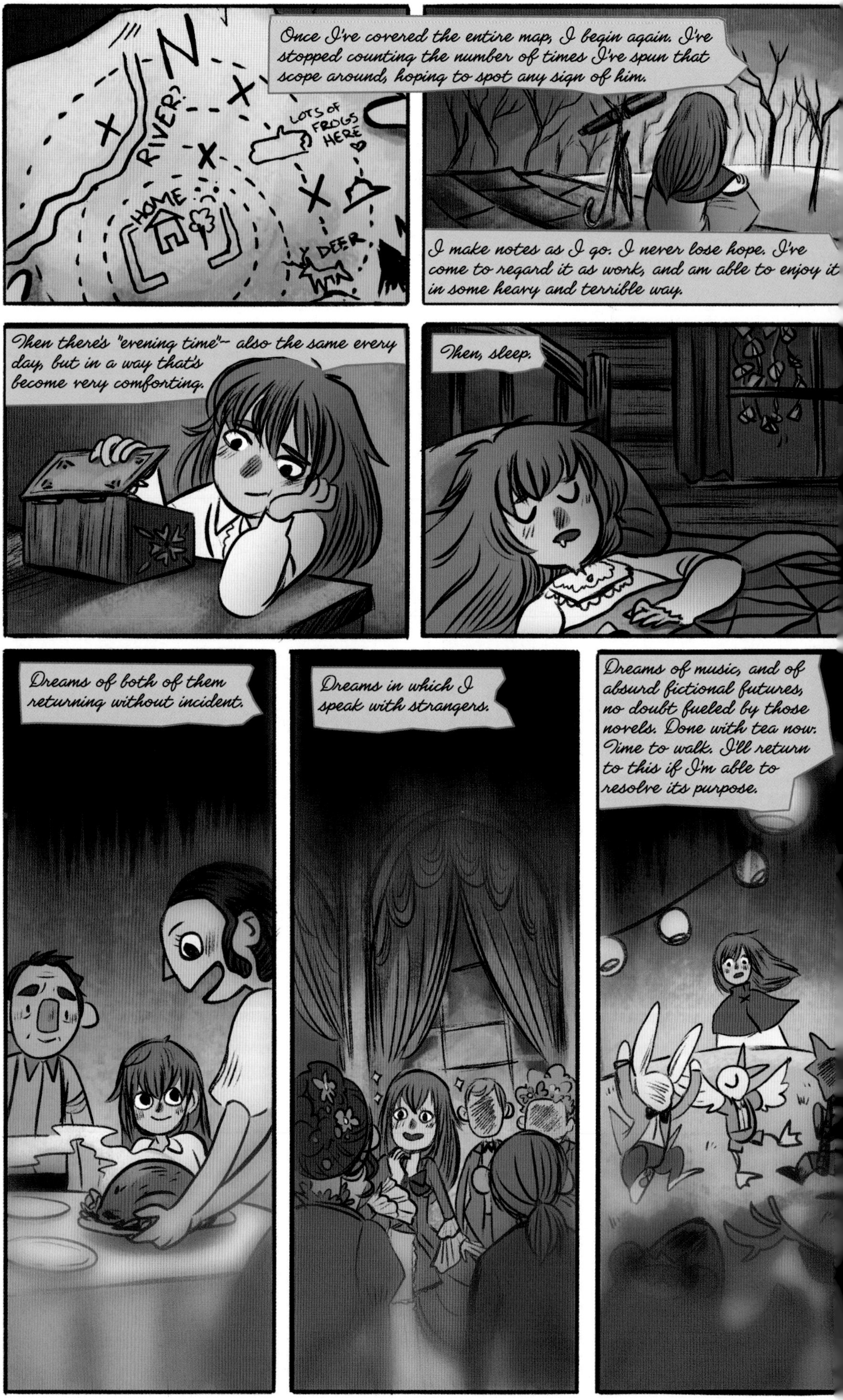
N
RIVER?
LOTS OF FROGS HERE
HOME
DEER
Once I've covered the entire map, I begin again. I've stopped counting the number of times I've spun that scope around, hoping to spot any sign of him.
I make notes as I go. I never lose hope. I've come to regard it as work, and am able to enjoy it in some heavy and terrible way.
Then there's "evening time"– also the same every day, but in a way that's become very comforting.
Then, sleep.
Dreams of both of them returning without incident.
Dreams in which I speak with strangers.
Dreams of music, and of absurd fictional futures, no doubt fueled by those novels. Done with tea now. Time to walk. I'll return to this if I'm able to resolve its purpose.

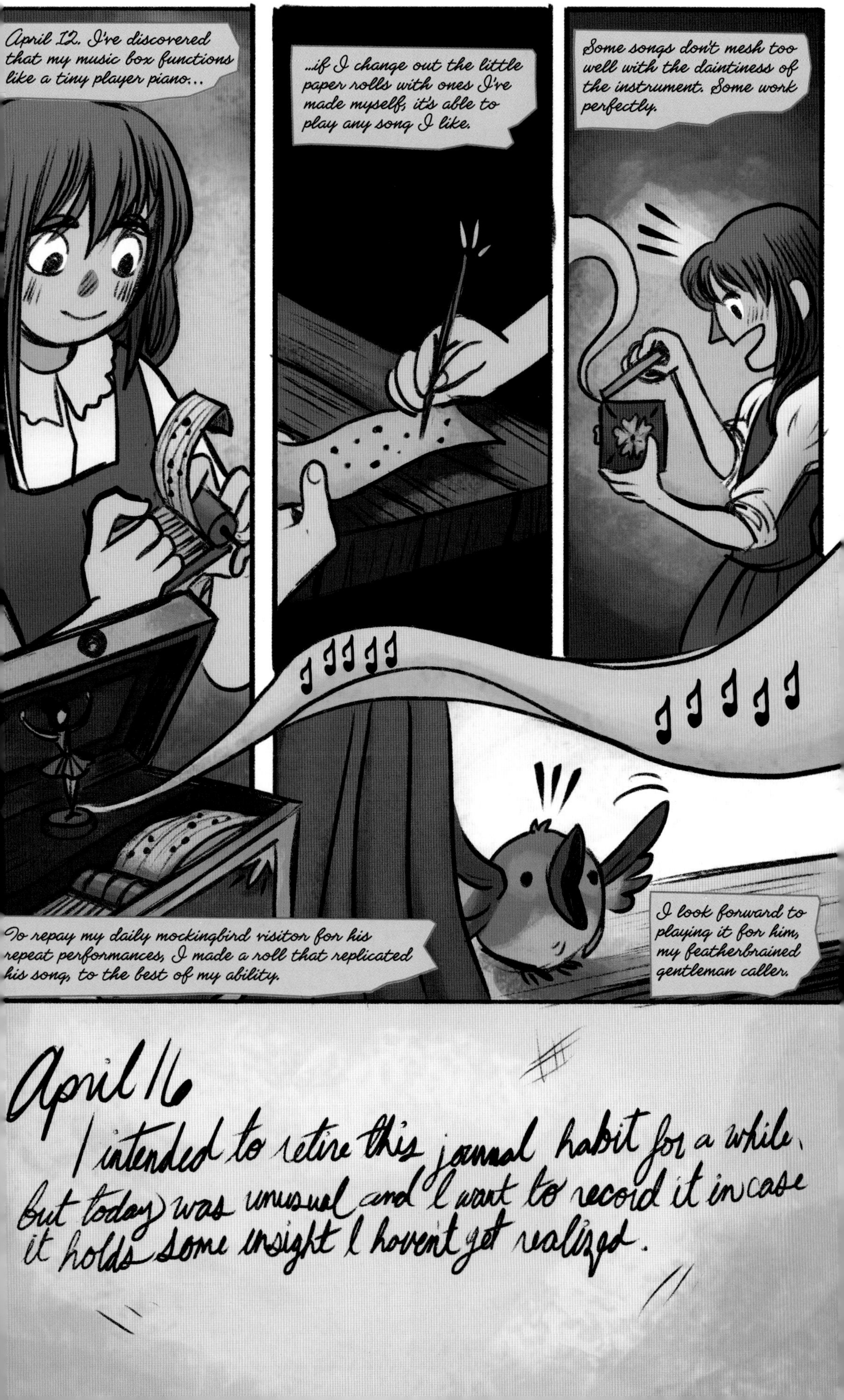
April 12. I've discovered that my music box functions like a tiny player piano...
...if I change out the little paper rolls with ones I've made myself, it's able to play any song I like.
Some songs don't mesh too well with the daintiness of the instrument. Some work perfectly.
To repay my daily mockingbird visitor for his repeat performances, I made a roll that replicated his song, to the best of my ability.
I look forward to playing it for him, my featherbrained gentleman caller.
April 16
I intended to retire this journal habit for a while, but today was unusual and I want to record it in case it holds some insight I haven't yet realized.

All telescope observations passed without incident. Halfway through my rounds, though, I spotted...something.

Other times I've noticed some life stirring in the forest~ plenty of creatures and the occasional wanderer~

~and once, some sort of celebration that I nearly investigated. But it would have been foolish. I've let caution dictate my choices, as Father would wish.

Lately, though, every time the telescope indicates a sign of some-one~anyone~I freeze. I've dismissed the sensation as fear, but I know it now as a sort of alarm set off by my loneliness.

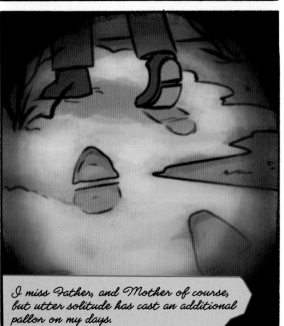

I miss Father, and Mother of course, but utter solitude has cast an additional pallor on my days.

I feel it deeply, a dearth that infiltrates the simplest moments with a disgusting sort of longing for even the smallest restige of connection with another person. Today the feeling got the better of me.

From my scope, I spotted a young couple about to stroll into a part of the woods from which it would have been difficult to return.

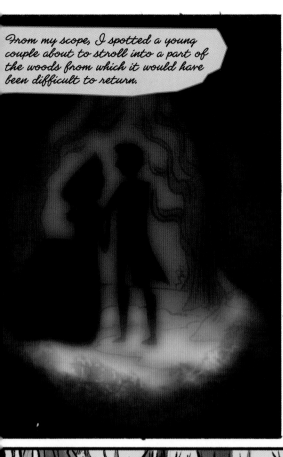

I ran. In my haste to reach them, I tumbled and tripped, making quite a mess of myself—

When I reached them, I hid.

They were, of course, in no danger.

There was no dark patch in the woods.

Finally desperate for conversation, my eyes had tricked me.

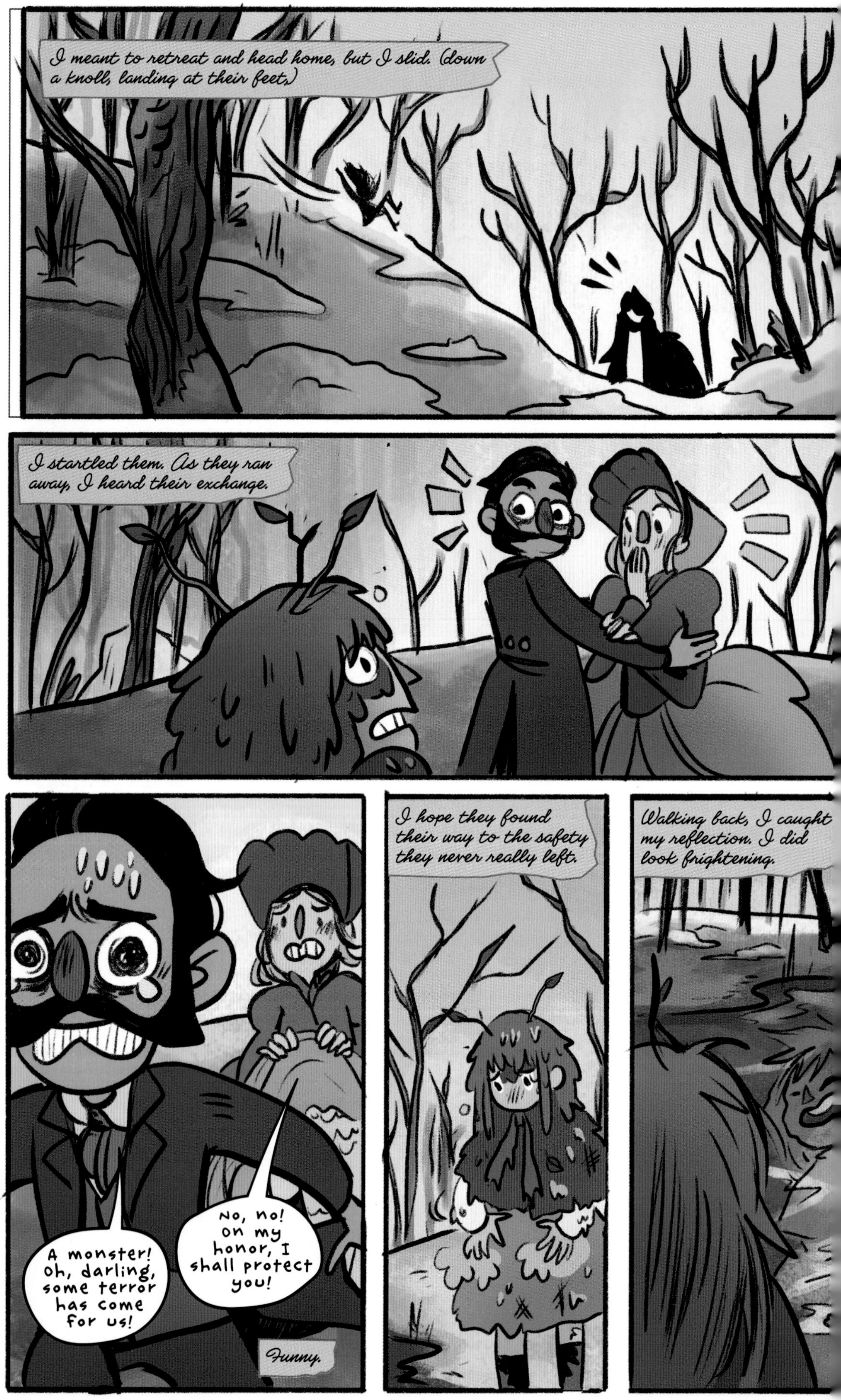

I meant to retreat and head home, but I slid. (down a knoll, landing at their feet.)
I startled them. As they ran away, I heard their exchange.
A monster! Oh, darling, some terror has come for us!
No, no! On my honor, I shall protect you!
Funny.
I hope they found their way to the safety they never really left.
Walking back, I caught my reflection. I did look frightening.

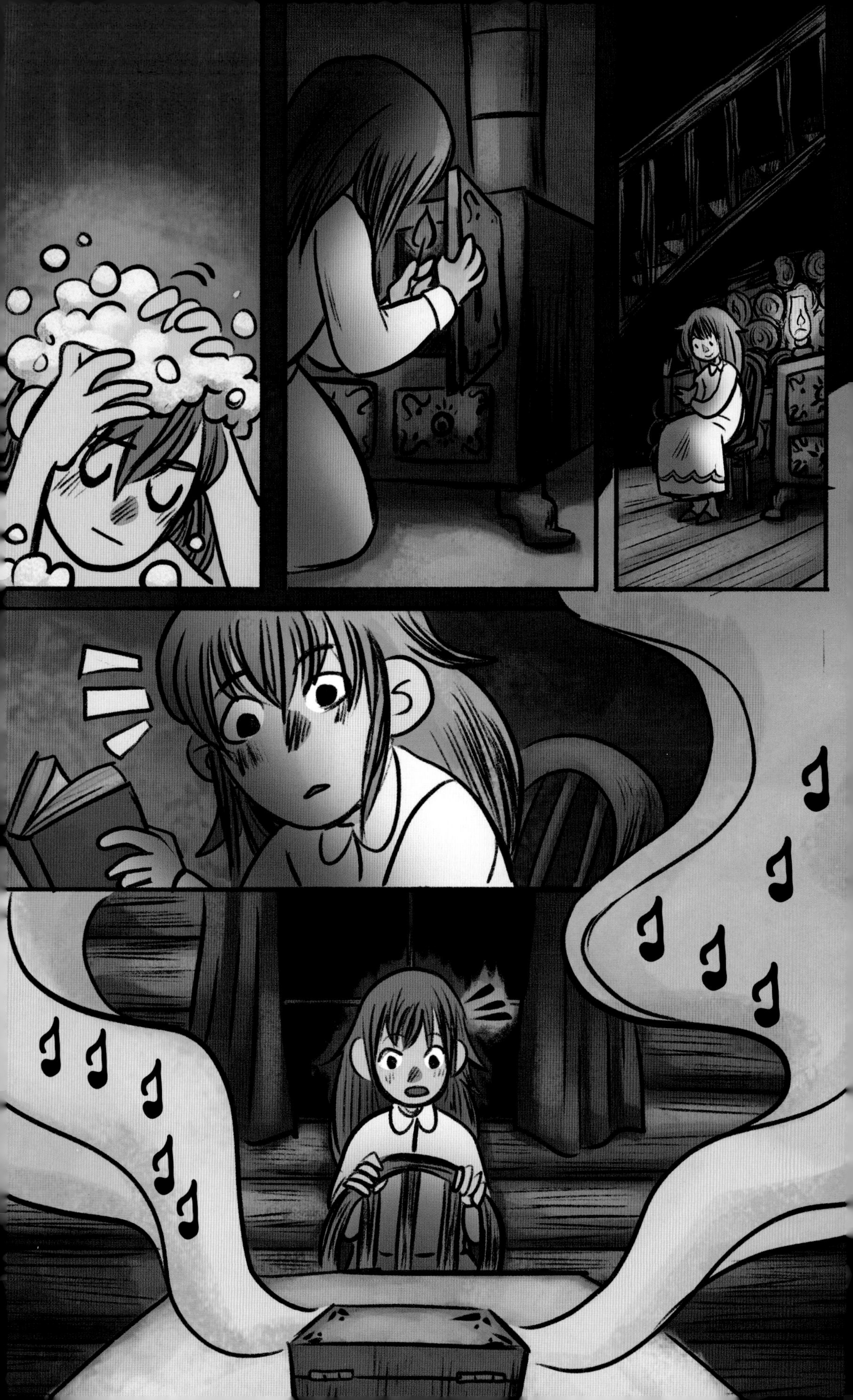

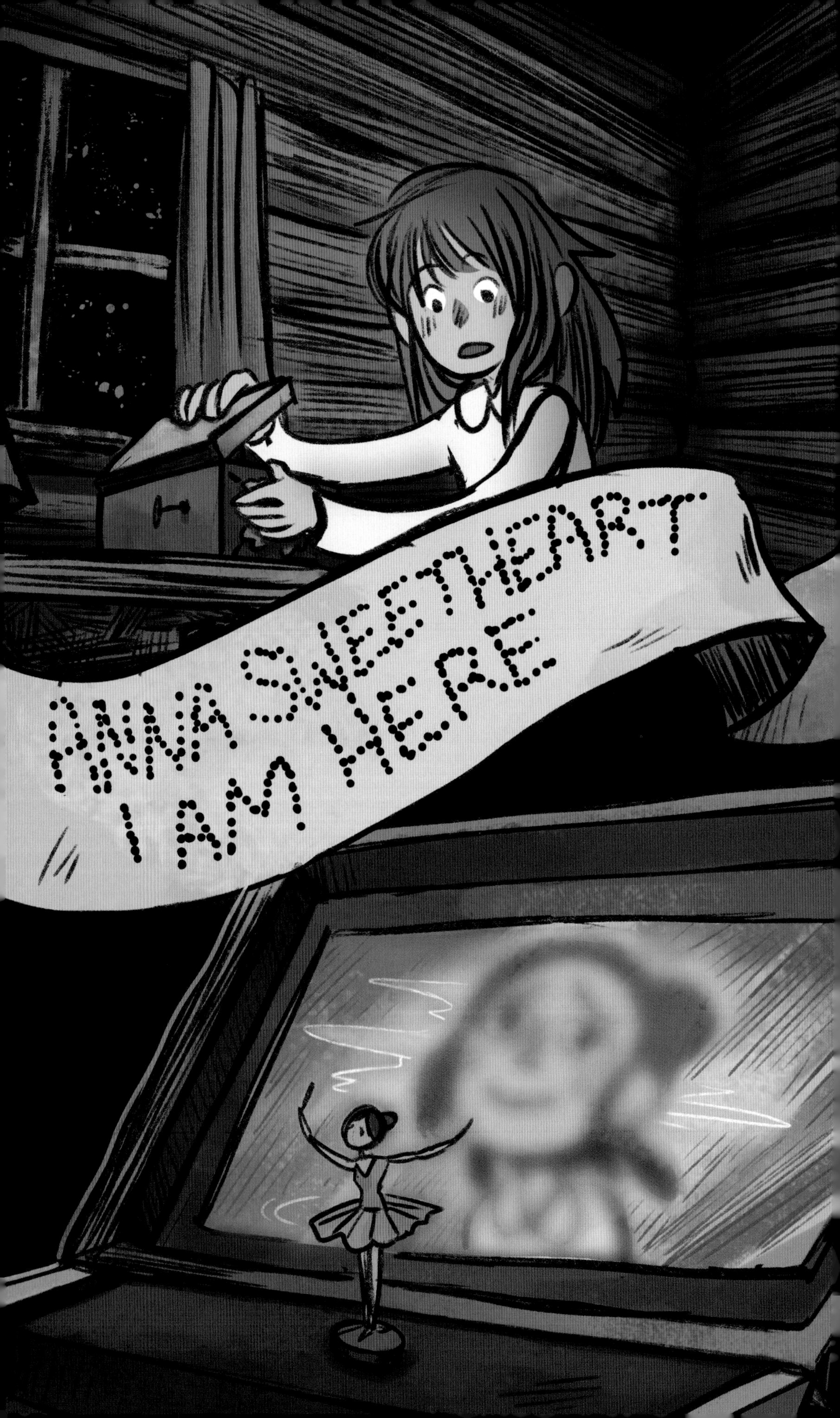
ANNA SWEETHEART
I AM HERE

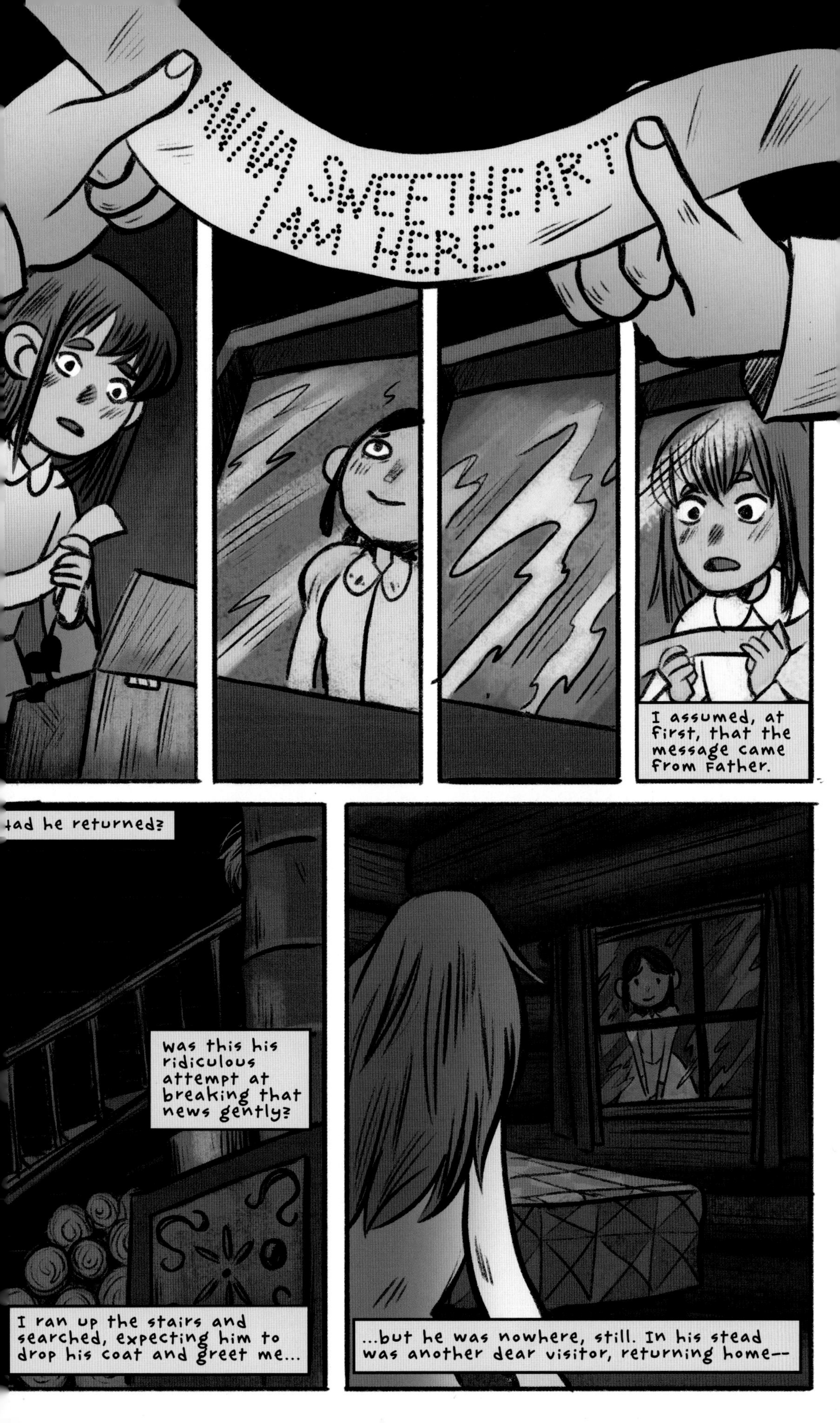
ANNA SWEETHEART I AM HERE
I assumed, at first, that the message came from Father.
Had he returned?
Was this his ridiculous attempt at breaking that news gently?
I ran up the stairs and searched, expecting him to drop his coat and greet me...
...but he was nowhere, still. In his stead was another dear visitor, returning home--

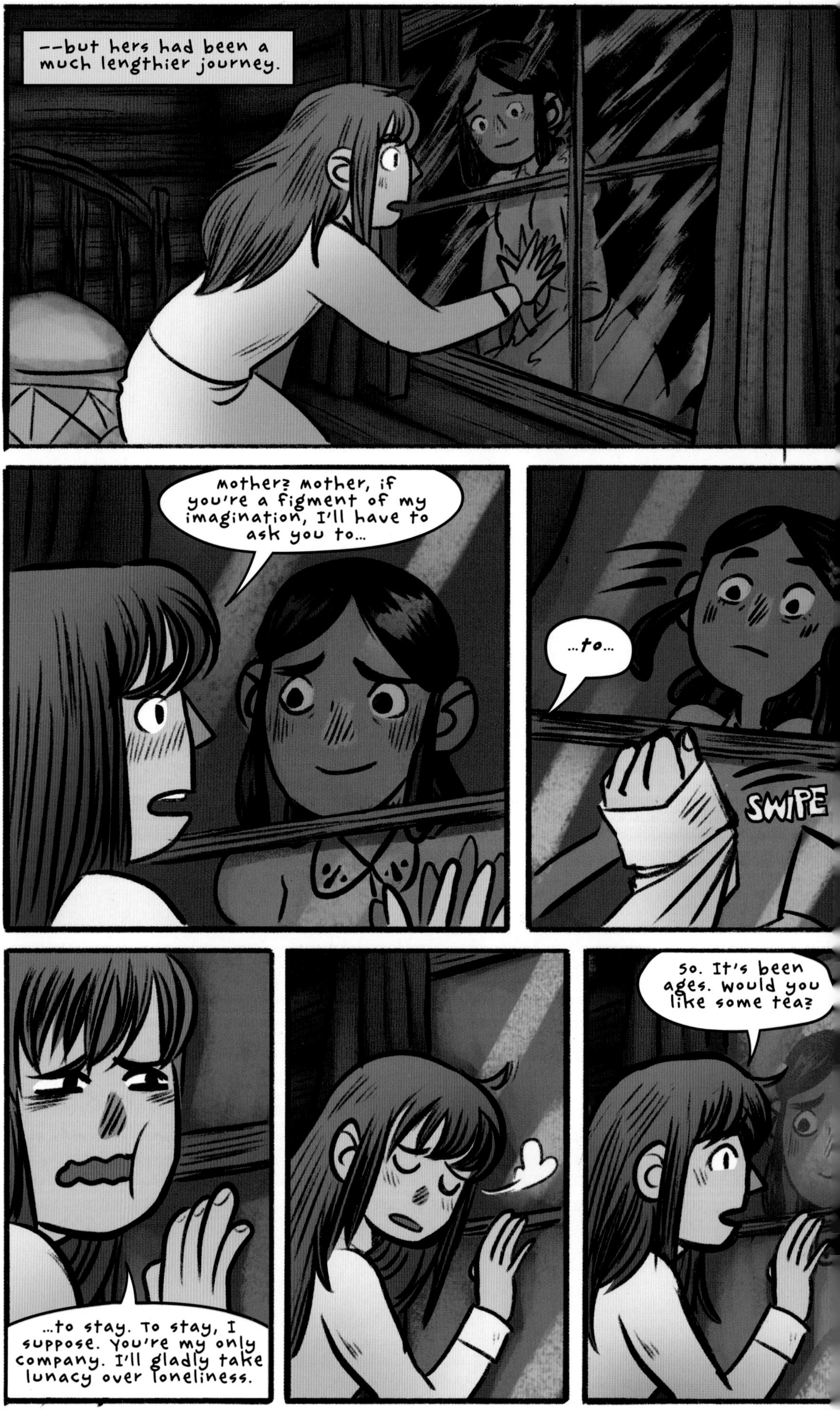
--but hers had been a much lengthier journey.
Mother? Mother, if you're a figment of my imagination, I'll have to ask you to...
...to...
SWIPE
...to stay. To stay, I suppose. You're my only company. I'll gladly take lunacy over loneliness.
So. It's been ages. Would you like some tea?

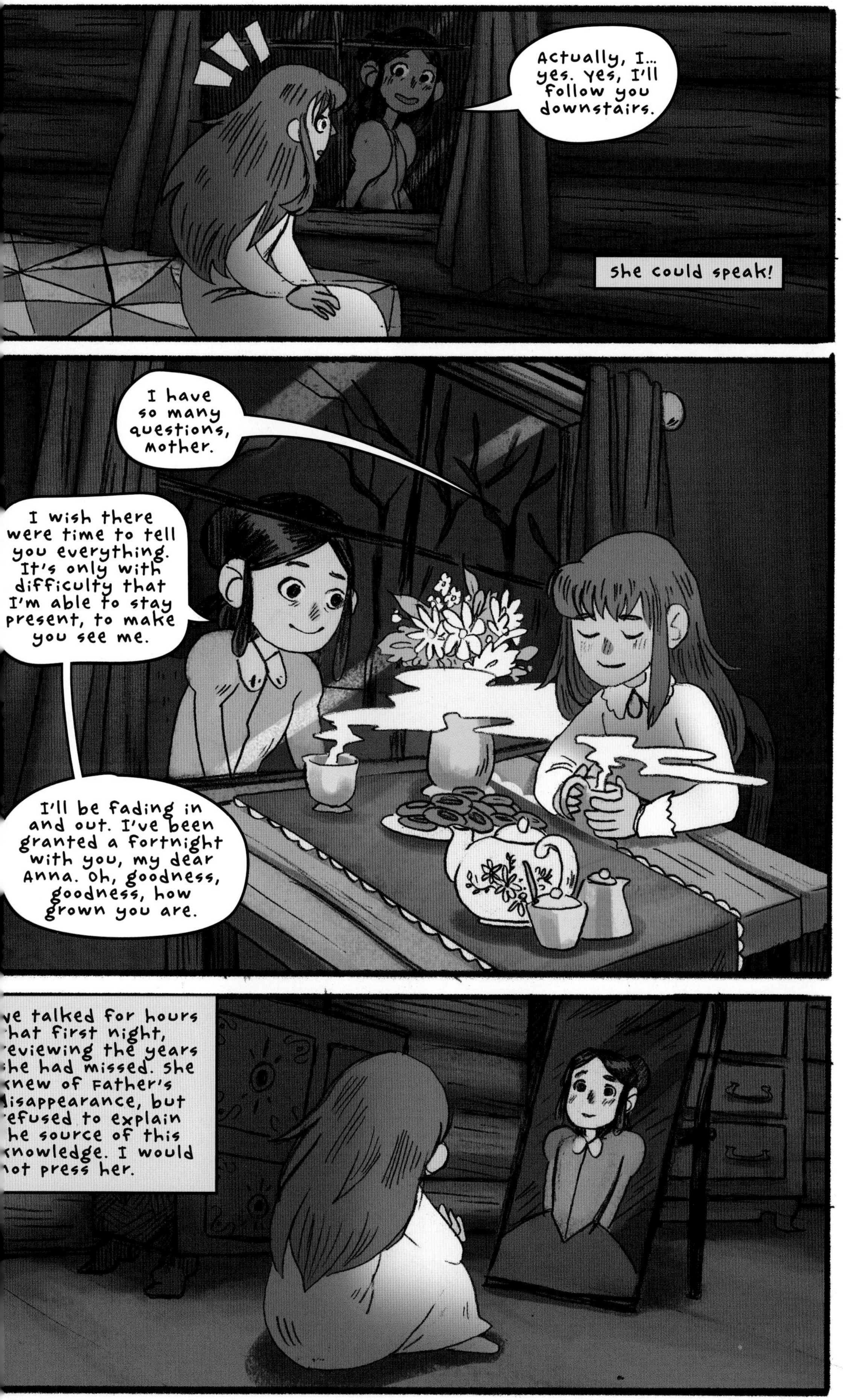

Actually, I... yes. Yes, I'll follow you downstairs.
She could speak!
I have so many questions, mother.
I wish there were time to tell you everything. It's only with difficulty that I'm able to stay present, to make you see me.
I'll be fading in and out. I've been granted a fortnight with you, my dear Anna. Oh, goodness, goodness, how grown you are.
We talked for hours that first night, reviewing the years she had missed. She knew of Father's disappearance, but refused to explain the source of this knowledge. I would not press her.

She insisted that we focus. There was so much time lost, and so much ground to cover, lessons she wished she had been able...present...to impart to me.

Are those brambles in your hair?

This belonged to my grandmother. But I replaced the metal brush pins with boar bristles. From a boar I caught myself. Ever caught a boar, dear?

Raccoon paws pressed in forest floor. Will lead you to the dullest boar.

Mother, I've missed your rhymes more than I can say.

Oh, sweetheart, stay sharp. You're stalking a feral hog.

Did you see the way those cowbirds fell?! They looked like cast-iron artichokes. Thud, thud--

--thud.

Oh. Gone.

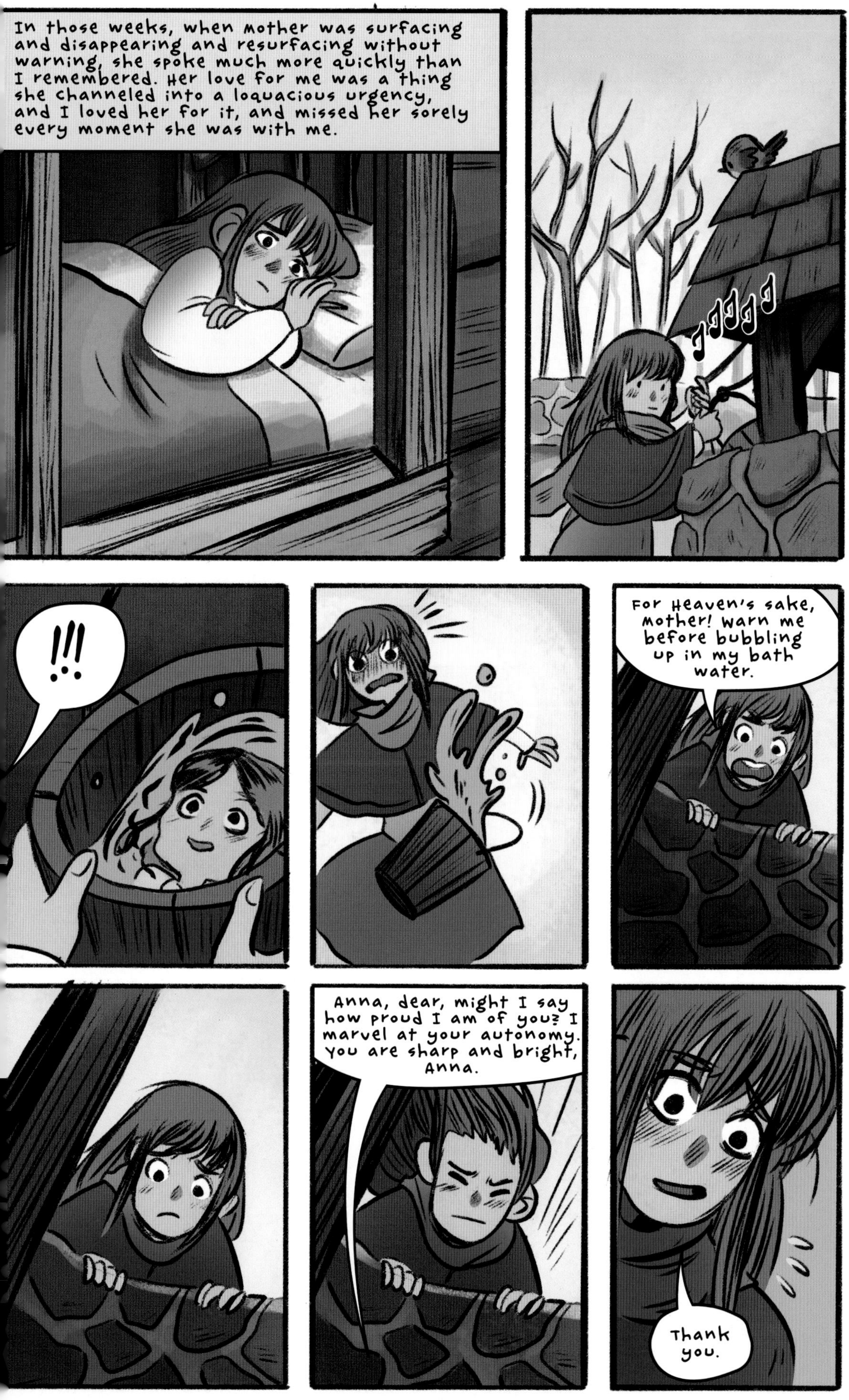
In those weeks, when mother was surfacing and disappearing and resurfacing without warning, she spoke much more quickly than I remembered. Her love for me was a thing she channeled into a loquacious urgency, and I loved her for it, and missed her sorely every moment she was with me.
!!!
For Heaven's sake, mother! Warn me before bubbling up in my bath water.
Anna, dear, might I say how proud I am of you? I marvel at your autonomy. You are sharp and bright, Anna.
Thank you.

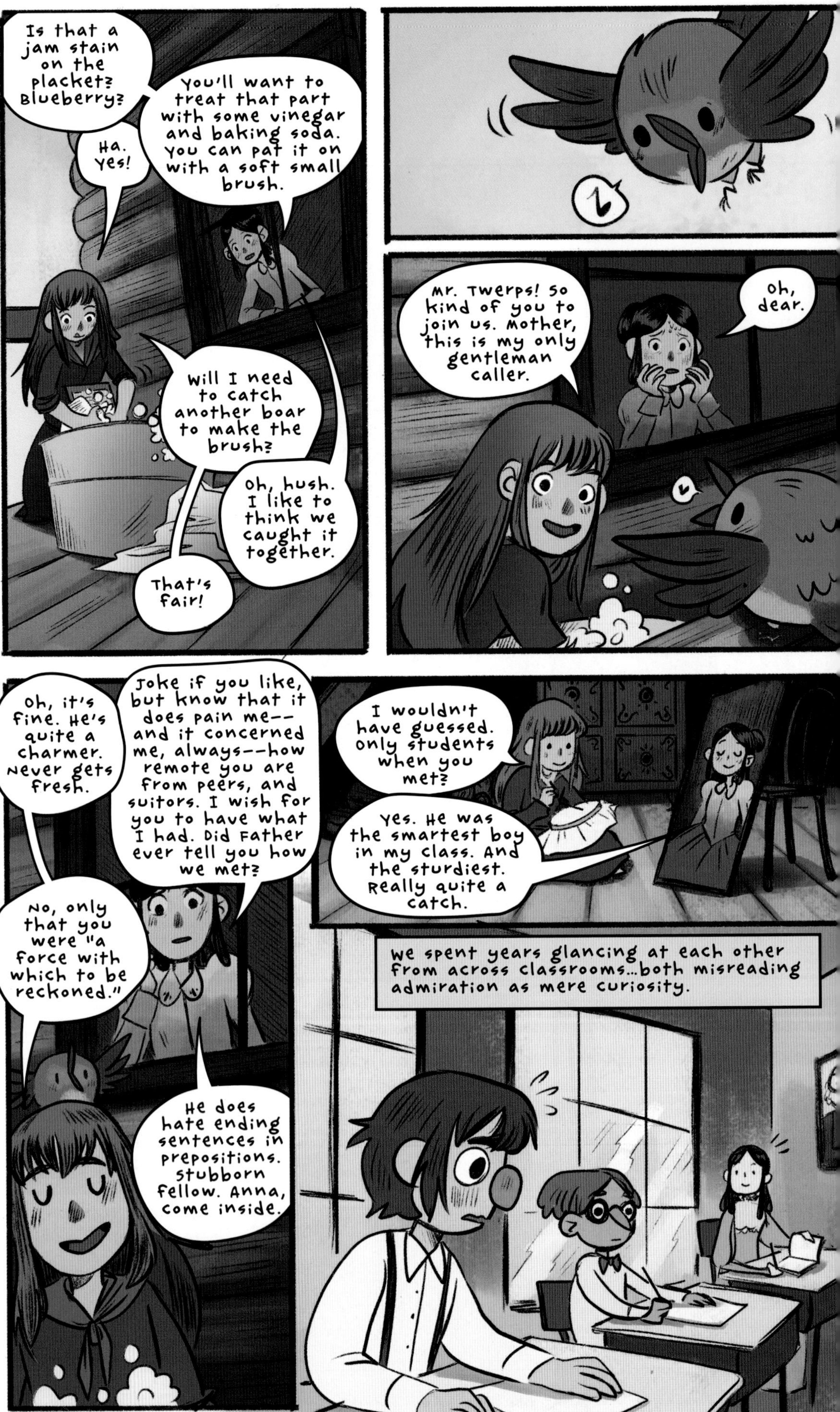
Is that a jam stain on the placket? Blueberry?
Ha. Yes!
You'll want to treat that part with some vinegar and baking soda. You can pat it on with a soft small brush.
Will I need to catch another boar to make the brush?
Oh, hush. I like to think we caught it together.
That's fair!
Mr. Twerps! So kind of you to join us. Mother, this is my only gentleman caller.
Oh, dear.
Oh, it's fine. He's quite a charmer. Never gets fresh.
Joke if you like, but know that it does pain me-- and it concerned me, always--how remote you are from peers, and suitors. I wish for you to have what I had. Did Father ever tell you how we met?
No, only that you were "a force with which to be reckoned."
He does hate ending sentences in prepositions. Stubborn fellow. Anna, come inside.
I wouldn't have guessed. Only students when you met?
Yes. He was the smartest boy in my class. And the sturdiest. Really quite a catch.
We spent years glancing at each other from across classrooms...both misreading admiration as mere curiosity.

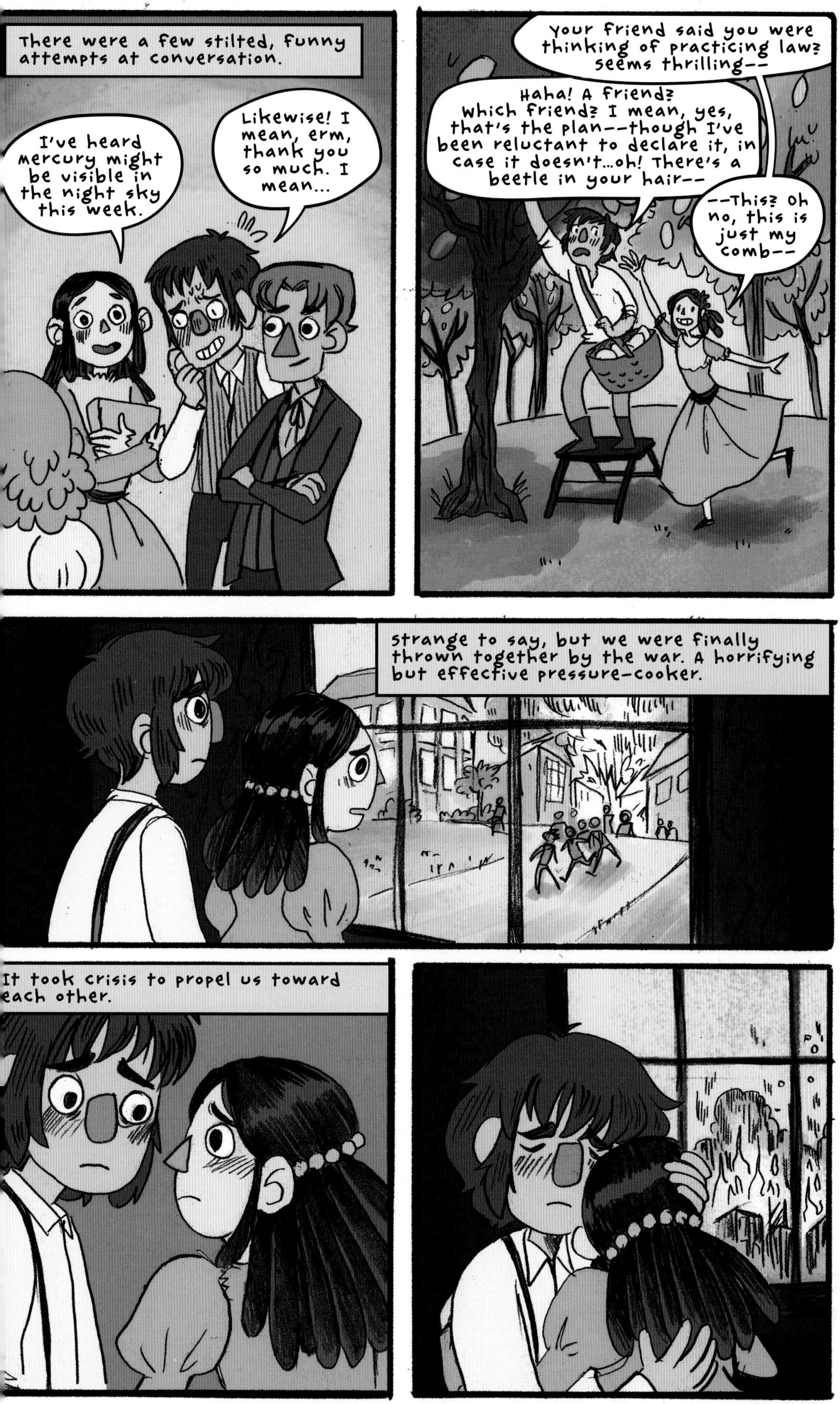
There were a few stilted, funny attempts at conversation.
I've heard mercury might be visible in the night sky this week.
Likewise! I mean, erm, thank you so much. I mean...
Your friend said you were thinking of practicing law? seems thrilling--
Haha! A friend? Which friend? I mean, yes, that's the plan--though I've been reluctant to declare it, in case it doesn't...oh! There's a beetle in your hair--
--This? Oh no, this is just my comb--
strange to say, but we were finally thrown together by the war. A horrifying but effective pressure-cooker.
It took crisis to propel us toward each other.

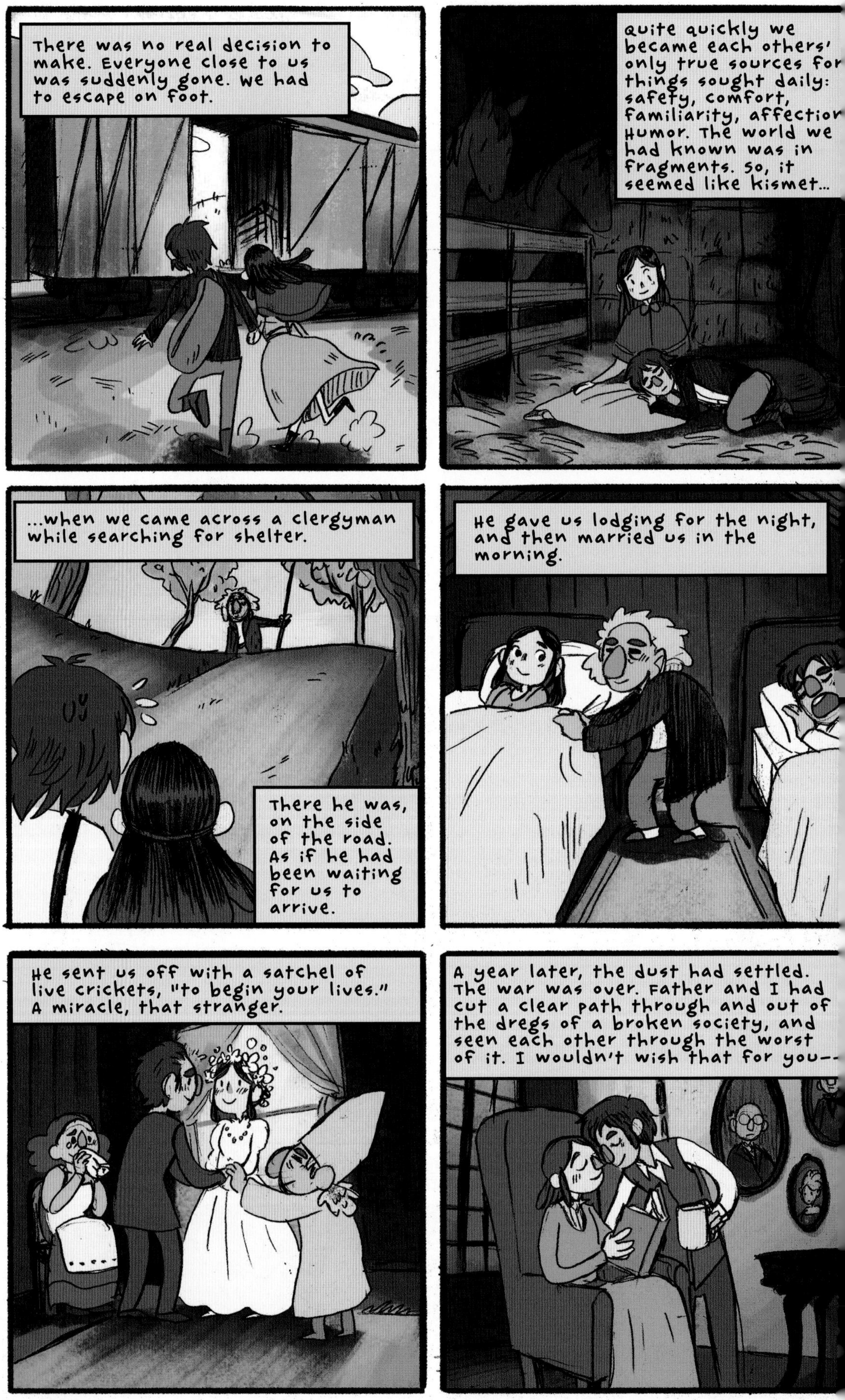
There was no real decision to make. Everyone close to us was suddenly gone. We had to escape on foot.
Quite quickly we became each others' only true sources for things sought daily: safety, comfort, familiarity, affection, humor. The world we had known was in fragments. So, it seemed like kismet...
...when we came across a clergyman while searching for shelter.
There he was, on the side of the road. As if he had been waiting for us to arrive.
He gave us lodging for the night, and then married us in the morning.
He sent us off with a satchel of live crickets, "to begin your lives." A miracle, that stranger.
A year later, the dust had settled. The war was over. Father and I had cut a clear path through and out of the dregs of a broken society, and seen each other through the worst of it. I wouldn't wish that for you--

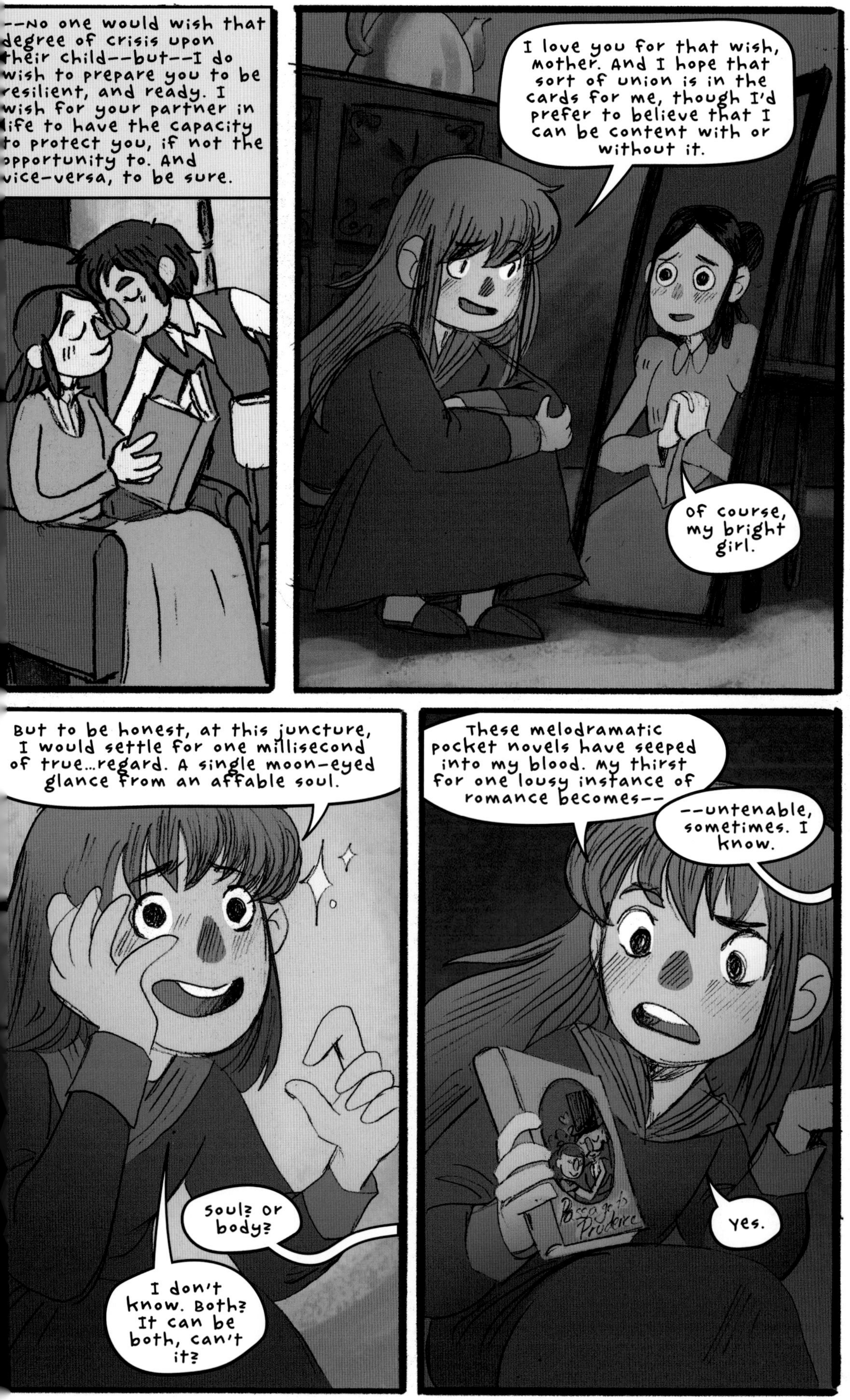
--No one would wish that degree of crisis upon their child--but--I do wish to prepare you to be resilient, and ready. I wish for your partner in life to have the capacity to protect you, if not the opportunity to. And vice-versa, to be sure.
I love you for that wish, mother. And I hope that sort of union is in the cards for me, though I'd prefer to believe that I can be content with or without it.
Of course, my bright girl.
But to be honest, at this juncture, I would settle for one millisecond of true...regard. A single moon-eyed glance from an affable soul.
Soul? Or body?
I don't know. Both? It can be both, can't it?
These melodramatic pocket novels have seeped into my blood. My thirst for one lousy instance of romance becomes--
--untenable, sometimes. I know.
Yes.
Passage to Prudence

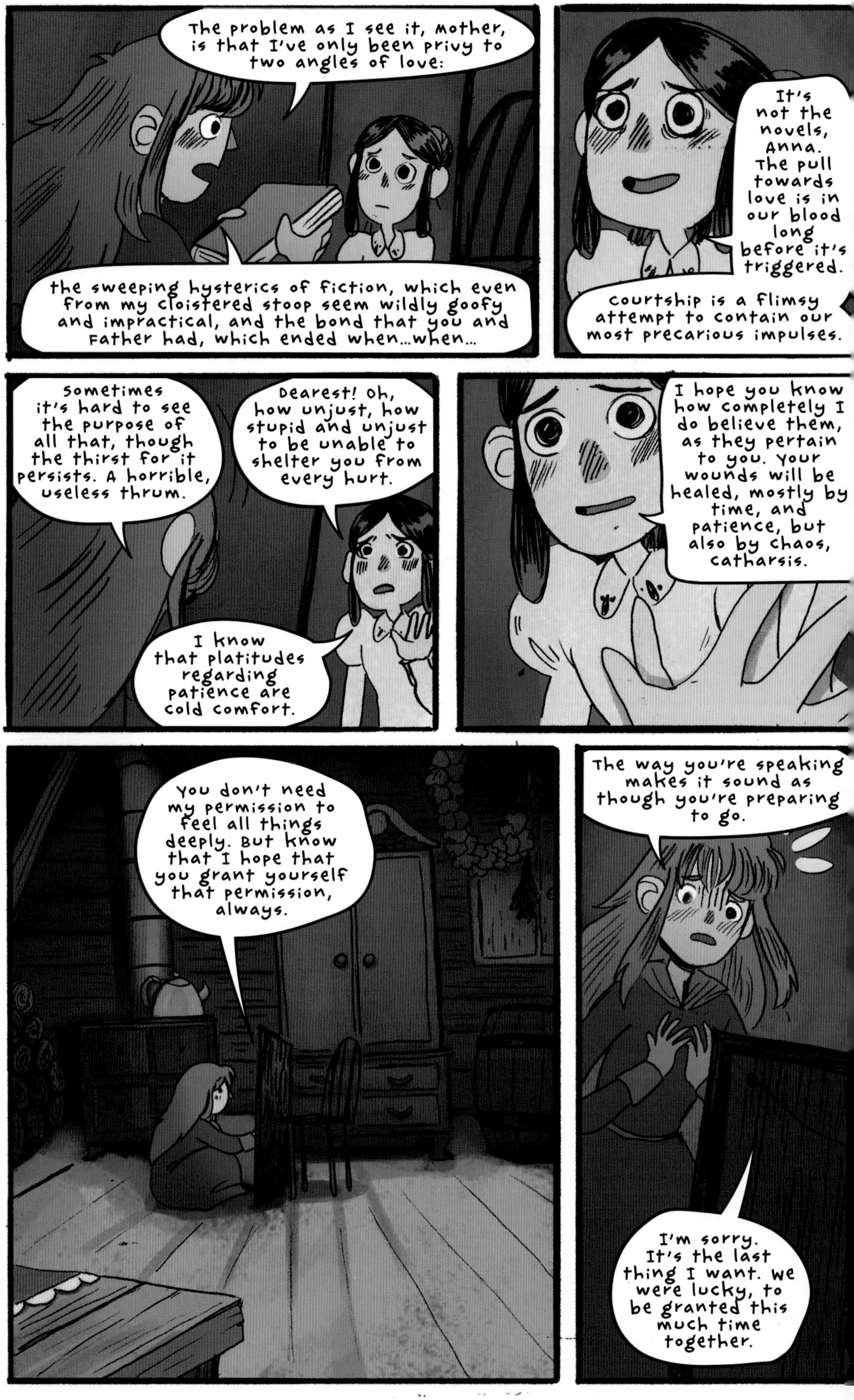
The problem as I see it, mother, is that I've only been privy to two angles of love:
the sweeping hysterics of fiction, which even from my cloistered stoop seem wildly goofy and impractical, and the bond that you and Father had, which ended when...when...
It's not the novels, Anna. The pull towards love is in our blood long before it's triggered.
Courtship is a flimsy attempt to contain our most precarious impulses.
Sometimes it's hard to see the purpose of all that, though the thirst for it persists. A horrible, useless thrum.
Dearest! Oh, how unjust, how stupid and unjust to be unable to shelter you from every hurt.
I know that platitudes regarding patience are cold comfort.
I hope you know how completely I do believe them, as they pertain to you. Your wounds will be healed, mostly by time, and patience, but also by chaos, catharsis.
You don't need my permission to feel all things deeply. But know that I hope that you grant yourself that permission, always.
The way you're speaking makes it sound as though you're preparing to go.
I'm sorry. It's the last thing I want. We were lucky, to be granted this much time together.

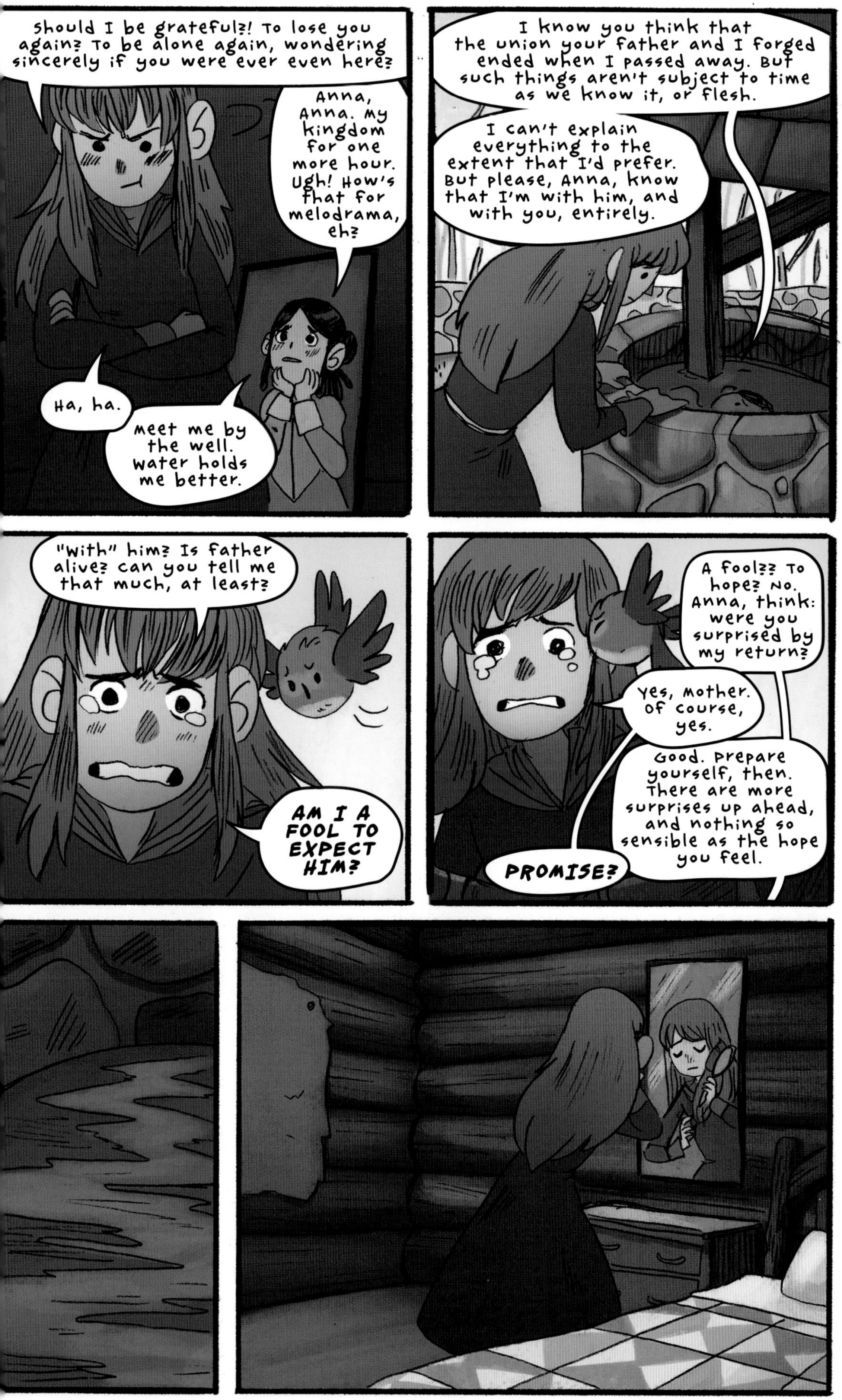
Should I be grateful?! To lose you again? To be alone again, wondering sincerely if you were ever even here?
Anna, Anna. My kingdom for one more hour. Ugh! How's that for melodrama, eh?
Ha, ha.
Meet me by the well. Water holds me better.
I know you think that the union your father and I forged ended when I passed away. But such things aren't subject to time as we know it, or flesh.
I can't explain everything to the extent that I'd prefer. But please, Anna, know that I'm with him, and with you, entirely.
"With" him? Is father alive? Can you tell me that much, at least?
AM I A FOOL TO EXPECT HIM?
A fool?? To hope? No. Anna, think: were you surprised by my return?
Yes, mother. Of course, yes.
Good. Prepare yourself, then. There are more surprises up ahead, and nothing so sensible as the hope you feel.
PROMISE?

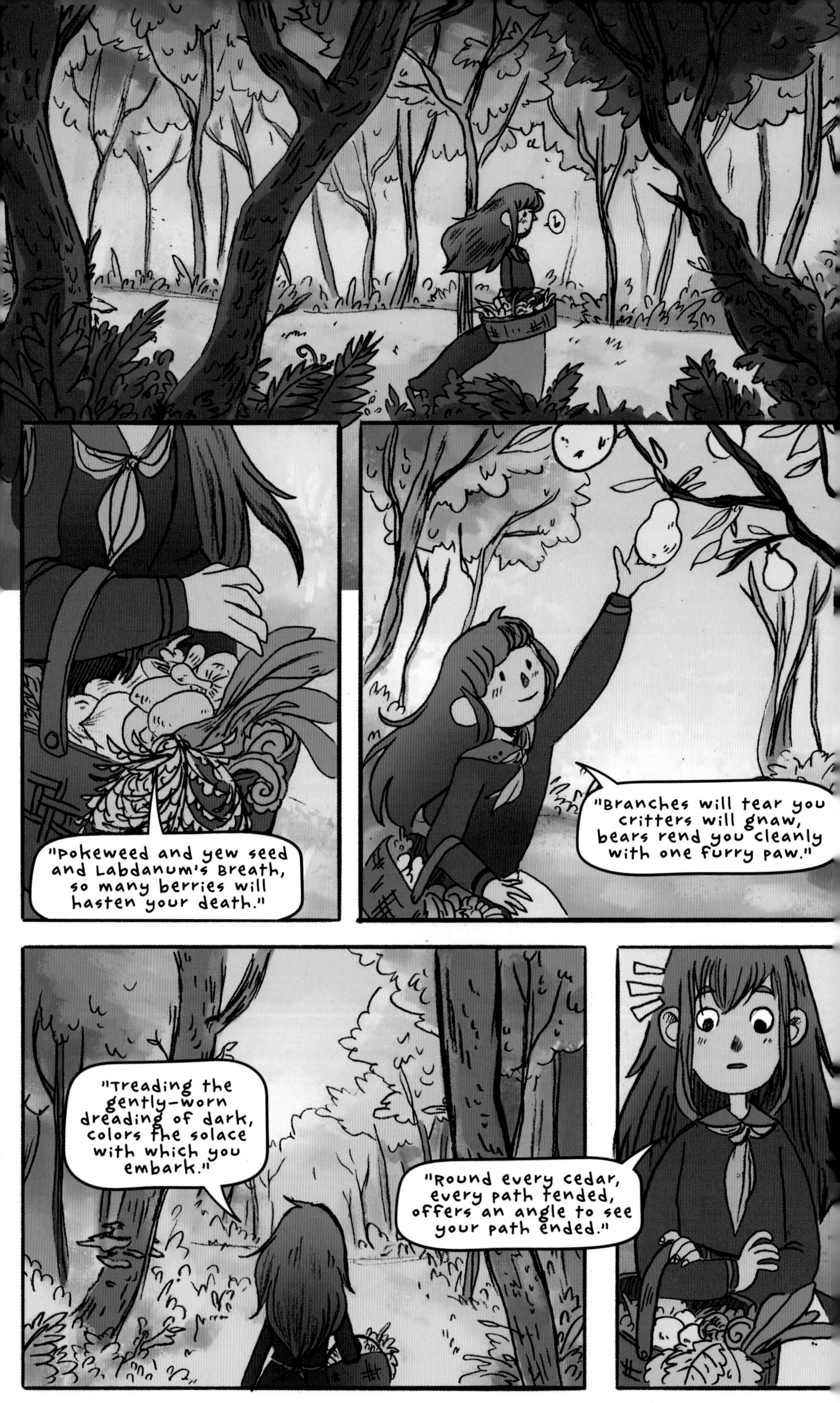
"Pokeweed and yew seed and Labdanum's Breath, so many berries will hasten your death."
"Branches will tear you critters will gnaw, bears rend you cleanly with one furry paw."
"Treading the gently-worn dreading of dark, colors the solace with which you embark."
"Round every cedar, every path tended, offers an angle to see your path ended."

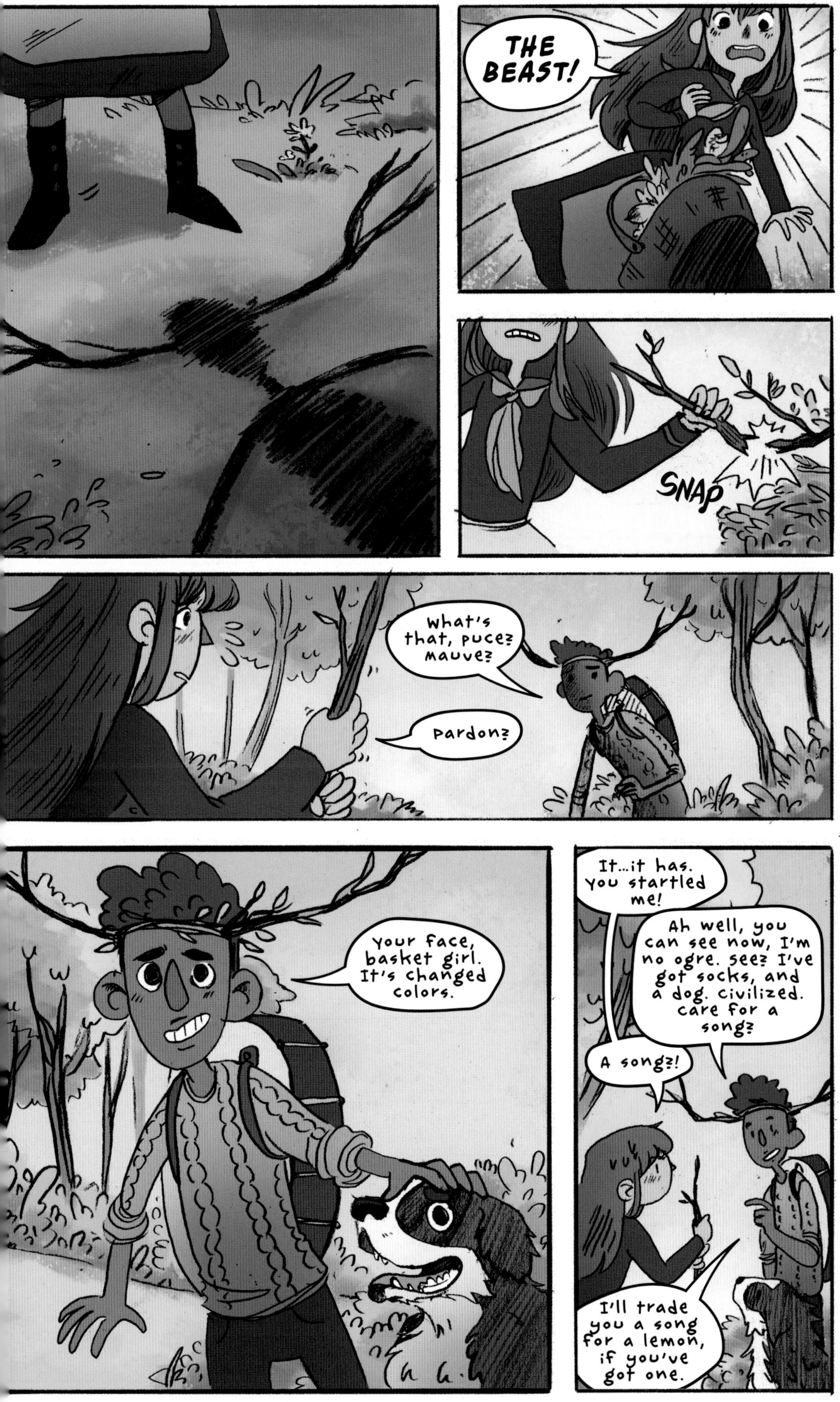
THE BEAST!
SNAP
What's that, puce? mauve?
Pardon?
Your face, basket girl. It's changed colors.
It...it has. You startled me!
Ah well, you can see now, I'm no ogre. see? I've got socks, and a dog. civilized. care for a song?
A song?!
I'll trade you a song for a lemon, if you've got one.

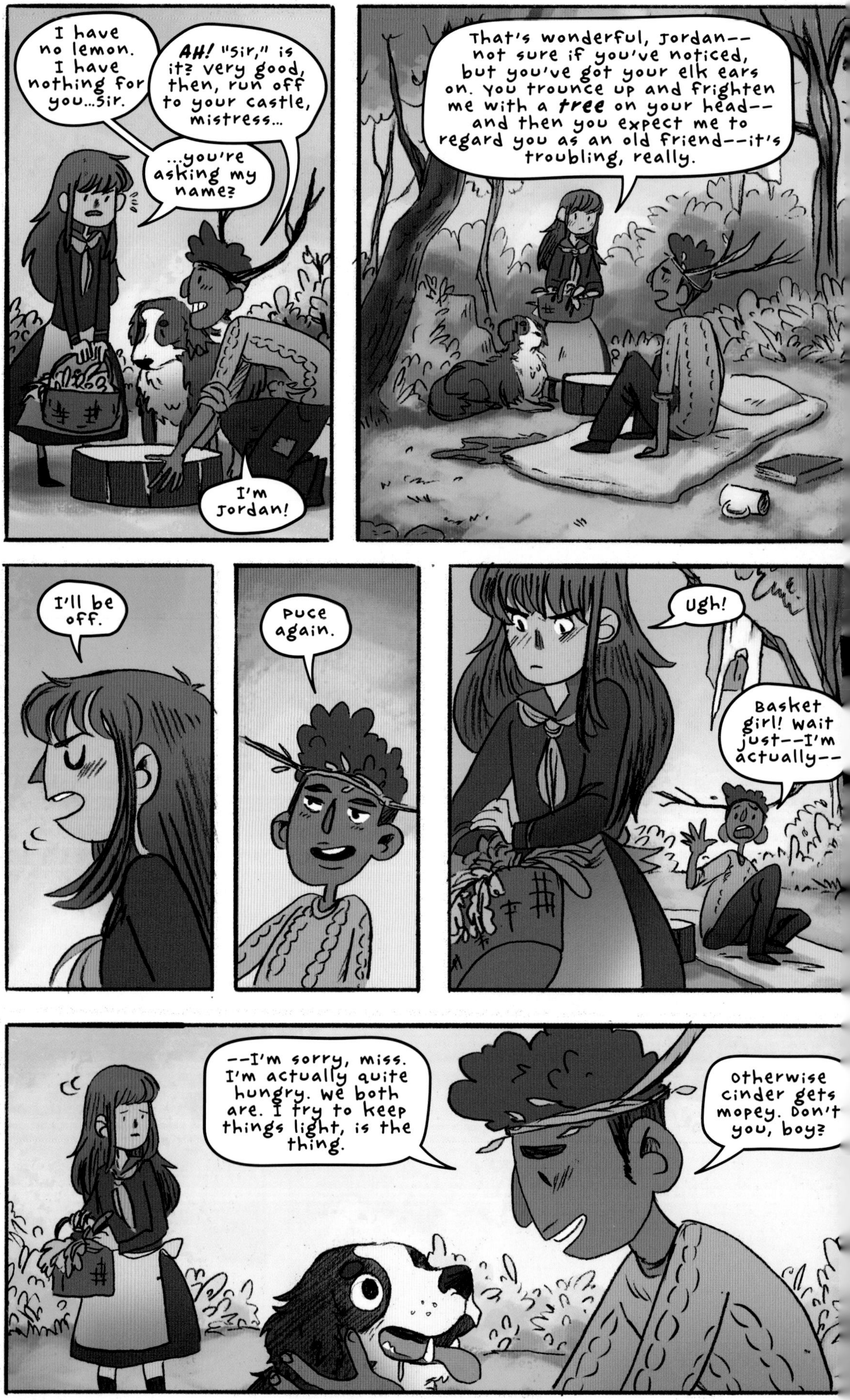
I have no lemon. I have nothing for you...Sir.
AH! "Sir," is it? Very good, then, run off to your castle, mistress...
...you're asking my name?
I'm Jordan!
That's wonderful, Jordan--not sure if you've noticed, but you've got your elk ears on. You trounce up and frighten me with a tree on your head--and then you expect me to regard you as an old friend--it's troubling, really.
I'll be off.
Puce again.
Ugh!
Basket girl! Wait just--I'm actually--
--I'm sorry, miss. I'm actually quite hungry. We both are. I try to keep things light, is the thing.
Otherwise Cinder gets mopey. Don't you, boy?

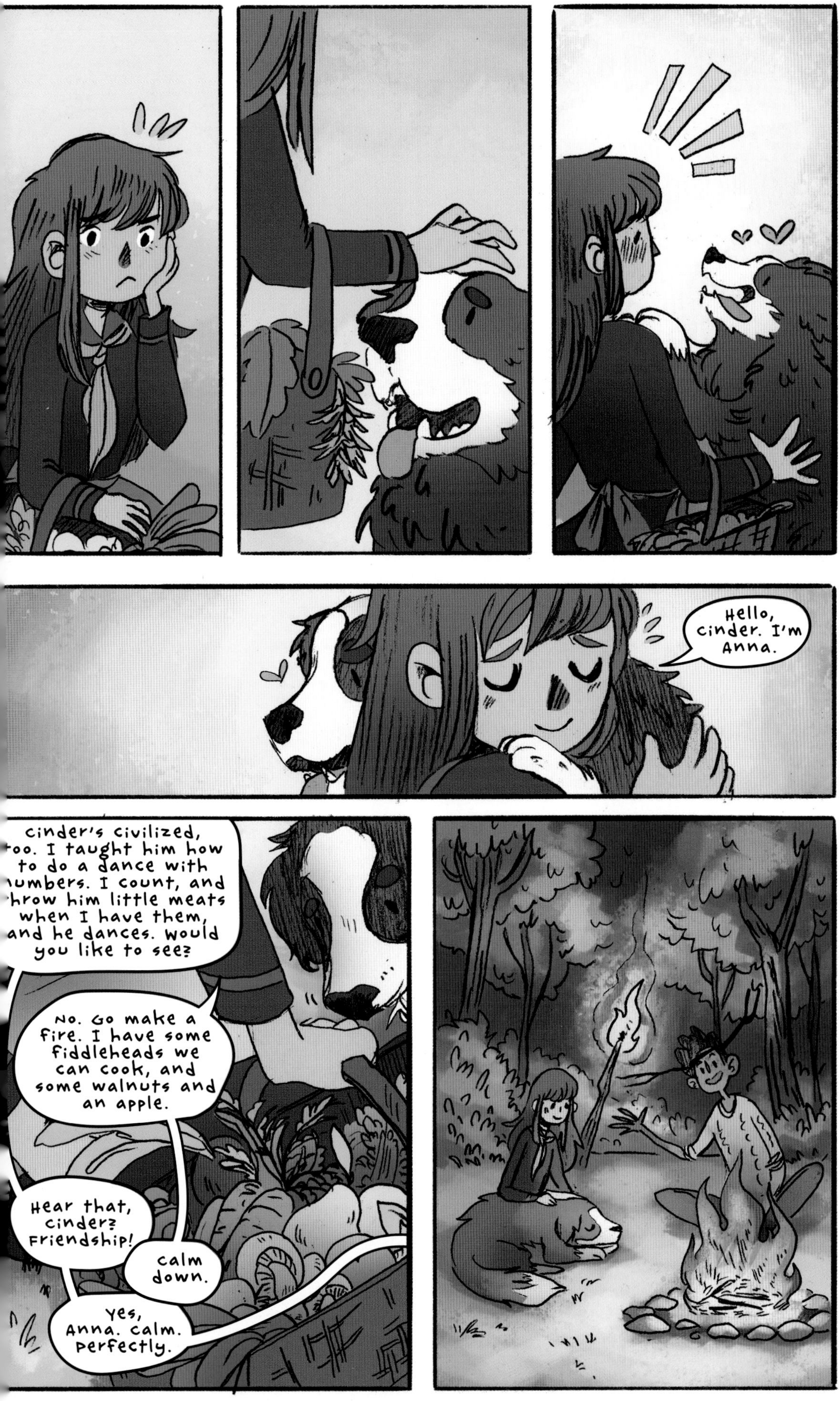
Hello, cinder. I'm Anna.
cinder's civilized, oo. I taught him how to do a dance with umbers. I count, and hrow him little meats when I have them, and he dances. would you like to see?
No. Go make a fire. I have some fiddleheads we can cook, and some walnuts and an apple.
Hear that, cinder? Friendship!
calm down.
Yes, Anna. calm. Perfectly.

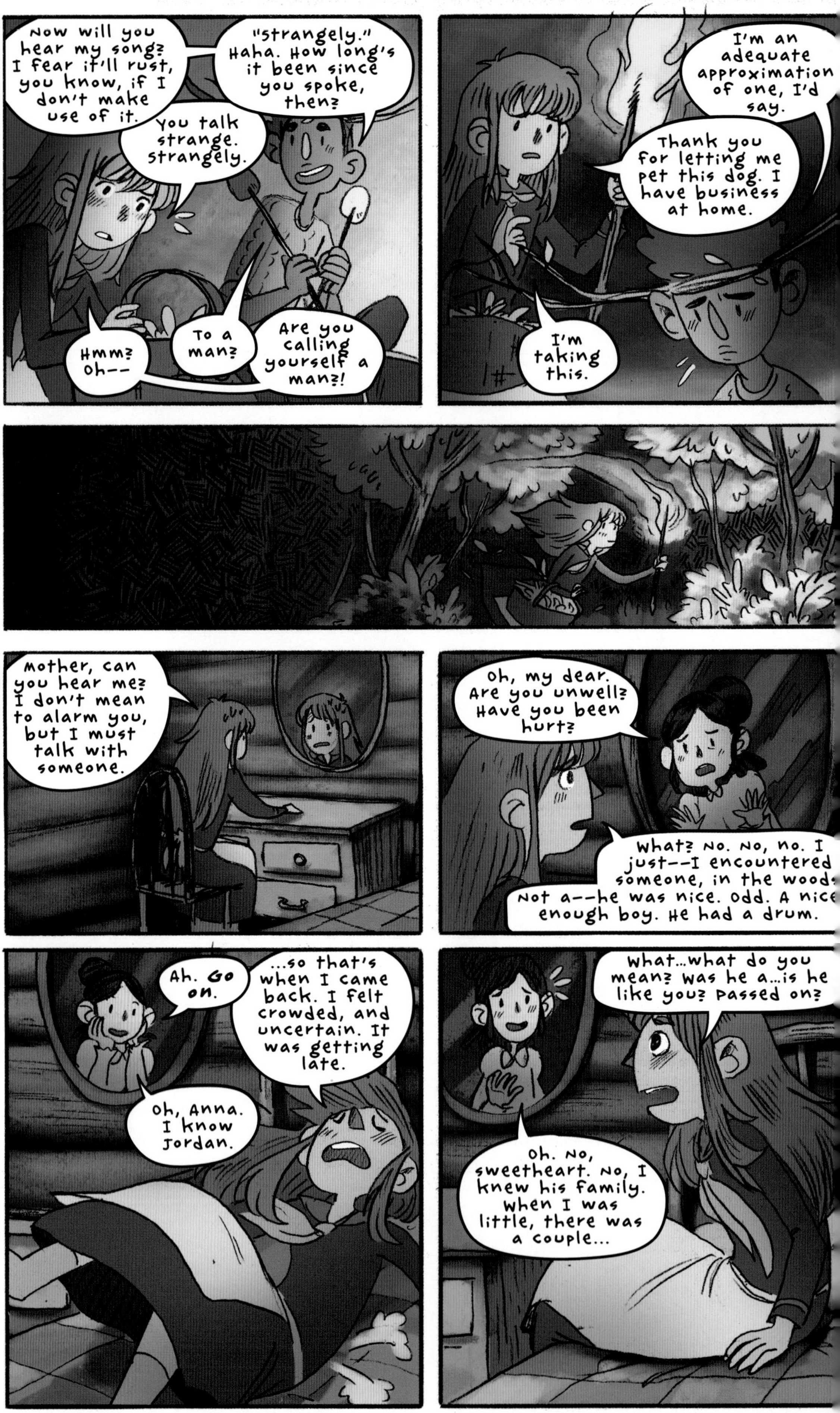
Now will you hear my song? I fear it'll rust, you know, if I don't make use of it.
"Strangely." Haha. How long's it been since you spoke, then?
You talk strange. strangely.
Hmm? Oh--
To a man?
Are you calling yourself a man?!
I'm an adequate approximation of one, I'd say.
Thank you for letting me pet this dog. I have business at home.
I'm taking this.
Mother, can you hear me? I don't mean to alarm you, but I must talk with someone.
Oh, my dear. Are you unwell? Have you been hurt?
What? No. No, no. I just--I encountered someone, in the woods. Not a--he was nice. odd. A nice enough boy. He had a drum.
Ah. Go on.
...so that's when I came back. I felt crowded, and uncertain. It was getting late.
Oh, Anna. I know Jordan.
What...what do you mean? was he a...is he like you? Passed on?
Oh. No, sweetheart. No, I knew his family. When I was little, there was a couple...

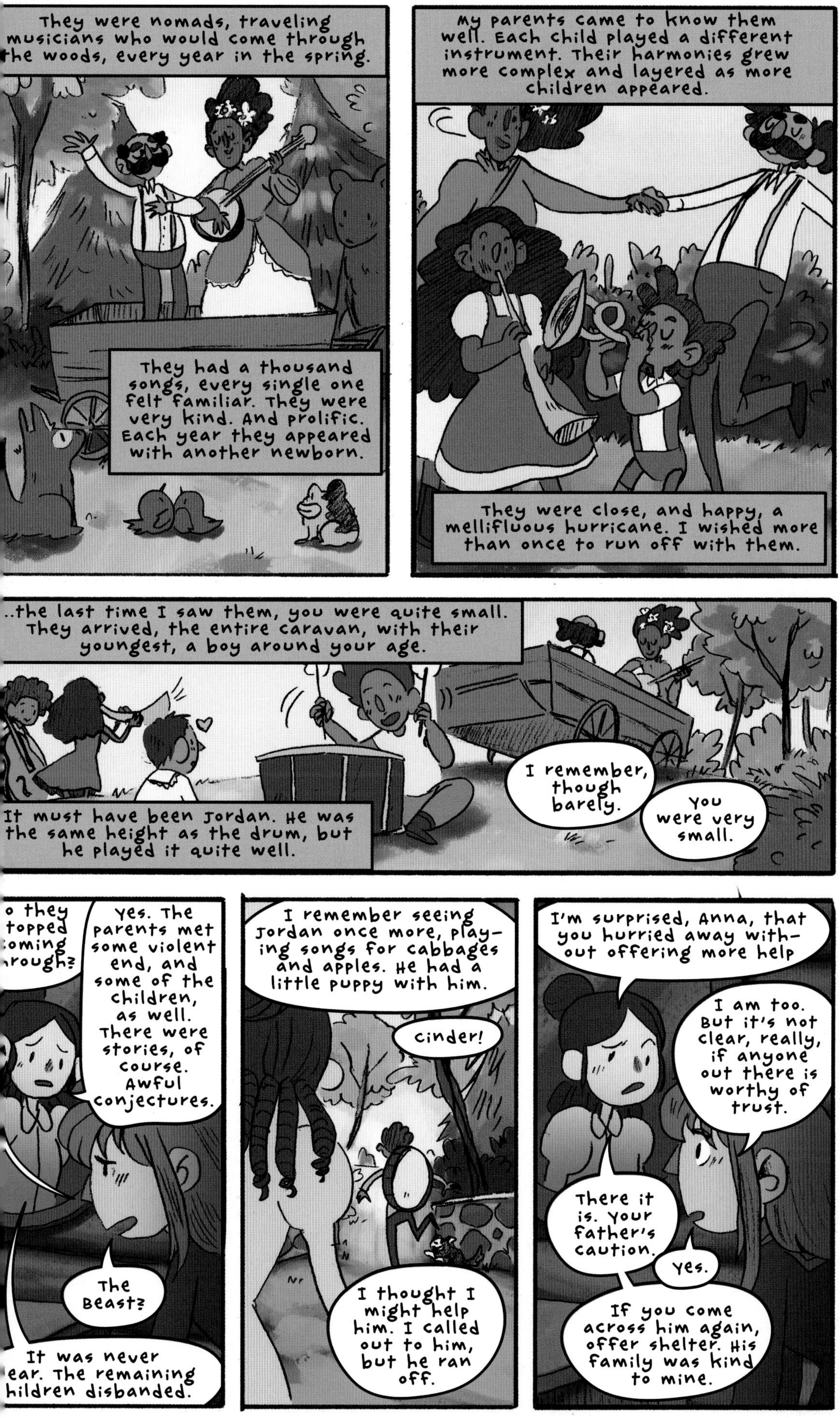
They were nomads, traveling musicians who would come through the woods, every year in the spring.
They had a thousand songs, every single one felt familiar. They were very kind. And prolific. Each year they appeared with another newborn.
My parents came to know them well. Each child played a different instrument. Their harmonies grew more complex and layered as more children appeared.
They were close, and happy, a mellifluous hurricane. I wished more than once to run off with them.
..the last time I saw them, you were quite small. They arrived, the entire caravan, with their youngest, a boy around your age.
It must have been Jordan. He was the same height as the drum, but he played it quite well.
I remember, though barely.
You were very small.
o they topped coming rough?
Yes. The parents met some violent end, and some of the children, as well. There were stories, of course. Awful conjectures.
The Beast?
It was never ear. The remaining hildren disbanded.
I remember seeing Jordan once more, playing songs for cabbages and apples. He had a little puppy with him.
Cinder!
I thought I might help him. I called out to him, but he ran off.
I'm surprised, Anna, that you hurried away without offering more help
I am too. But it's not clear, really, if anyone out there is worthy of trust.
There it is. Your father's caution.
Yes.
If you come across him again, offer shelter. His family was kind to mine.

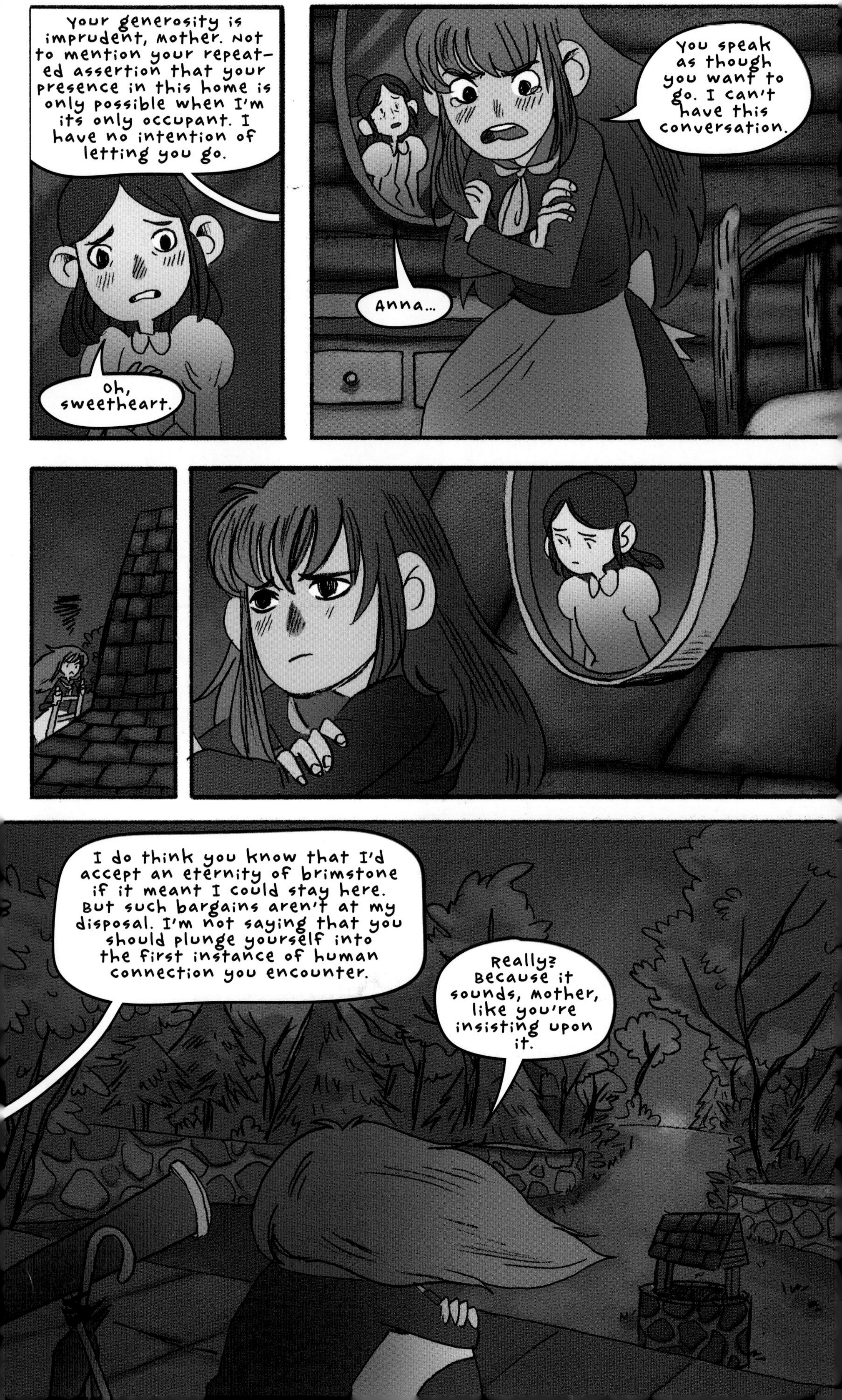
Your generosity is imprudent, mother. Not to mention your repeated assertion that your presence in this home is only possible when I'm its only occupant. I have no intention of letting you go.
Oh, sweetheart.
You speak as though you want to go. I can't have this conversation.
Anna...
I do think you know that I'd accept an eternity of brimstone if it meant I could stay here. But such bargains aren't at my disposal. I'm not saying that you should plunge yourself into the first instance of human connection you encounter.
Really? Because it sounds, mother, like you're insisting upon it.

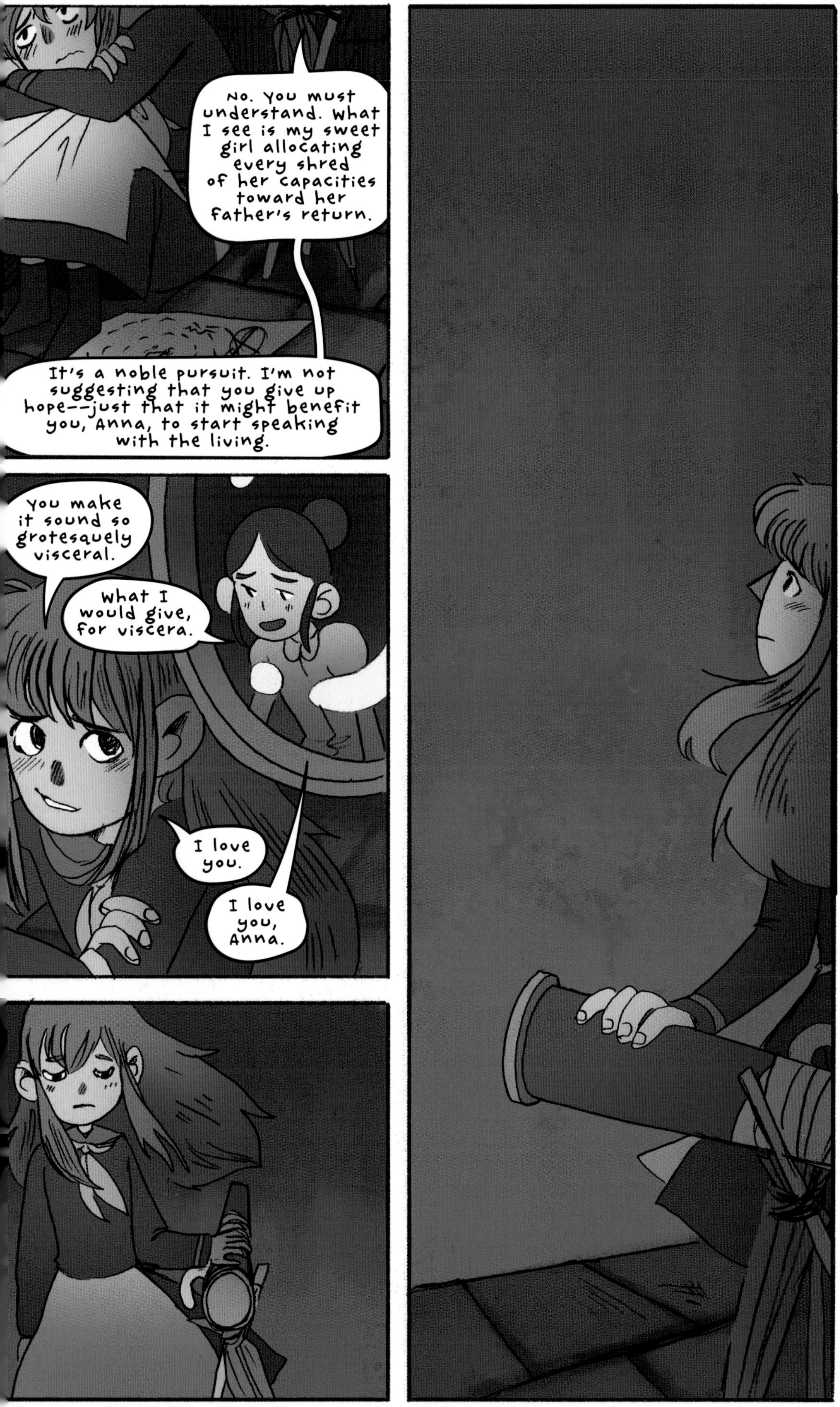
No. You must understand. What I see is my sweet girl allocating every shred of her capacities toward her father's return.
It's a noble pursuit. I'm not suggesting that you give up hope--just that it might benefit you, Anna, to start speaking with the living.
You make it sound so grotesquely visceral.
What I would give, for viscera.
I love you.
I love you, Anna.

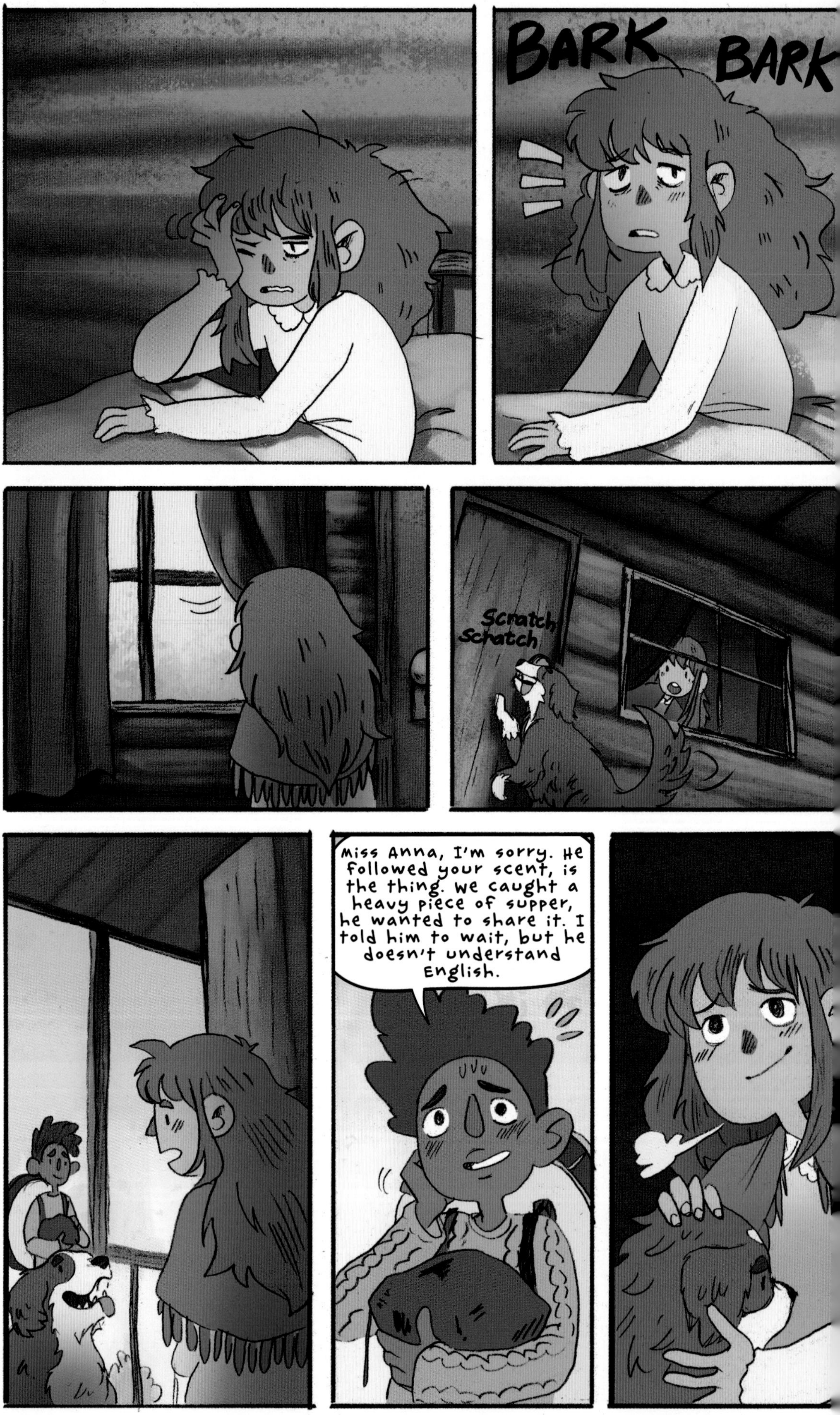

BARK
BARK
Scratch
Scratch
Miss Anna, I'm sorry. He followed your scent, is the thing. We caught a heavy piece of supper, he wanted to share it. I told him to wait, but he doesn't understand English.

come in.

Jordan! what's that tune? I've heard it before.

my brother wrote it, the eldest one. Zacky.

Are...you certain? There was a mockingbird that came by here often, early in the winter. That was his song.

Ah, must have been my brother. I've been wondering what form he took.

That...sounds like a much longer story.

sure, lots to tell. But we've got time, yah? How long's it take this stew to cook?

Six... seven hours...

superb. We can help you do the chores today, if you like.

Thanks. Thank you, that sounds... yes.

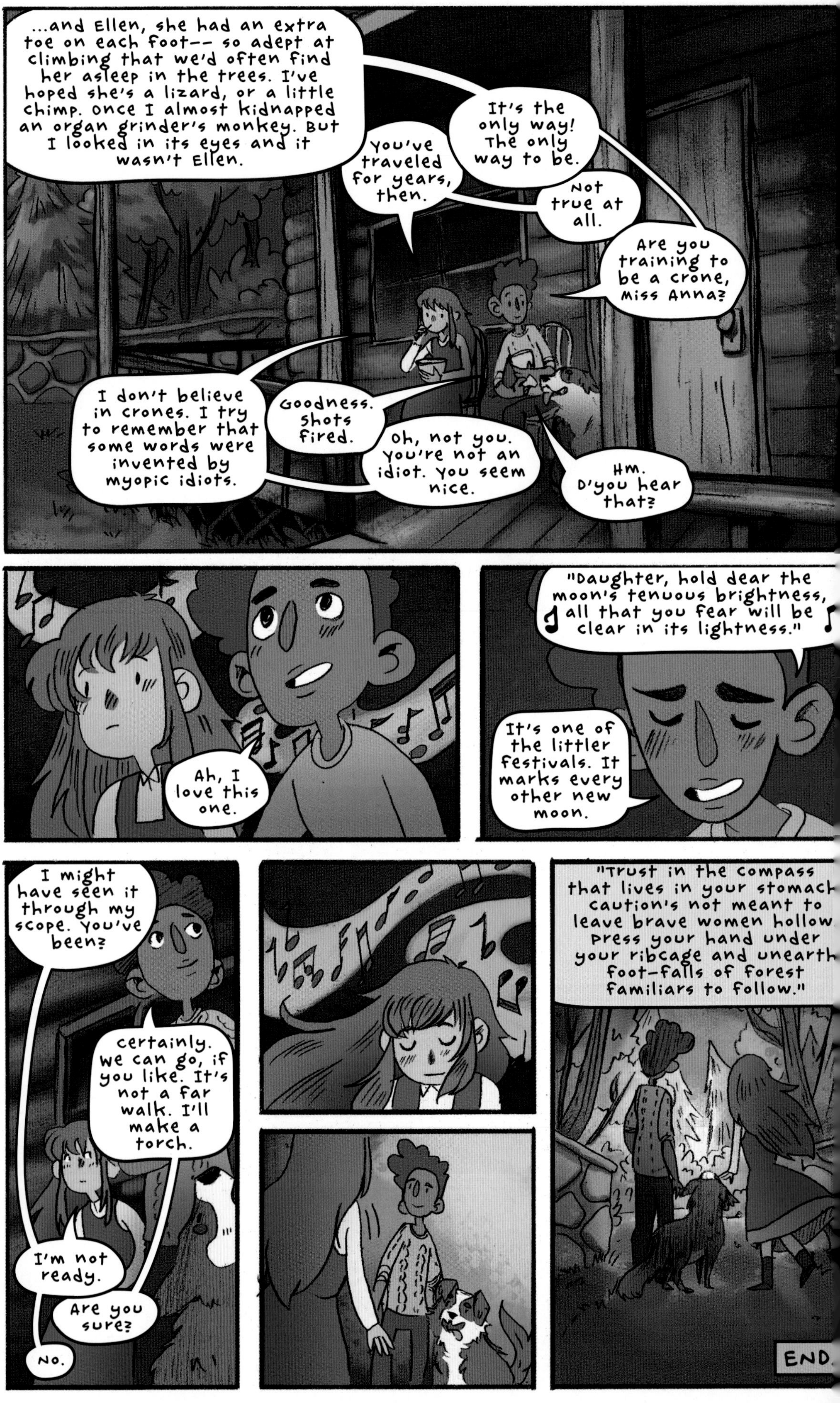

...and Ellen, she had an extra toe on each foot-- so adept at climbing that we'd often find her asleep in the trees. I've hoped she's a lizard, or a little chimp. Once I almost kidnapped an organ grinder's monkey. But I looked in its eyes and it wasn't Ellen.
You've traveled for years, then.
It's the only way! The only way to be.
Not true at all.
Are you training to be a crone, Miss Anna?
I don't believe in crones. I try to remember that some words were invented by myopic idiots.
Goodness. Shots fired.
Oh, not you. You're not an idiot. You seem nice.
Hm. D'you hear that?
Ah, I love this one.
"Daughter, hold dear the moon's tenuous brightness, all that you fear will be clear in its lightness."
It's one of the littler festivals. It marks every other new moon.
I might have seen it through my scope. You've been?
Certainly. We can go, if you like. It's not a far walk. I'll make a torch.
I'm not ready.
Are you sure?
No.
"Trust in the compass that lives in your stomach caution's not meant to leave brave women hollow press your hand under your ribcage and unearth foot-falls of forest familiars to follow."
END.

❧ Cover
Gallery ❧

ISSUE ONE COVER
JIM CAMPBELL

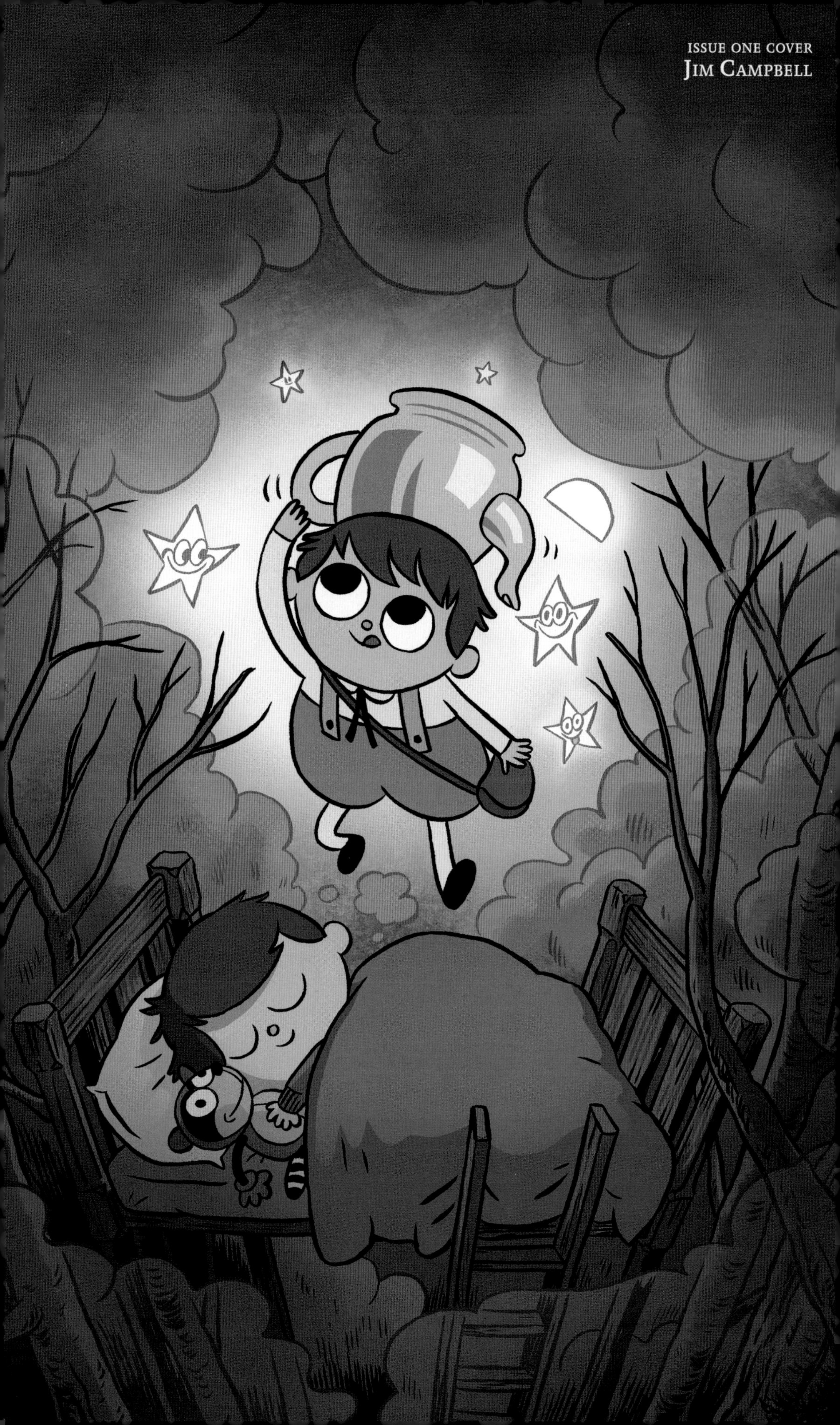

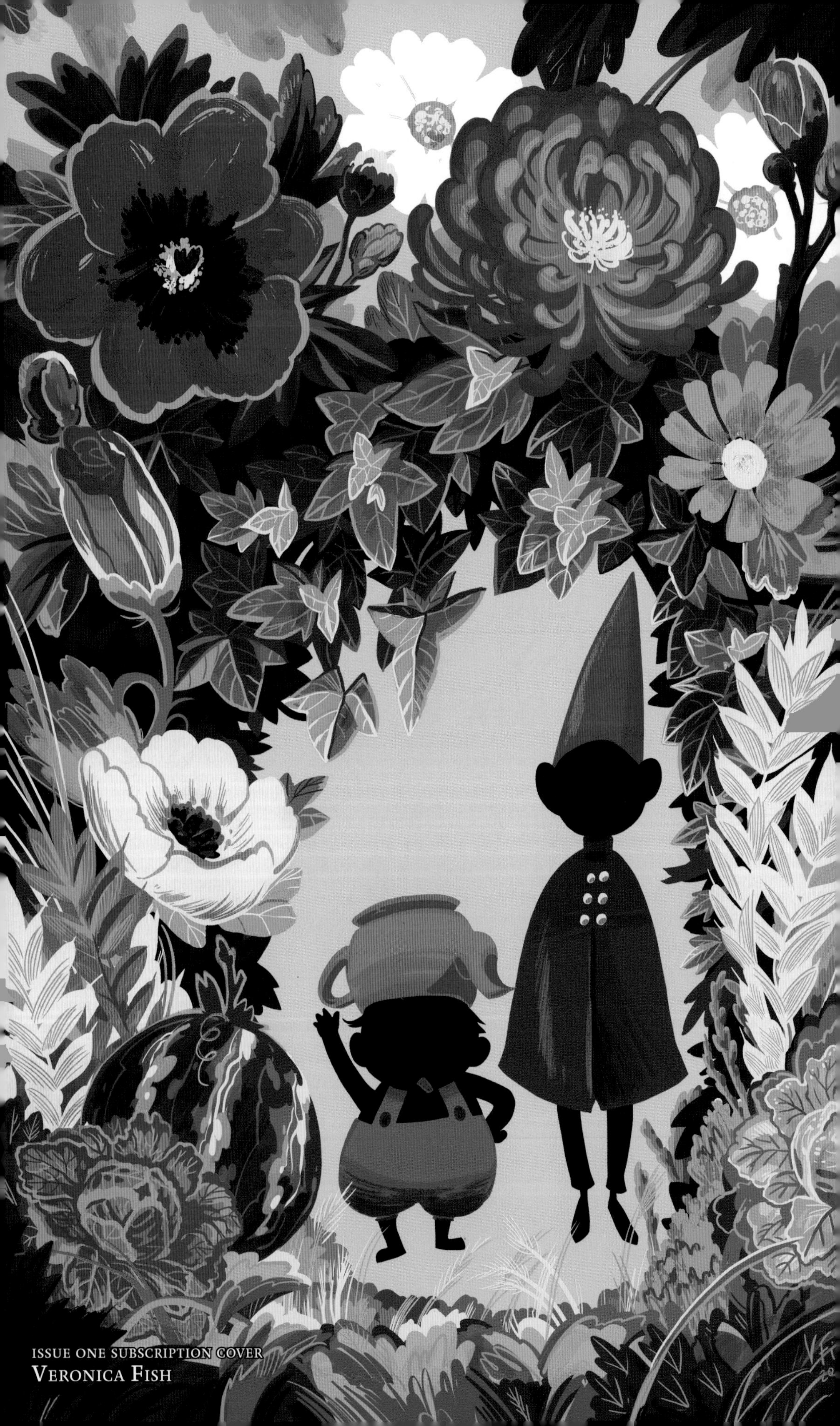

ISSUE ONE SUBSCRIPTION COVER
VERONICA FISH

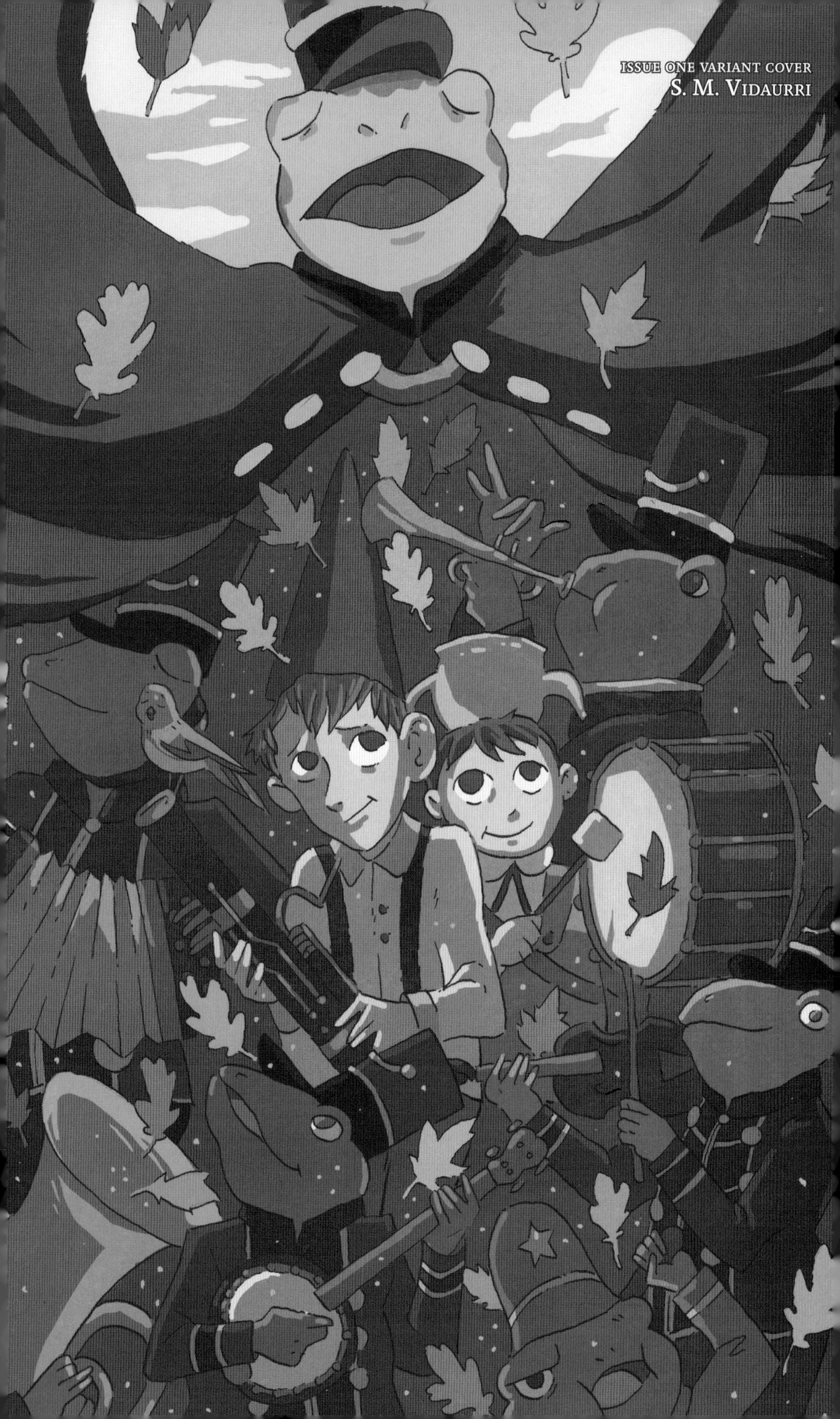

ISSUE ONE VARIANT COVER
S. M. VIDAURRI

ISSUE ONE RETAILER APPRECIATION COVER
RACHEL SAUNDERS

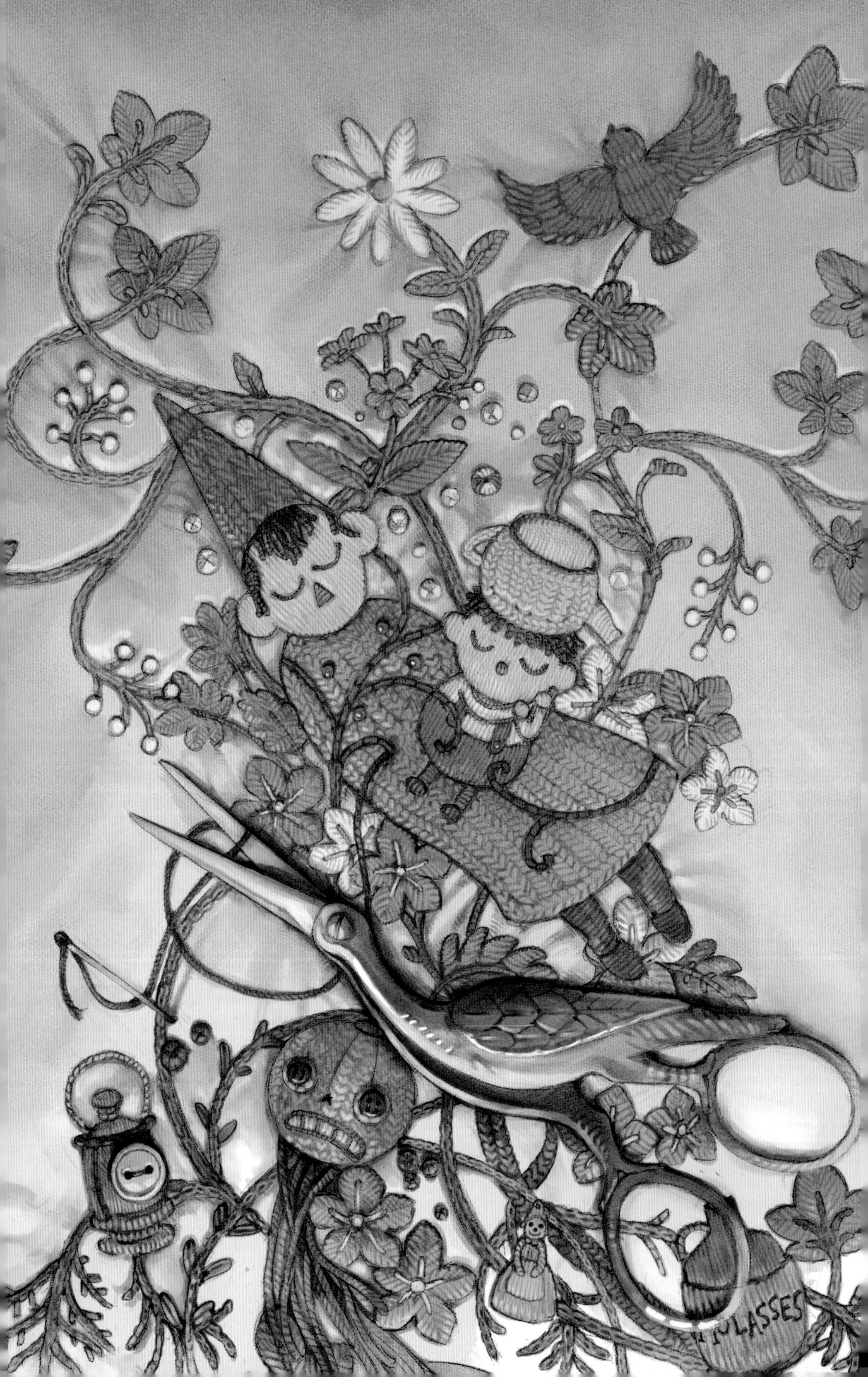
MOLASSES

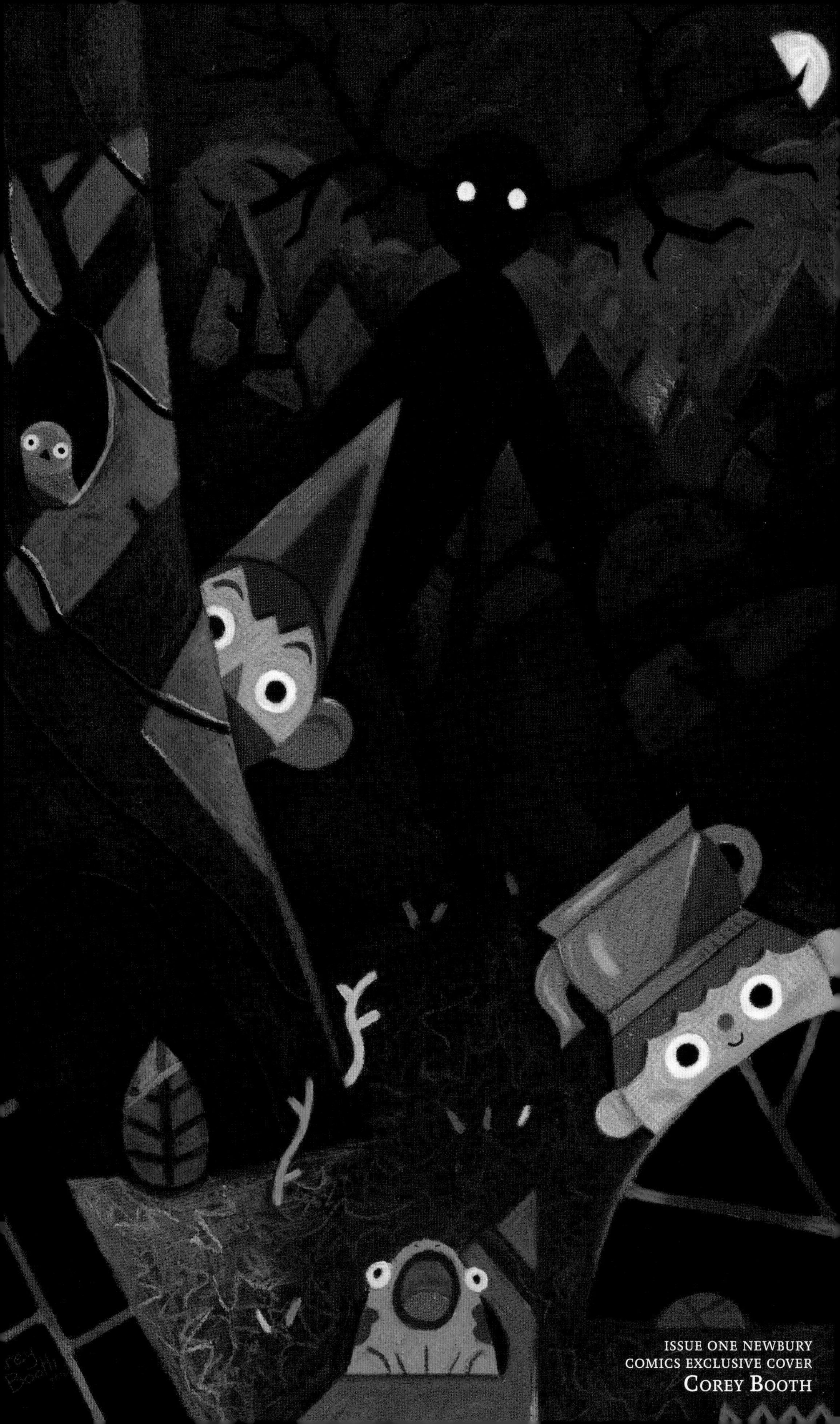

ISSUE ONE NEWBURY
COMICS EXCLUSIVE COVER
COREY BOOTH

ISSUE ONE SAN DIEGO COMIC-CON
EXCLUSIVE COVER
REX HACKLEBERG

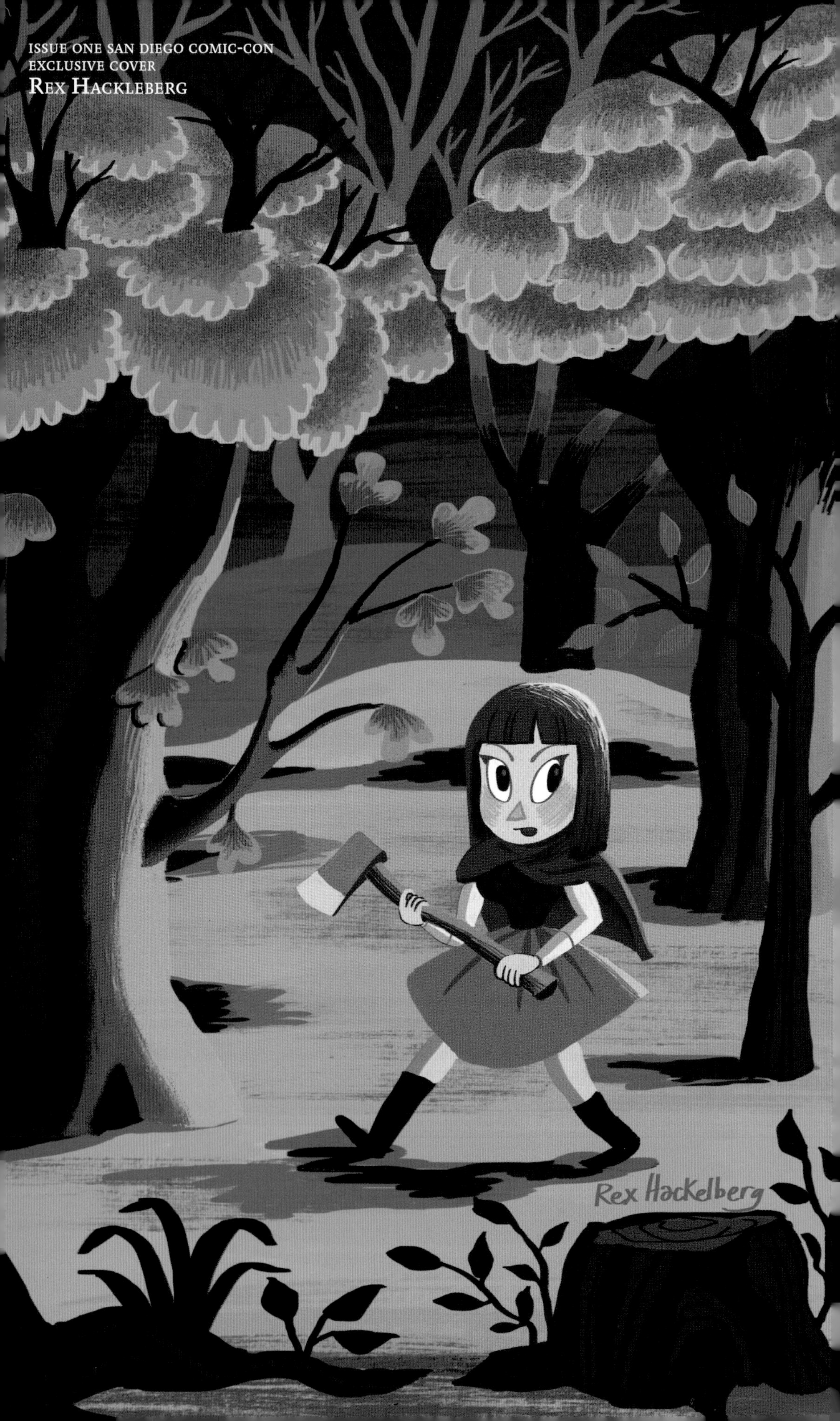
Rex Hackelberg

ISSUE ONE SECOND
PRINT COVER
JONATHAN REINCKE

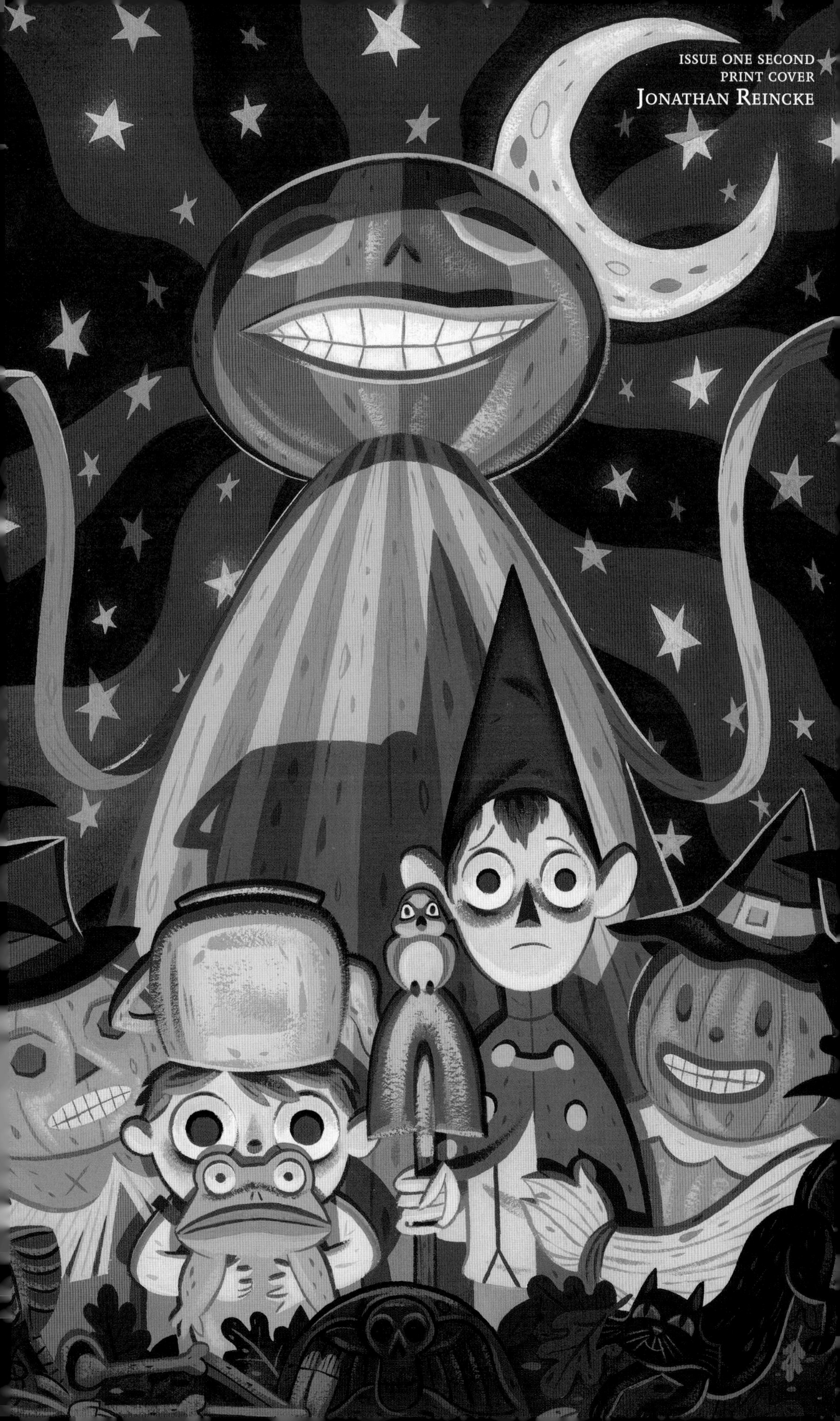

ISSUE TWO COVER
JIM CAMPBELL

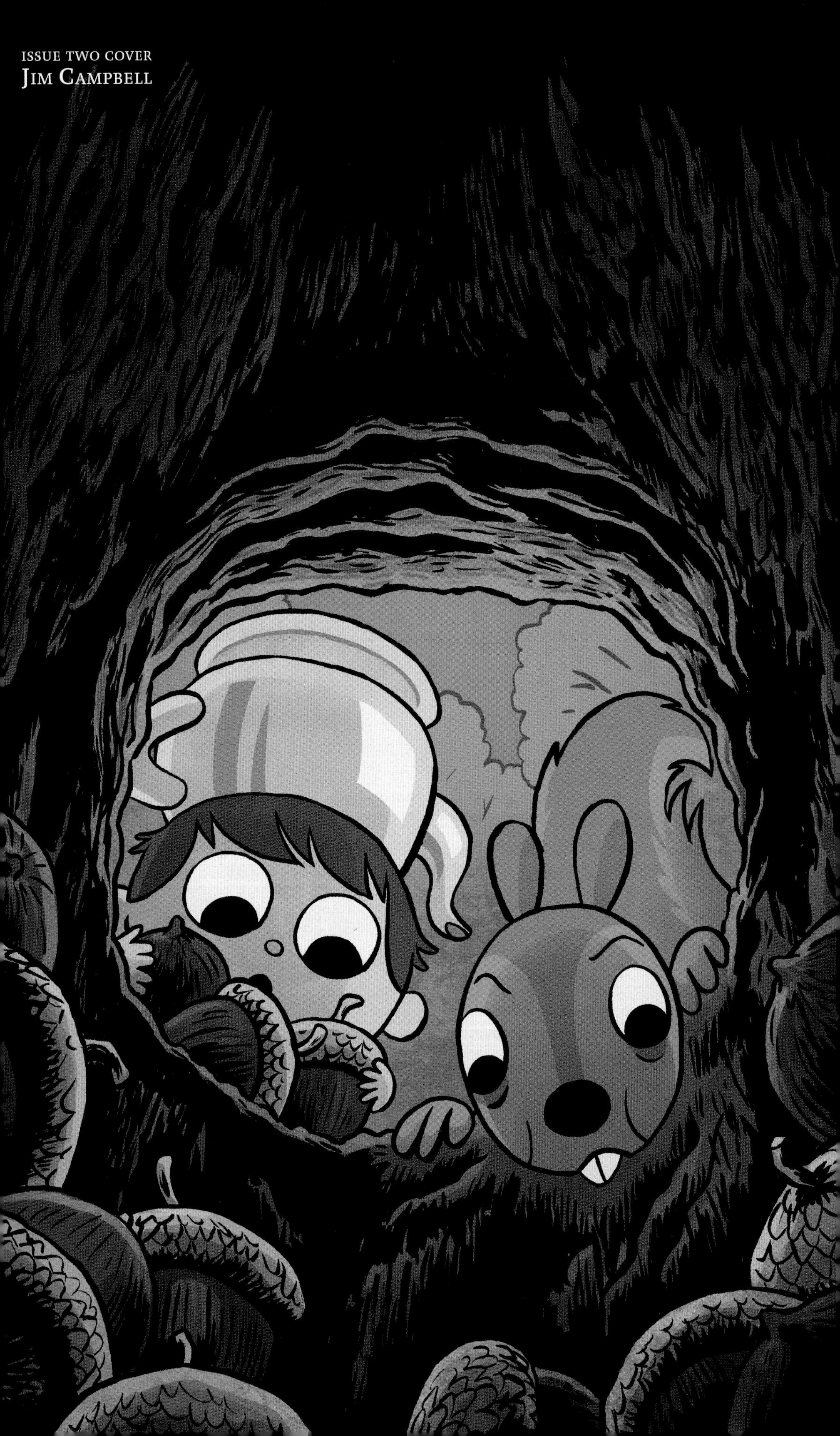

ISSUE TWO SUBSCRIPTION COVER
ANNA CRAIG

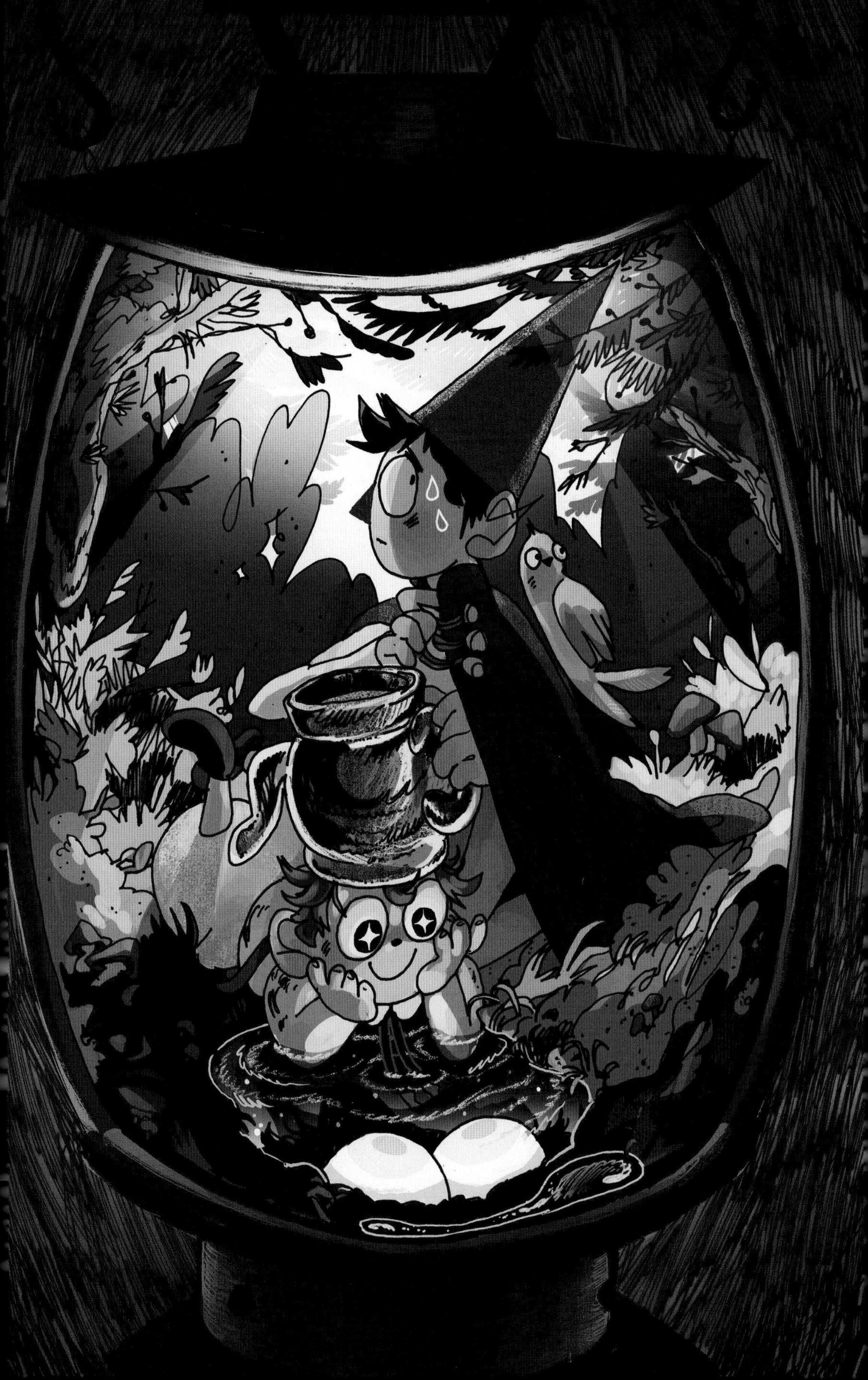

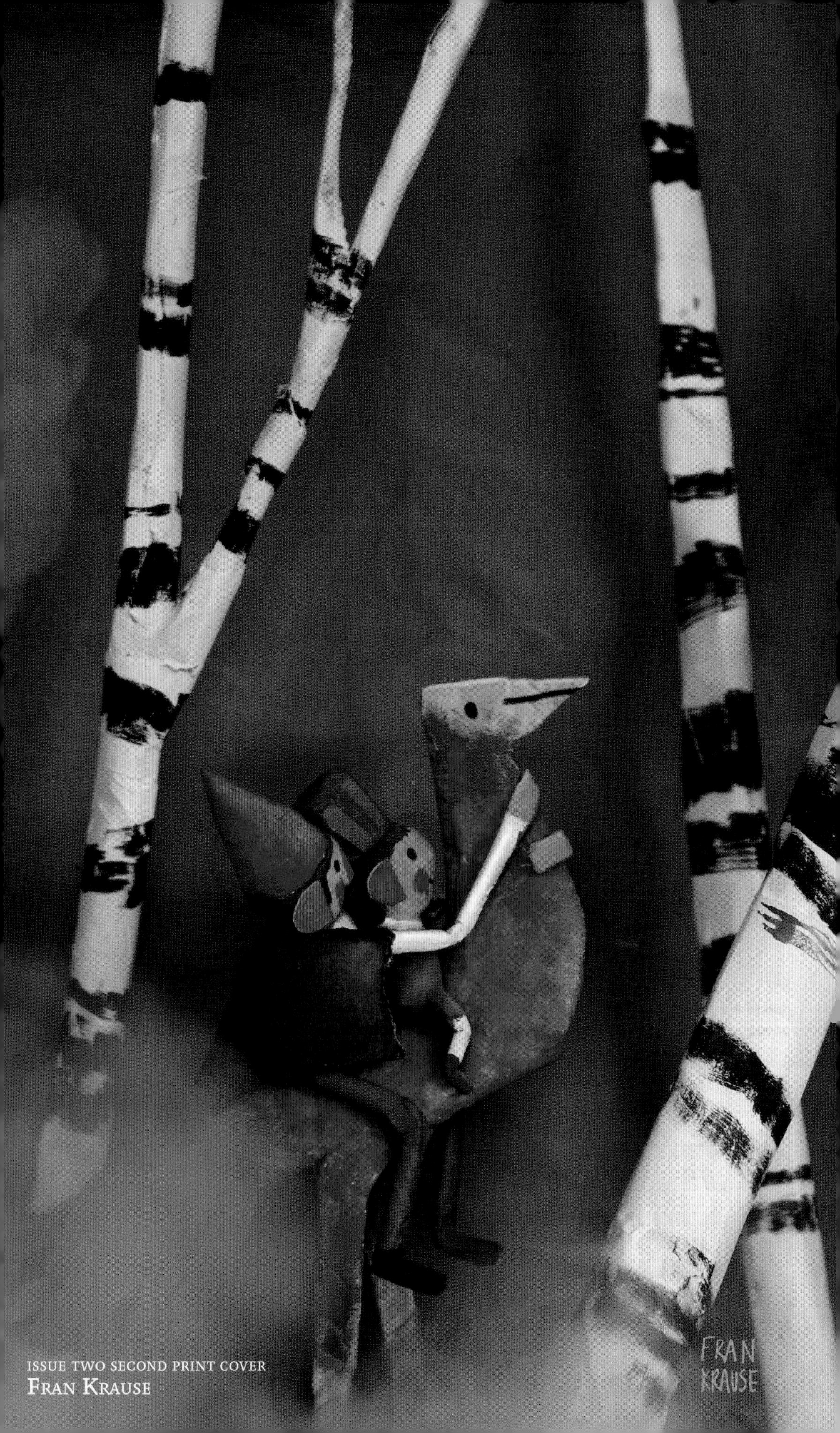
FRAN
KRAUSE

ISSUE TWO SECOND PRINT COVER
FRAN KRAUSE

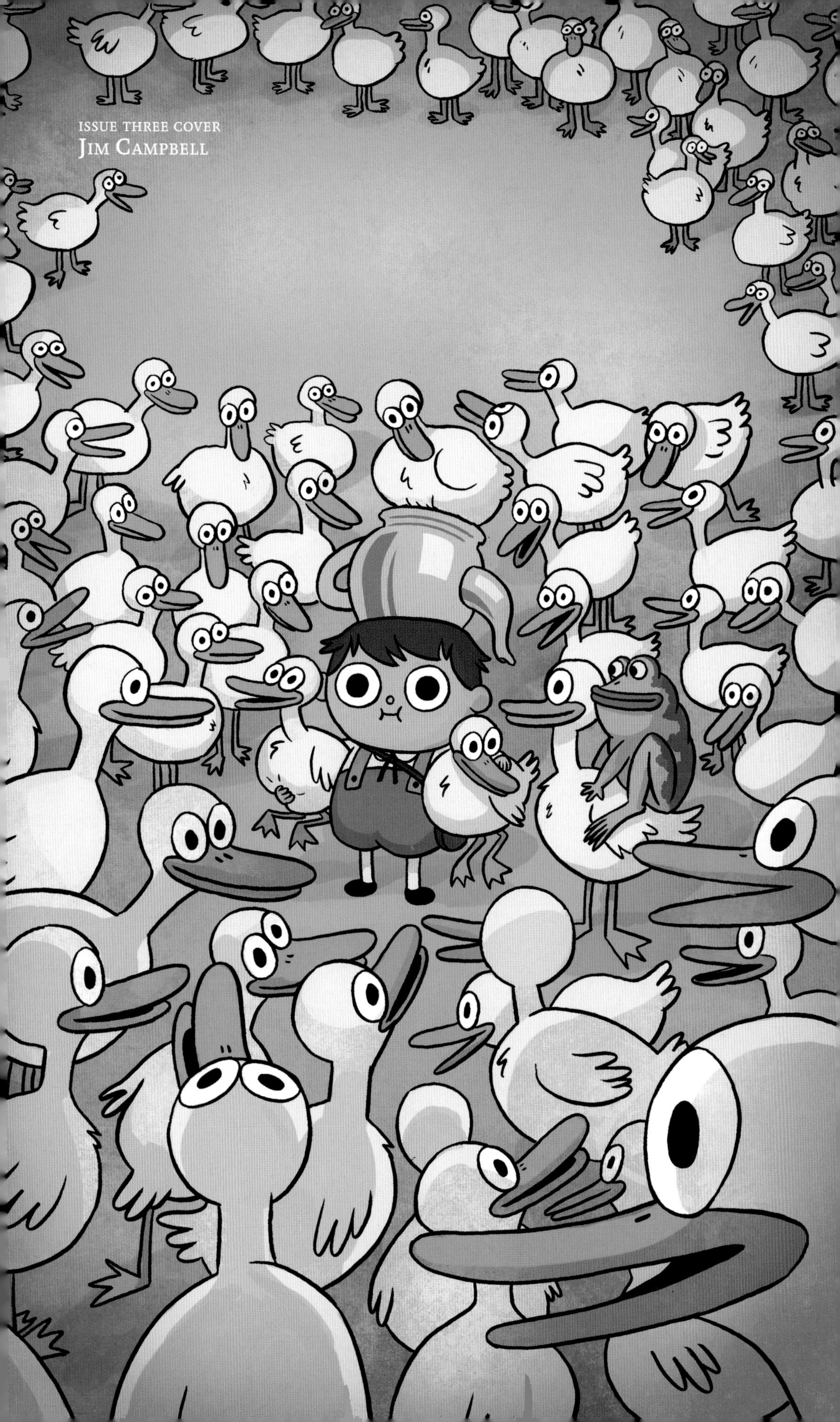

ISSUE THREE COVER
JIM CAMPBELL

ISSUE THREE SUBSCRIPTION COVER
KEVIN JAY STANTON

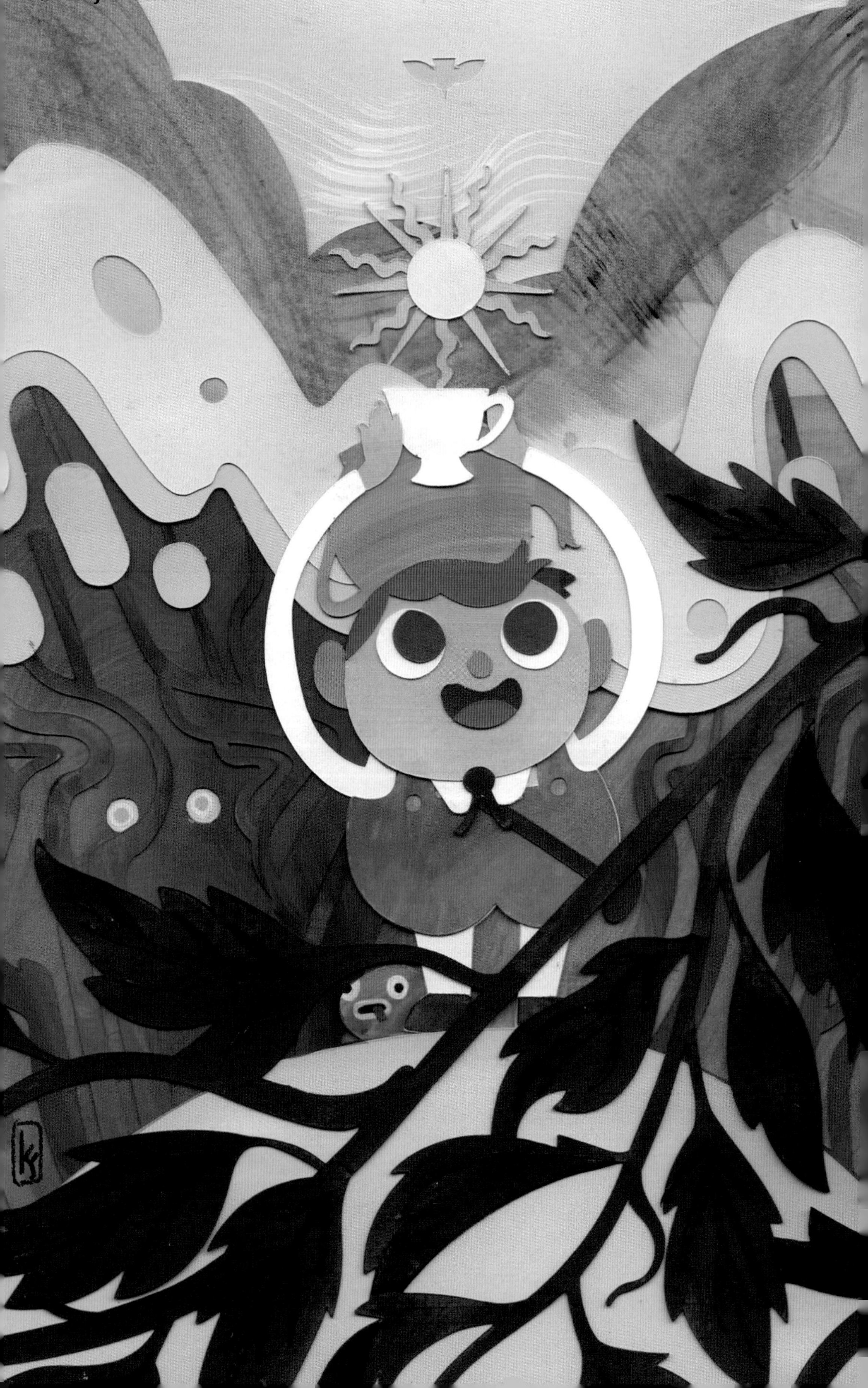

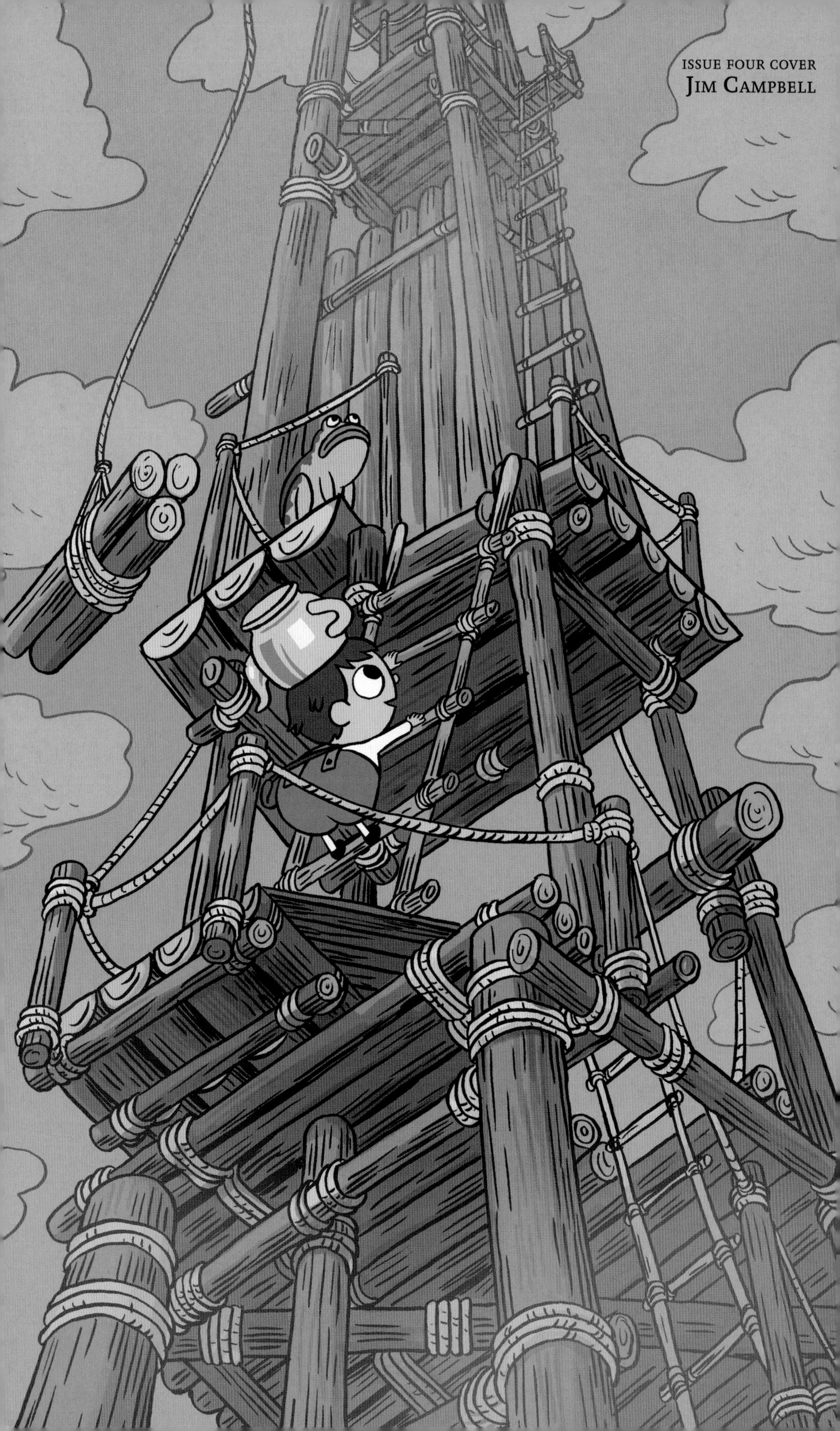

ISSUE FOUR COVER
JIM CAMPBELL

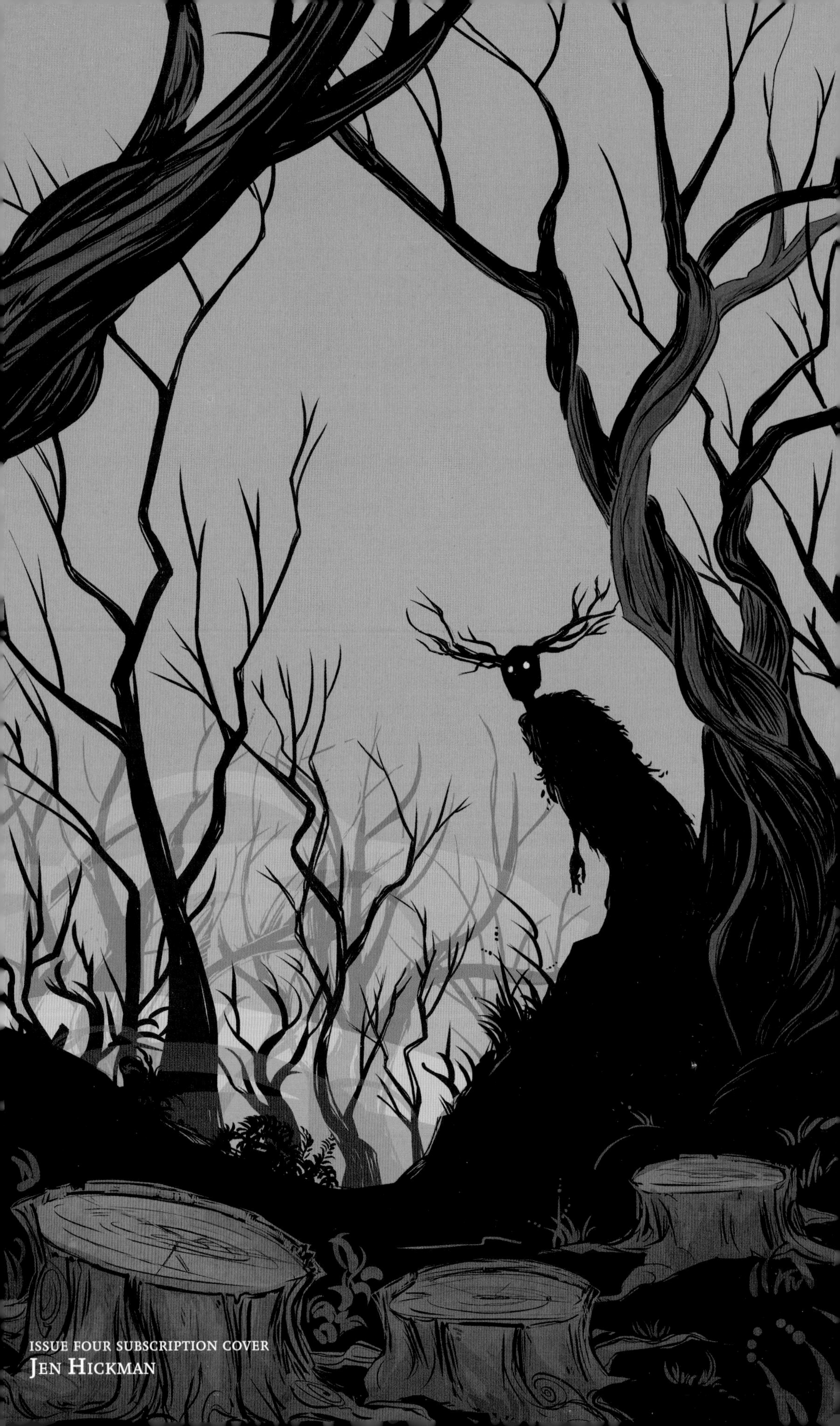

ISSUE FOUR SUBSCRIPTION COVER
JEN HICKMAN